Love on Deck

ALSO BY KASEY STOCKTON

Contemporary Romance

Cotswolds Holiday

I'm Not Charlotte Lucas

Falling in Line

His Stand-in Holiday Girlfriend

Regency Romance

Properly Kissed

Sensibly Wed

Pleasantly Pursued

Honorably Engaged

Love in the Bargain

All is Mary and Bright

A Noble Inheritance

The Jewels of Halstead Manor

The Lady of Larkspur Vale

Scottish Historical Romance

Journey to Bongary Spring

Through the Fairy Tree

The Enemy Across the Loch

Love on Deck

AN ARCADIA CREEK ROMANCE

KASEY STOCKTON

GOLDEN OWL PRESS

For those who love spreadsheets, fresh notebooks, and the smell of sharpened pencils. I see you.

CHAPTER ONE

LAUREN

PREPARING for a warm cruise to the Caribbean when it was cold outside my Texas apartment was a puzzle my logical brain struggled to solve. What was I supposed to wear to the airport when Dallas was dipping down to the forties—the equivalent of freezing for me—yet the plane would land in Miami, where it was too warm for long leggings? My clothes for the cruise were all laid out on my bed in neat, organized piles, along with the perfectly aligned shoes and two swimsuit options—which suddenly didn't seem like enough—but my traveling outfit evaded me.

My eyes darted to the shimmery pink dress smoothed out on the end of the bed, playing its own little game of *which of these things is not like the other?* against the array of grays, tans, and whites that made up my day-to-day wardrobe. Did my closet resemble a J. Crew ad? Perhaps. They did supply more than two-thirds of my wardrobe. It was clothing that lasted and was worth the investment. As a business professional in the hospitality industry, it was entirely reasonable to own so many things that fell in the neutral color scheme. I wanted my clothing to be good quality, comfortable, and professional.

Which was why I was fairly positive my sister had chosen the bright pink maid of honor gown just to get under my skin. Since I was up for promotion from assistant events manager to *the* events manager now that my boss was making her maternity leave permanent, I didn't take anything lightly—clothing choices included. It was going to be a close call between Jerry and me for the promotion, despite my seniority, and I wasn't giving the Hunnam Hotels Group any reason not to pick me. I had long taken my career seriously, and my array of unremarkable pencil skirts proved that.

My phone rang, pausing the cozy mystery that had been feeding into my earbuds, and I tapped to answer. "Lauren Foley."

"You don't have to put on the work voice for me, Lo," my baby sister crooned through the speaker, all light and fluffy, a vocal embodiment of her personality. She acted like your stereotypical elementary school music teacher, and was—in my wise twenty-eight-year-old opinion—much too young to be getting married.

"That's what you get for putting me in this awful color," I teased. Only, it was more like a half-joke. A quarter-joke? Fine. I meant it.

"You'll thank me when you see the wedding pictures. That pink is going to make your skin glow."

"Didn't you quit the whole personal shopper gig because you realized it *isn't* your calling to decide what looks good on other people?"

"Maybe. But we're practically identical, and I know how to shop for myself. Just trust me on this."

Which was right where she lost me. Accepting that Amelia was not totally off base by providing me with a bright pink dress involved *trust*, and that wasn't something I gave out freely. Besides, we were identical in everything except our skin tones. She was blessed by the sun in that regard, and I was a slave to the moon. "I love you enough to wear it, so that has to count for something, right?"

Amelia growled. "I wish you would just see yourself the way I see—"

"I don't have time." My stomach tightened as I fended off the pep talk. "I need to run into the office before I head to the airport."

She sighed. "The office? Seriously? I don't know anyone who needs to be surgically removed from work like you do. If my wedding is too much of a burden—"

"I never said this trip was a burden." It *was*, but I never actually said that to her. I searched for another truth before she could read my tone and ferret out my real feelings. "I would never miss your wedding."

"Well, duh," she agreed with triumph. "This week is going to be exactly what you need to breathe for a minute. To take out that ridiculously tight knot and let your hair loose."

My hand slipped to the base of my neck and smoothed over my perfect honey-brown chignon. This was a week of falling behind at work and slipping in the ranks against Jerry. To say nothing of the mountain of things that would be waiting to be dealt with once I returned, since he couldn't seem to do anything without handholding. I had a plan to sneak away and check in with the office every morning using the Wi-Fi package the cruise line offered, but Amelia didn't need to know that.

"I like my French twists. They make me look professional."

I could practically hear her eyes roll. "At work, yeah. Not on a boat in Nassau."

"I promise not to wear a French twist when we dock at Nassau."

"Thank you," she said kindly, as if I had offered to supply her with a stack of magazines and endless piña coladas instead of discussing my hair style choices. "So, there's something I need to talk to you about. I was going to wait until you got to Florida for this, but I feel like maybe it's better if you have the plane ride to prepare yourself."

A cold, icy stone dropped to the pit of my stomach and made a home there. If she thought I needed two hours to prep my emotions, this couldn't be good. "What is it?"

"You know how I told you Jack wasn't going to be able to make it because of a work thing?"

"Yes." It had been the best news I'd heard in months, and I'd immediately run to my portal to request time off work for the cruise. When Jack had potentially been in the running to attend this ridiculously small wedding party with us, I'd been tempted to tell my own sister I couldn't make it to her elopement. *That* was how badly I wanted to avoid her fiancé's best friend.

"Well . . ." Amelia drew the word out like she was dangling a moldy carrot in front of me.

"Don't say it, Ames."

She was quiet, and even the silence sounded unsure. "You don't want to know?"

No. Oh, who was I kidding? The unknown was far worse than what I was imagining. It had to be.

Amelia read my silence for acquiescence. "Now Jack's coming."

"Jack Fletcher?" I squeezed my eyes closed, hoping beyond reason that Amelia knew two Jacks.

"Yes, Lauren," she said flatly. "The same Jack Fletcher whom I can't *uninvite* because he's my fiancé's best friend and for some reason you still hate—"

"Hey!" I said in defense, bending over my bed to pull piles of clothes toward me and layer them smoothly in my suitcase.

She sighed softly, and my immediate bite-back died on my tongue. The hatred between Jack and me was mutual. The blind date Amelia and her fiancé had set us up on was awful for both of us. We had barely made it through the entire meal before Jack pretended to get sick and ditched me to make out with the waitress.

"I'll admit, that blind date wasn't his best move," she said, conceding. But I didn't want her to concede, and I didn't want to be the reason she was stressed right before her wedding.

Time to pull up my big girl pants and be a mature adult. Though, to be fair, saying it wasn't Jack's best move was an understatement. No, I think his best move was when he'd accidentally called me later that night, complaining about our awful date to his roommate in a five-minute voicemail. Or maybe it was after that, when he couldn't seem to be around me for five seconds at Kevin's birthday party without telling me how uptight I was.

Big girl pants.

"That date was two years ago. I'm really fine with Jack being there."

Amelia was silent. Was she suspicious of my motives? She knew I had every reason to hate Jack Fletcher—including the voicemail still saved to my phone that expounded on the greater reasons about why he couldn't stand me—but this was her wedding. I wasn't going to be the one to ruin it.

Besides, she couldn't help it if her fiancé had terrible taste in friends.

"It's really in the past. I don't have any problem with him being on the cruise," I said, mining the words from my chest one chink at a time. I arranged my shoes in the suitcase to give my hands something to do. For the next week, I could put aside my well-founded hatred for Jack and make this the best wedding cruise Amelia could possibly hope for. She was my priority here, and I wasn't going to let anything get in the way of that.

"This sounds too good to be true, but I'm going to choose to believe you, because I've been so stressed about y'all being together on this cruise."

"Well, you have nothing to worry about. Seriously, Ames. *Nothing.*"

"You can't know what a relief that is." She blew out a breath, and I could practically feel her shoulders lower away from her ears. "We have a few activities in mind for the first half of the week, but after the wedding, your time will be your own."

That meant four days. Four days of faking that I was fine being around my nemesis before I could sneak away and find a quiet chair away from the sun to read and listen to the waves lap against the boat. Did waves lap against a giant cruise ship? I guess I was about to find out. My shoulders relaxed a little. Maybe this trip would be good for me, after all.

"I need to get going," I said. "I'll see you tonight."

"Yeah! Bachelorette night, baby!"

I laughed. Amelia had specifically requested no bachelorette party, so I had come up with a pre-cruise spa night in our hotel with her sole bridesmaid, Cara. It was the perfect way to relax and refresh right before getting on the boat. And hopefully to detox my bad energy so I would be able to handle Jack and his negativity. No matter what happened, I wasn't about to let anyone ruin my baby sister's big day.

EVERYONE at the office was surprised to see me when I showed up a half hour later. Jerry, especially, looked up from his desk with suspicion. "I thought you were off for the next two weeks."

"Eight days," I corrected. "And I plan to check in daily, so don't worry. It won't feel like I'm gone at all."

He gave me a grimacing smile. "Great."

"Is Hal in his office?"

Jerry nodded. "Not in a great mood though, fair warning."

When was Hal ever in a good mood? He'd only been our interim manager for the last few months, but it was long enough to understand the type of boss he was. I knocked at his office door and pushed it open when he called me in.

He looked up from his computer. "Didn't expect to see you today."

"Just wanted to check in before I left, sir." I hovered behind the chair opposite his desk. "Preparations for Fantasy Con can still come my way, and I'll make sure to respond to every necessary email within twenty-four hours."

He looked at me shrewdly. "I thought you were going to a wedding."

"I am." Did my willingness to be reachable make me seem cold and heartless? I thought my diligence would be impressive. "But there will be a lot of downtime, and I know how important this event is for the hotel."

"Not anymore."

I froze. Fantasy Con had been Camila's project the last few years, and I'd shadowed her heavily. Now that she no longer planned to return from maternity leave, this was my chance to take the project on and prove my worthiness. "Is there a problem with the conference?"

"There is no more conference," Hal said bitterly. He smoothed his fingers over his mustache. "They canceled. I guess they found facilities they believe are better quality and better priced, so they pulled from the contract."

"How can they get away with that?" Our contracts were pretty ironclad.

"They found a clause. It doesn't matter now," he said, waving his hand. "You can put your efforts into something else."

But there wasn't anything else, not at the caliber of Fantasy Con. Nothing that took as much facilitating and gave me the chance to prove I was worthy of the promotion. Except for maybe the lawyer conference we had coming up in a few weeks. It wasn't the same level as the nerdy conference, but it was the next best thing. "Maybe the law—"

"Jerry has that well in hand," Hal said. "But you can assist him."

Assist? I would not be formally *assisting* Jerry in anything. That would secure me in Hal's head as second-best.

"I believe my talents are put to better use elsewhere, sir."

"Probably true, but there isn't anything else until July."

Which was a problem for me because Camila's maternity leave was up at the end of April. The promotion decision would be made by then.

"I can canvass," I offered. "Find a new conference. Or maybe work on Fantasy Con's guild a little—"

"Lauren," Hal placated. "I don't need you to do any of that. I need you to take your break, breathe a little sea air, and clear your mind for a few days. I promise your job will be waiting here when you return."

My job would, yes, but maybe not my promotion. My five-year plan was already mapped out in a detailed spreadsheet on my laptop. I couldn't afford to put this promotion off any longer. I'd already been stagnant for too long. I looked through the window where Jerry's desk was visible and found him watching us, his forehead shiny underneath the fluorescent lights. That little shark was planning to swoop in and steal the promotion I'd given four years of my life to obtain, and I wasn't about to let that happen.

Hal rose, indicating our meeting was over. Since I stood across from him in tan LuLu Lemon knockoff joggers and a plain white shirt, I was inappropriately dressed for the office anyway.

"Go to Florida, Lauren," Hal said. "And do me a favor."

"Yes?"

His caterpillar eyebrows lifted. "Enjoy yourself."

Jack's stupidly handsome face flashed in my mind, the deep creases from his years of consistent smiling and sparkling green eyes under dark brown hair. Ugh, so gross. I was *not* going to enjoy myself, and that was just a plain fact.

I felt the promotion slipping further from my fingers as Hal ushered me out his door and past Jerry's desk. Panic edged in. I needed this promotion. I needed to be rewarded for my years of hard work and sacrifice and all the time Camila put into training me to take her place. If this didn't come to me now, it would knock everything in my spreadsheet down a cell, which would mess *everything* up. When Hal was brought in as interim events coordinator and given the role of choosing Camila's successor, I'd thought I had it in the bag, but watching him praise Jerry over recent weeks had given me a wriggle of doubt. Now I was growing more and more insecure.

He walked me to the elevator and pushed the button, then herded me inside. Stepping back into the hallway, he slung his hands in his pockets. "See you in a couple weeks."

I swallowed against a dry throat and grappled for understanding. Before I could say anything, plead my case, *beg* even, the elevator doors slid closed, shutting down my dreams.

CHAPTER TWO

JACK

IT WAS the picture of my brothers together at Gigi's Diner that did me in. Their arms were thrown over each other's shoulders, their smiles bright beneath the beaming pendant lights. The diner was crammed past capacity, people spilling from the booths, others leaning between occupied stools at the long counter. I could practically feel the sticky linoleum under my feet as if I was there, smell the potatoes frying in the back and the sizzle of energy in the room. Everyone in town had shown up for Wyatt's birthday party.

Everyone but *me*. Which was fair, I guess, since I didn't live in Arcadia Creek anymore. But I didn't even get an invitation, despite the fact that Wyatt was my cousin and once my closest friend. Dallas was only an hour away from my hometown. I could have driven out for a birthday party.

Except I was about to get on a flight to Florida for Kevin's elopement cruise. So *technically* I couldn't have made it to Wyatt's party last night, since I was packing and tying up last minute work things to make this trip possible. He and Kevin had never been big fans of each other—Wyatt, my small-town best friend, and Kevin, my grad school roommate turned best friend, had never clicked. Telling Wyatt I couldn't be there because of a commitment to Kevin would have been worse.

So maybe it was a good thing they didn't want me at the party anyway.

I clicked off my phone so Instagram wouldn't show me any more pictures of my family hanging out without me. Overhead, an airline worker made a staticky last call for a flight to Chicago, and I pulled out my AirPods to cancel the noise. I was boarding in twenty-five minutes, and I planned on spending every last minute watching downloaded episodes of *Redone*. It was only the best renovation show HGTV had to offer. You didn't have to be middle-aged or a woman to appreciate a good renovation.

Which was a blessed thing, since I was a late-twenties man who couldn't seem to get enough of the fixer upper shows. (Yes, I'd been down to Waco. I'd pretended I was too cool for it, yet I'd geeked out internally, like a twelve-year-old who'd just been given his first paintball gun.)

It was the best thing my dad ever taught me—how to strip paint and stain old furniture, how a new set of hardware and a little polish could completely transform a dresser from a mid-century nightmare to modern and chic. My Dallas apartment didn't have a work shed though, so I had to satisfy myself by watching other people do it for now.

A woman walked past me, catching my attention. I recognized that low, tight bun and the concentration on her brown eyebrows, bunched so tight they were causing canyons to develop in the lines on her forehead. Lauren Foley, sister of the bride. She was just as pretty as I remembered and looked just as stern. She could be holding a stick, ready to rap kids' knuckles or walk slowly down the library aisles, searching for people to shush.

When Kevin and Amelia set us up on a blind date, it had started well enough. She was intelligent, and I'd thought of her as a breath of fresh air compared to the women I typically saw. She could actually discuss things of value and had insight to share. None of that breathy, fluttering crap with Lauren. She'd felt authentic.

To say nothing of the fact that she was beautiful, her hazel eyes bright, her lips full. She had the same high cheekbones as her sister, but despite their similarities, Lauren was clearly older than Amelia. Mature, like a good cheese. Which was exactly what every woman wanted to hear.

Just call me a charmer.

Like an utter creep, I watched her settle on a seat a few rows ahead of me and felt the briefest temptation to go sit by her. Rip off the Band-Aid, get it over with, let her know we were on the same flight from Dallas to Miami. But the woman was a little crazy. Like, ditched-our-date-before-it-was-even-over crazy. To be fair, things were tense before I'd felt a little queasy and got up to go to the bathroom, but she'd never told me why she used that opportunity to sneak out. The few times we'd seen each other since that awful night left no mystery as to how she felt about me.

It didn't make me like her all that much either.

Which was a shame, because I think we might have gotten along if she didn't have a ruler stuck up her butt. From what Amelia had said about her, she didn't know how to have fun, which I could readily believe.

My phone rang, and I answered it. "What's up?"

"Hey man, you on your way?" Kevin asked. I could hear that he was outside. He'd gotten to Florida already. Amelia had a few errands she wanted to run before guests arrived.

"About to get on the plane."

"Okay, cool. Cool." The silence stretched.

This was not a good sign. "What's wrong? I got my room squared away. The cruise line let me add on to Lucas's—"

"No, it's not that." He cleared his throat. "You know Amelia's friend Sydney . . ."

My stomach shifted into a hard, solid rock. *Friend* wasn't really an accurate descriptor. That woman breathed drama. "You told me she wasn't invited."

"She wasn't. But after Amelia saw how easily they let you join Lucas's room, she asked Sydney. She didn't expect her to be available at the last minute. I don't think she has a job," he added as an afterthought.

"And now we all get to put up with her for a week."

"Listen, at least you don't have to deal with my Aunt Nona getting handsy. There *are* benefits to eloping."

True. She'd been a little too fresh during that Fourth of July BBQ last year. But she would still be better than Sydney.

"Can you call it eloping when you've had the wedding planned for months?" I asked.

"I can when none of my family knows about it. I'm going to return home a married man, and I don't even have to put up with all the typical wedding crap. Just a cruise, a ceremony on the beach, and my best friends."

"Your mom is going to kill you," I said, cringing.

"Maybe. But she doesn't want this wedding to happen anyway, so I'm saving her from needing to witness it."

And saving his fiancée from having to put on a face and try to please in-laws who would only ruin the day for her. This way, Amelia got to enjoy her wedding without being called a gold digger. Which she clearly wasn't, or she wouldn't be teaching music to kindergarteners. "Honestly, I thought you were just being lazy, man. But it's kind of sweet you're sparing Amelia from your mom."

"Just call me Tenderheart."

"I can call you *what?*"

"It's a Care Bear—you know what? Don't worry about it. Elementary school stuff."

Kevin, six-foot-two and all brawn, knowing the names of the Care Bears? His fiancée had obviously impacted his life. Why wouldn't Mr. and Mrs. Dougherty want her in their lives? Unsolved mysteries of the Texan oil tycoons. "This is a side of you I've never seen."

"Ames makes me a softy." He must have moved the phone away from his face because he shouted something unintelligible and then came back to the speaker. "Gotta go. We're grabbing food at six."

"I won't make it in time for that."

"Okay. See you at the hotel?"

"That's the plan."

We hung up. I glanced up to find Lauren still sitting there, chewing on one of her nails. She looked stressed, her focus on her open laptop. Maybe a little break would be good for her. Lighten her up a little. Prepare her for the cruise crowd.

I put my AirPods away and gathered up my backpack before making my way toward her. I hoped she would look up at some point, but her attention was on the computer, her concentration unbreakable.

Well, let's test that theory.

I plopped down on the chair next to hers and immediately felt her stiffen. She glanced over at me and the concentration on her face morphed into irritation, but only for a second.

"Hey there, Sunshine." I put on my best smile just to lighten her up.

"Jack." I didn't realize my name could sound like a condemnation, but here we are.

"Looks like we're on the same flight."

"What luck."

She dropped her attention back to the computer. Dismissed. She just needed a sweater and a pair of glasses because she had the cranky librarian attitude down. I looked at her tightly wound bun at the base of her head and wondered what it would look like undone. If I reached over and pulled it out of its somehow magically held together knot thing, would she loosen up?

The impulse was weird, and I shook it off. Despite her schoolmarm-ness, she was so pretty. I bet she'd be even prettier if she liked me.

Creating a civil space between us was going to be tougher than I realized. I turned up my charm a little. "Maybe we'll get lucky and our seats will—"

"Be on opposite ends of the plane?"

"Ouch." Okay, noted: impervious to charm.

She lifted one eyebrow but still didn't remove her gaze from the computer. I hoped this wasn't how the entire cruise would go. Maybe, for the sake of Kevin and Amelia, we could come to a truce now.

Her focus on the spreadsheet drew my attention there, and I looked at the file name at the top of the screen. *Dougherty_Wedding_Naussau*

Hold up. Lauren had made a spreadsheet for her sister's elopement? Didn't that take away from the feeling of running away or the magic of eloping? Next she was going to produce a list of acceptable restaurants and timetables of the various island tides. "I didn't realize we had a schedule."

Lauren shut her laptop, frowning. "This is personal."

"A personal spreadsheet?" Good grief, she was more rigid than I realized. "For your sister's wedding."

"It's all my information in one place and a perfectly reasonable thing to have before a vacation."

"So explain the outfits tab, then. You intending to consult the spreadsheet before you get dressed? Actually looking through your suitcase isn't good enough?"

Lauren narrowed her eyes. "At least I have a plan for coordinating my outfits." She gave me a gentle sweep I felt to my toes.

What was wrong with my shorts and tee? So what if my

yellow shirt was a little loud. This was a vacation. "There's nothing wrong with color."

Her raised eyebrows spoke differently. "Of course not. Everyone wants to be picked out of a crowd by how badly their shirt is burning retinas."

"At least I won't blend into the sand."

She glanced at her own khaki joggers and white tee. "It's called sophistication. Look it up."

"So right next to strict, right? Or is it closer to stiff? Stern? Stringent?"

"Wow. You know a lot of words."

I was impressed with myself as well. "I also know spontaneity. Google that one, Sunshine."

Lauren's hazel eyes spit fire. Maybe coming over here wasn't such a good idea after all. We had to spend the next week together for Amelia and Kevin's wedding, and I didn't want our mutual hostility to ruin anything for them. Time to suppress my innate desire to hogtie the woman and try to make peace. "Listen, Lauren—"

"It's okay, you know." She slid her laptop into its case and proceeded to put it away. "We don't have to do this."

Do this? Do *what*, exactly? Fight or try to make up?

"I'll see you in Florida." She stood, muttering, "Unfortunately." She shot me a brief smile before walking away. I watched her buy a water bottle in the mini mart across from our gate—DFW really needed to get with the times and provide water bottle refill stations—and snag a bag of Chex Mix.

She chomped away at her snack while waiting in line to board and ended up sitting about five rows ahead of me on the plane.

No, I wasn't a creep. I didn't know why I couldn't help clocking her movements after the solid rejection she'd delivered. Something in me was ignited by her. Was it the challenge? Or just the fact that her dislike rubbed me wrong? It felt so unjustified.

Not everyone has to like you, Jack. Which was true, but also, usually they had a good reason. Lauren, from what I could tell, didn't have any. Oh well. I had eight days with the woman and a new goal: she was going to be my friend by the end of it.

CHAPTER THREE

LAUREN

THE ENTIRE FLIGHT between DFW and Miami was taken up with scheming to fill the empty slot created by Fantasy Con pulling out of our hotel, but still I got nowhere. Major conferences were booked out months, sometimes years, in advance, and I didn't know what I could pull in to make up for the loss of the fantasy nerds. There were *a lot* of them, and they showed up in droves to meet their favorite authors and actors.

Brainstorming was made more difficult by the knowledge that my nemesis was somewhere behind me on the plane, but I refused to turn around and see where he'd sat. Jack was best left off my mind.

He had clearly picked up the message, too, because I didn't see him after landing. Not at the baggage claim, or waiting in the humid heat for my Uber, or at the hotel check-in desk.

It was like Jack never got off the plane in Florida . . . which was just too good to be true.

My employee discount with the Hunnam Group had gotten us a good set of rooms for tonight, and I reached the suite before anyone else. The whole bridal party was already in town, but they had gone to dinner while I snacked on pistachios and set up for Amelia's bachelorette party. It wasn't that I was anti-social, exactly. It was that I didn't quite vibe with Amelia and Kevin's friends. They were all sorority girls and frat guys who were still stuck in that Greek mentality three years after leaving college. We just didn't enjoy the same things.

Except for pampering. Everyone loved to be pampered.

Chocolate-covered strawberries, drinks, and an empty ice bucket sat on the little table next to an array of nail polishes, buffer blocks, face masks, lotions, and creams. I'd called to see about a massage therapist, but Amelia vetoed it quickly and told me she and Kevin had a couple's massage booked on the cruise already.

When everything was set up, I cued up *The Proposal* on my phone and connected the Bluetooth to the TV, tuning into the beginning to make sure it would work. Loud, feminine voices carried down the hall outside my door, and a tightness in my stomach proved exactly how eager I was for the party to descend on me. I liked Cara, my sister's college roommate, but she could get a little loud and sloppy, and we just didn't mesh super well.

For being sisters who looked almost identical despite the four-year age gap between us, Amelia and I could not be more opposite —including our choice in friends. But I could endure anything for my sister. It had only been me and Amelia for so long anyway. We were each other's rocks, our family, and our sole support system.

Amelia must have picked up her key from the front desk, because there was a beep and the door swung open to the sound of many girls hollering their excitement.

When I said many girls, I meant *three*, but it was one girl more than I'd expected, and the new addition had the pipes of four hyped-up cheerleaders. Sydney Browne—Amelia's longtime friend and bane of my existence—followed Cara into the room, dying from exaggerated laughter. I immediately wanted to ram a chocolate strawberry into each ear.

Amelia waved at me but turned back to talk to Kevin at the door for a minute. I couldn't hear what they were saying, but they both stopped to listen to someone hanging back in the hallway. Even from this distance I would recognize that terrible, low, smooth-like-a-chocolate-fountain voice anywhere. Jack freaking Fletcher. *Again*. It wasn't enough that he'd had to pounce on me at the airport. He was going to be here the entire trip.

My body had an involuntary physical reaction to the man. It clenched and screamed to flee while outwardly I froze and suppressed my unreasonable reactions. I had been warned, and *still* I reacted like this every time he was around. I'd had the entire plane ride to come to terms with the fact that the man I most despised would now be part of this wedding weekend. And I was determined to pretend he didn't bother me. So *why* couldn't I get a grip on myself?

Before I could get another glimpse of my nemesis, though, Amelia closed the door and pivoted to face me, throwing up her arms in the air and squealing until she had me in her tight grip. "Sissy!"

Oh gosh, how I hated that term. "Ames!" I said, squeezing her tightly. "And then there were *four!*"

"Oh, yeah." Amelia stepped back, squeezing my upper arms. "We called the cruise line and they let us add Sydney to Cara's room! Isn't that great news?"

"Fantastic!" Maybe I had this sorority girl thing down. I just had to say everything enthusiastically and smile extra brightly, even when I wanted to rip my hair out, right? Immediately my brain started working around the dilemma of adding a fourth woman to festivities that were carefully planned for three. We could each squeeze a bit of our face mask out for the fourth. Everyone would sacrifice a little, but there would be enough to go around, surely.

Fifteen strawberries didn't divide evenly into fours, but I could have three and the other girls could each have four.

Everything would work out. It just required a bit of math.

Cara tossed her bag onto the foot of one of the beds and unzipped it. "I don't know what to wear tonight! I should save my best dresses for the ship, right? I feel like it's a better investment to look good then. We'll be seeing the same people for seven days."

"You can wear one of them twice though," Sydney said. "The only people who will see you in it twice are the guys."

I sat on the edge of the other bed, reworking the evening while adding an extra woman to our plans, but my head popped up at this. "The guys?"

"Kevin, Lucas, and Jack," Cara said, rummaging through her bag and pulling out different dress options.

I swung my attention to my sister. The guilt splashed over her pinking cheeks was proof that I was not going to like what I was about to hear. "We were thinking of going out tonight!" she said. "Wouldn't that be fun? Kev and I don't want traditional bachelor/bachelorette parties, so we figured we would combine them. What do you think?"

I thought that I had—as the maid of honor—been granted full authority over this evening and had proceeded to plan the spa night my sister specifically requested. A night out in Miami sounded awful.

What did one even wear to go clubbing? That was *so* not my scene.

But Amelia's eyebrows were drawn together in worry, and it was my job to keep those eyebrows perfectly in line. I sucked in a breath, ready to lie. "Oh, of course! So much fun!" There was that enthusiasm. So! Many! Exclamation points!

Amelia's shoulders deflated in a relieved exhale. "Good. You had me worried. You've already put so much effort into this."

She swept her hand toward the chocolate-covered strawberries and face masks.

I reached for the remote to power off the TV before she noticed that too. "No, not at all. You're the bride. You'll only get married once."

"Hopefully," Sydney muttered.

Cara laughed and slapped her on the arm.

"I mean, you never know!" Sydney said, flipping back her long, black hair.

Cara hushed her, and Amelia laughed lightly, but it was still such a weird thing to say. I really wished whatever reconciliation that had permitted Sydney on the trip hadn't happened so it could still have been just the three of us tonight. Sydney was such a wildcard, and this wedding would be difficult enough for Amelia to manage emotionally. It was sure to bring up the grief of not having either of our parents or our grandma here, all three of whom had died far earlier than they should have.

"You know," Amelia said gently, "if you'd rather stay in, Lauren, that's fine. I'm not even getting married tomorrow. We could do our pre-wedding spa night on the boat at an actual spa. This can just be going out for fun."

Hope curled into my chest like a beacon of sunlight. "I can't stay in, Ames. I'm here for you."

"But you hate going out like this. It's really fine." She widened her eyes, staring at me like she could see through my face. "I mean it. We'll be spending the entire week together."

I wouldn't read too much into her assurances, because it almost felt like she'd prefer I didn't go . . . and I knew that wasn't the case. I was her sister. These other women were friends of hers, but I was her *sister*. There was no trumping me when it came to the important people in her life—except Kevin, of course. We were literally all each other had when it came to family.

"Okay. I'll finish up my work here so I don't have to worry about it on the ship."

Amelia looked almost relieved. "Good. I'm glad you aren't coming out of obligation. We'll have loads of fun on the ship."

"And *we'll* have loads of fun tonight," Cara said, shimmying.

Sydney stripped down and pulled on a gold sequined dress. I averted my gaze while they all got ready for the club. I picked up one of the face masks and my pajamas—a button-down cotton shirt with matching shorts. "If y'all are done in here, I'm going to shower."

They all confirmed it was fine. I took the opportunity to scrub the airplane from my hair. I pulled on my sensible cotton pajamas, threw my hair up in a towel, and leaned close to the steamy mirror to apply the lime green face mask. It had said all natural ingredients on the front of the package, but I imagined that wasn't the case. No avocados were this bright unless they were made out of fabric or adhered to a preteen girl's water bottle.

The room was blissfully silent when I got out of the bathroom, and I felt guilty for being slightly relieved I didn't have to attend the party tonight. But never mind that. I would watch *The Proposal*, rejuvenate my t-zone, stuff my face with strawberries, and keep searching for a solution to my promotion problem.

But first, ice. I grabbed the bucket and my key card, slid my feet into my flats, and left the room in search of the ice machine. It really wasn't the end of the world that half of the wedding party were people I didn't like. It was only seven days, and I could handle anything—including screeches that masqueraded as voices—for seven days.

The ice machine was at the end of the hall. I found it easily and filled my bucket. Before I made it back to my room, the door next to mine swung open and a man stepped out, colliding with me and my freshly filled bucket of ice. The bucket flew out of my hands and swung through the air, sending thick ice cubes all over the carpet.

"I'm so sorry," he said.

"It's fine—" My words lodged in my throat when I lifted my head from the ice massacre and leveled my gaze on the perpetrator. *Of course* it would be Jack. His dark eyebrows jumped up on his forehead, and I was grateful for the crusty, half-dried spa mask covering my skin, because lime green sludge was bound to hide the blush bleeding into my cheeks.

"Ah. So you opted not to join the girls?" he asked, in a tone that said *why am I not surprised?*

My excuse stuck in my throat. I didn't owe him an explanation. Instead, I picked up my ice bucket and went to move around him. "If you'll excuse me."

"Hold up." He put a hand up. His stupid-handsome face looked confused. He'd changed out of his earlier outfit and now wore fitted chino shorts and a short-sleeved button-down. It accentuated his bicep just below the sleeve. A bicep I would not pay any more attention to. "What's that about?" he asked.

"What's what about?"

He seemed to weigh his words for only a second. "Have I done something to offend you?"

"Are you joking?" The image of him making out with the waitress in the middle of our date flashed through my mind. In his defense, I guess he might not know I'd seen him with her. Five minutes after he'd excused himself for the restroom, I had gotten up to take a phone call. When I was heading back to the table, I saw them in the narrow hallway at the back of the restaurant. He couldn't have seen me, since he'd been otherwise occupied. But when he returned to our table to find me gone, that should have been a giveaway that he'd been caught, right?

Both of his hands were up now. "I realize we didn't exactly hit it off when Kevin and Amelia set us up—"

"That might be the biggest understatement of the year."

"—but we're stuck together now for a week. We can let the past stay in the past, right?"

I pressed my lips firmly together. For Amelia? Yeah, I could pretend I didn't hate this guy for seven days. I'd already planned on doing exactly that, but then I faced him and irritation oozed from me like a runny nose. I know that's gross. So is Jack.

"Oh my *gosh*, I'm so glad I caught you!" The high-pitched voice grated over my skin, and I didn't have to turn around to know Sydney was walking our way. It was a point of pride for me that I wasn't comparing my cotton pajamas, lime green face, and towel-covered hair to her clubbing dress.

"Heyyy, Sydney," Jack said. The strain in his voice was like ClingWrap pulled so tight over a bowl of leftovers it was a miracle it didn't rip. "What's up?"

She slinked closer, and her eyes were doing all sorts of speaking that her mouth wasn't. Mostly they were saying *I want you.*

Well, there was clearly history here.

"I came back to the room for my phone. Silly me. Totally forgot it." She laughed. "Want to share an Uber over to the club? Everyone else has gone on already."

Her story was too much. If I was the detective type, which I totally was—*hello* cozy mysteries—I would deduce Sydney sent everyone else along so she could ride over to the club with Jack. And Jack clearly wanted nothing to do with this scenario.

"You know, on second thought," he said, stepping back and sliding his arm around my waist so seamlessly I was shocked into silence. "I think I'll hang back tonight. I don't want Lauren to be lonely. What kind of boyfriend would I be then?"

CHAPTER FOUR

LAUREN

WHAT? I sputtered, choking on my own shock and spit. Jack Fletcher, spawn of the devil himself, had just called himself my boyfriend.

"Sorry, babe," Jack said, cradling me to him and softly hitting my back. "Did you swallow your gum again?" He looked up at Sydney and added endearingly, "She's always doing that."

I think my surprise was blocking my ability to speak, because I couldn't form the words to call out his lies.

Not that it mattered. Sydney appeared to believe we were dating as much as she believed I had just swallowed my nonexistent gum. "You two?" She pointed between us. "Together?"

"Yeah. Cute, right?" Jack sighed lightly. Overacting, much? "But do me a favor and don't say anything to Amelia. We haven't broken the news yet."

She looked even less believing then. "Sure."

"What a relief." Jack grinned, squeezing me, his warm fingers digging into my arm. "We didn't want to steal the spotlight this weekend, so we weren't planning on saying anything until the wedding was over."

Sydney narrowed her gaze. "Okay. I'm going to leave now."

She turned away from us to go back the way she came, and we stood in utter silence until she disappeared around the corner to where the elevators were.

I dislodged myself from his hold and spun to face him. "What the heck was that?"

His arms went up in defense. "I don't know. I panicked."

I opened my door, stepping over half-melted ice cubes and carrying my empty bucket.

Jack followed me into the room and closed the door behind himself. "I should probably wait until she's gone for real before I head back to my room."

"She never actually came in here for her phone, so she could show up at any second."

"We both know the phone thing was fake. It's probably in her purse right now."

I lowered my voice. "But if it's not, and she wasn't lying, then she'll be back any second. I suggest you keep your voice down before you make both of us look like lying scum."

He shook his head softly. "Man, you really don't like me, do you?"

I stared at him. Could his memory be that short? "I was under the impression the feeling was mutual."

Jack's eyebrows lifted. He slid his hands into his shorts pockets and looked far too good in that casual pose. "Well, then. I guess you won't be helping me keep up this ruse all week, huh?"

Laughter bubbled from my chest, but his expression didn't shift, his green eyes locked on me. I swallowed. "Oh, you were serious?"

He pointed back at the door. "We both know the first thing Sydney will do when she sees Amelia is ask her if we're dating."

"And Amelia will tell her we aren't because she knows how much I can't stand—" I cleared my throat. "How incompatible we are."

His mouth turned up on one side in a half smile. "Nice almost save."

The door beeped, and Jack jumped toward me, his arms going around my waist and pulling me close. He was like a romance ninja finding ways to get me into compromising positions in the blink of an eye. He tilted his face down to look at me, and my breath caught. He was so close I could see the varying shades of green in his eyes, smell whatever cologne he'd lightly applied. His breath was coming quickly, his hands stilling on my back. Despite the fact that I loathed this man, the way he held me now felt . . . really good. Like, far better than I would've ever expected it to. I almost couldn't blame that waitress now for making out with my date when his touch sent so much warmth coursing through my body.

"Oh my gosh," a woman said. Only, it wasn't Sydney. My eyes widened, I tilted my face to better look at Jack, and my nose bumped his.

"Amelia," I whispered. She must have been waiting for Sydney downstairs after all.

Jack swore softly.

"Sydney was telling the truth?" Amelia asked. "I didn't believe her."

I stepped back from Jack, but he didn't release me. Instead we both turned to face Amelia with guilty expressions, his arms around me possessively.

"We can explain—"

"But should we?" Jack asked. "I mean, now that the secret is out, we don't really have to hide anymore."

I looked at him sharply. His eyes widened infinitesimally. He was practically begging me with just a look.

Kevin stepped into the doorway behind Amelia, laughing. His dark blond hair was cut close on the sides and styled on top. He had more muscle in his arms than I possessed in my entire body. But despite looking like a meathead, he was a softie. "You two? I never would have guessed. Especially not after y'all suffered through that terrible date."

I laughed awkwardly, so unsure about the current situation. I owed Jack nothing, but his desperation made me feel for him a little.

Not that he deserved mercy after the way he talked about me after our date. *Uptight. No fun. It's no wonder she's single.*

That last one still stung.

"Why did you try to keep it from us, though?" Amelia asked.

"We didn't want to steal your thunder," Jack said.

She looked at me.

"It's your wedding week," I added, before I could think better of it. "It's all about you."

There was a beat of silence when she looked from me to Jack, then she sagged as though someone had lifted the weight of ten cozy mysteries from her shoulders—hardback editions. "Oh my gosh, what an utter relief! Now I understand why you were so weirdly okay with him being on the cruise when I called to warn you. I still thought this week was going to be a disaster with the two of you, but now I don't have to worry."

Excuse me? Disaster? My spine straightened. I was the most put-together twenty-eight-year-old on the planet. I was exactly the opposite of a disaster. But her relief was almost palpable, and something about that struck a chord within me.

"So you're both staying in?" Kevin asked, slipping his arm around Amelia's waist.

"Yeah," Jack said. "I think I'll hang back. Sorry, man."

"It's all good. Lucas is here, anyway. We'll catch you later."

They turned to go, but not before Amelia gave me another long look, tilting her head to the side. "I'm so glad, Lo. I really love this for you."

My stomach churned. "Thanks."

When the door closed behind them, Jack and I remained

frozen for a little while, listening to the voices trail down the hall.

"It looked like Sydney couldn't even wait until they left the lobby to spill the news," Jack said, his arms still around me.

I stepped out of his hold, his fingers dragging over my waist while I put distance between us. "Didn't she say she sent them ahead to the club? It looks like she lied about more than just leaving her phone behind."

"Sounds accurate," he muttered. He ran a hand through his messy brown hair and dropped on the edge of the bed. A bright green spot marred the tip of his nose, and I suppressed a laugh. "What?" he asked.

I fetched a washcloth and got it damp with warm water, then handed it to him. "You have a little something on your nose."

"You have a little something all over your face." He wiped his nose, then handed me the washcloth.

I tossed it on the table. "I'll get it later. We need to talk about this now."

"Talk about what?"

"Us! You've roped my sister into it now. I don't lie to her." As the adult figure in her life, it was a point of pride for me that I straddled the big sister and mom lines for Amelia so well. Honesty was a huge part of what made that successful.

"Don't think of it as a lie, then. You saw how relieved she was to see us together."

"Yeah, heaven knows why."

He lifted an eyebrow. "Less contention, clearly."

Was he joking? This was a nightmare dropped on us by the romcom gods so . . . what? We could suffer? I didn't deserve to be punished like this. "You sound like you actually want to pretend to date for the whole week."

"I do. What's the worst that can happen? Your sister is happy and I get to keep Sydney off my back. It's only seven days. Then we can part ways and never see each other again."

"Except your best friend is about to become my brother-in-law. I'm thinking this isn't the last time we'll be forced to interact."

"You're already really good at hating me. I don't think we'll need to worry about being believable exes."

He had a point there. But still. There was no reason for me to participate. "I can fix this. I'll just tell Amelia the truth. When I explain what happened in the hall, she'll get the whole misunderstanding."

"Oh, come on. Help a guy out? Sydney is freaking relentless. I broke up with her after a few weeks and she's never gotten over it. You'd think we were together for years by the way she acts."

So Sydney wasn't just into him . . . she'd dated him. That was different, but he still seemed a little desperate. "Then maybe when she comes onto you, you should tell her no." I got a fresh washcloth, rinsing it and wiping the green goop from my face. I scrubbed it away using all my pent-up energy until my skin was red and raw. I removed the towel from my head, ran my fingers through my wet hair and flipped my head back. When I looked back at Jack, he was staring.

"Okay, I know I look ridiculous, but you don't have to stare."

He swallowed. "I just didn't expect your hair to be so . . . much longer."

Weird. Why had he even been thinking about my hair? It was perfectly mid-length, too. Most people wouldn't call it long unless they were comparing it to a pixie cut. I shook it out and crossed my arms over my chest. "Why are you still here, anyway?"

"Because I'm trying to convince you to be my girlfriend for a week. I'll pay you."

"I don't want your money."

A grin spread over his lips. "I'll pay you in favors."

I flushed. "I don't want anything from you."

"Come *on*, Lauren. There has to be something I can give you."

"There's not. I really can't do this, Jack. I'm not a good liar. I'd give us away so fast, it's not even worth trying."

He stood up and dipped his head, holding my gaze. "Give me a day."

"What?" It was hard to think with the weight of his attention on me like this. I prided myself on my ability to be unfazed by hot men, but Jack was breaking down all my carefully erected walls right now with his smoldering eyes. He wanted this badly —like, *really* badly.

"Just the first day." He stepped closer, bringing a soft cloud of cologne that had no business smelling so good. "If we break up now, it'll be obvious that I made the whole thing up. Just give me one day—the first day on the boat—and we'll break up after dinner tomorrow night. Then I won't look like such an obvious liar."

I gazed at his beseeching eyes. Honestly, I didn't want to be caught in a lie, either. There was no mistaking how relieved Amelia was. How would she feel if I told her the truth? Maybe tomorrow night we could have an amicable break up in front of everyone and the focus could return to the wedding we were all there to celebrate.

"Fine. One day."

Jack grinned. His arms went around me and he laid a kiss on my cheek, but he backed up almost as quickly as he'd approached. "You're the best, Lauren. I owe you. Big time."

"Yes, you do." I stepped back so he couldn't touch me again. It sent a weird buzz through me that I didn't want to own. "And we will not forget it."

He dipped his head. "I'll be off then."

"Shouldn't we come up with a plan first?"

"For what?"

"For believability. How we got together. All of that." I'd seen enough movies to know that in fake dating relationships, this question *always* came up. "Or do you just want to wing it tomorrow?"

"No, you're right." He shifted closer. "We need to come up with our story. So? How did it happen?"

I studied the bit of collarbone peeking just out of his collar. "You felt awful about the way our date turned out, so you pursued me relentlessly until I agreed to go out with you again. Then you charmed me until I decided to give you a chance."

"Hmm." He bent his knuckle and lifted my chin so I was forced to look him in the eye. "We want it to be believable though, right?"

"Yes." I backed up and his hand fell. "Which is why there would have to be some serious effort on your part. Amelia knows how angry I was after our date."

Jack was quiet for a second. He folded his arms over his chest. "I really made that bad of an impression on you?"

Was he surprised by this? "That's a safe analysis."

"Can you put it behind us for a day? Just so we seem a little bit like we like each other?"

"We can't even come up with a believable story for how we got together, Jack. I don't know if we're going to fool everyone for an entire day."

He nodded softly, his eyes flicking over my face. "What if we say we just ran into each other?"

Literally. "It's the truth, I guess." Both at the airport and again here.

"Yeah. It is. So I ran into you and we got talking, and then boom . . . the next thing we knew, my arms were around you and the rest is history."

The image invoked warmth I shouldn't feel, so I shoved it aside. "That's . . . not actually a lie."

Jack grinned. "So maybe we can make it a little believable. I have faith in us, Lauren."

"That makes one of us."

"So, what are you doing tonight that kept you from going out with the girls?" His gaze swept the room and stopped on the nail buffer blocks and chocolate-covered strawberries.

I cringed. "Clubs aren't really my scene. I decided to stick with the original bachelorette party plan."

"Which was green goo and hygiene?"

"A spa night in, yes."

"Don't let me keep you from your exciting evening, then."

"Rejuvenating evening," I corrected, rolling my eyes. "Tomorrow my skin will *glow*."

Jack laughed, then paused at the door. "What, no good night kiss?"

"You would be so lucky."

"Yeah, I would." He quirked a smile at me and disappeared.

This was going to be interesting.

CHAPTER FIVE

JACK

KEVIN GROANED, rolling over on his bed until he hovered dangerously close to the edge of the mattress. I blinked away my sleepiness and checked the clock. 6:34. If I was back home in Central Time, it would be 5:34, and I'd be heading to the gym right now. Since I'd had an early night last night, I wasn't suffering for the early morning. It was just as well my body would wake up like normal.

I wondered if Lauren was awake now, too. She seemed like the kind of woman who woke up at the same time every day, ate the same bagel with a fresh smoothie, and logged an hour on the Peloton. Some sort of routine that led to a shower, very little makeup, and winding her hair so tight it suffocated the part of her brain that controlled relaxation or joy. I still wondered if loosening her hair would also loosen her personality, too.

Had she tried that?

"What time is it?" Kevin groaned again, his blond hair standing on end.

"Just after 6:30."

"Ugh. I have to meet Ames for breakfast in an hour." He

rolled over, burying his face in the pillow. "Do you think she'll still marry me if I don't show up?"

Since he was being rhetorical, I didn't respond right away. Lucas snored from the sofa bed, so I lowered my voice. "You could just tell her you aren't ready yet."

"I'll be ready by then."

"How about I shower first and give you ten extra minutes to sleep."

"You're the best, *best man*."

I saluted him, then unzipped my bag to get a change of clothes and my bathroom bag.

"You know," came his groggy voice. "I never would have put you with Lauren, but it kind of works."

So much for Kevin going back to sleep. He was clearly delirious. Foggy sleep brain or whatever. "You think so?"

"Dude, I don't know. I guess I'm just hopeful. Maybe if she's with you, she'll lighten up."

I laughed. "Unlikely. Lauren is . . . Lauren."

"Well, a man can hope." He rolled onto his back and scrubbed a hand over his face. "Amelia complains a lot about her. They don't really connect anymore, and it wears on her, you know? Lauren is always working, like even when they're together. She's permanently grafted to her laptop. Well, *you* would know, I guess."

Guilt swept through me. I didn't think I'd be too bothered lying to Kevin, because I didn't think he'd pay much attention to the fake relationship. He didn't usually care who I dated as long as she didn't screw up our poker nights, so his current investment in this—however slight—worried me. "Lauren's coming on the cruise, at least. That's putting her sister before her work."

"I bet she'll be in her room the whole time working, though. You know the girls don't have any other family, right? Lauren is all Amelia has. And she can't even put her computer away for five minutes to spend time with her."

"That's pretty sad." No other family? At all? I remembered when their grandma died a few years ago and how wrecked Amelia was, but I didn't realize family was such a rarity for her. When you grew up like I did, where it was impossible to go anywhere in town without running into someone you were related to, the idea of having no one was foreign.

"I know." He yawned. "If you could make her be a little more present, that would change Amelia's entire cruise."

"More present. Got it."

"Thanks, man."

I took my stuff into the bathroom and spent my shower worrying about how I was messing with the Foley family dynamics. Lauren cared about her sister, that much was plain. But even a workaholic would put her job aside for her sister's wedding, right?

When I got out of the shower, my shorts and T-shirt on and my hair a mess, I tossed my bathroom bag onto my suitcase. A door somewhere in the hallway closed with a thud, and I hurried over to the peephole just in time to see Lauren walk by.

My feet were sliding into my shoes before I had time to logically think through my decision. She was on her way somewhere —breakfast, maybe?—and I was going to put myself in her path.

"I'll catch you later," I said, grabbing my wallet and slipping out the door before Kevin could respond. The hallway was empty. I raced down it and saw the elevator doors slide closed. Shoot. Just missed her.

I hit the button and the second elevator opened right away. Guess I was going after her.

I stepped inside and hit the lobby button. Why was I putting myself in a position to spar with a woman who despised me? I didn't know.

But I couldn't get the lonely picture Kevin had painted out of my head, and I wanted to square our "relationship" away before everyone else woke up.

At least that's what I was telling myself.

CHAPTER SIX

LAUREN

I LEFT all three women sleeping like zombies when I went out in search of breakfast. My non-clubbing evening might have been a little less exciting than theirs, but at least I wouldn't be fighting bags under my eyes today. Amelia needed to monitor her sleeping over the next few nights if she wanted to look fresh for her wedding pictures.

I hit the button for the lobby and glanced at my reflection in the glossy elevator doors. My linen shorts revealed far more pale skin than I was used to—my legs were practically begging for a sunburn. I debated returning to the room to slather a preparatory layer of sunscreen over my legs, but my 85+ SPF was neatly packed away in my bag that was now waiting by the door. I could wait until we reached the ship for that. I couldn't be burned in a hotel cafe anyway. Probably.

The smell of coffee roasting and bacon sizzling reached me before I caught sight of the café. I hiked my computer bag higher on my shoulder and walked up to the counter.

"Good morning, Sunshine!" a voice called from behind me. Deep, smooth, and just like a glass of orange juice to the face.

I turned to find Jack approaching, his hands casually slung in his shorts pockets and his hair still damp from a shower. Could I have *some* peace before I had to perform for the rest of the bridal party later today? My shoulders bunched with tension, but my distaste seemed to go right over Jack's head. "Did you follow me?"

He flashed me a smile. "Do you smell like bacon? Because then *yes*, I did."

"Can I help you?" the barista asked. I was glad for the excuse to turn my back on Jack. I ordered a bowl of oatmeal with a glass of orange juice before snagging a booth. I pulled out my computer and powered it up.

Jack ordered his breakfast before coming to sit across from me.

I looked up from my computer when he slid onto the seat, my eyebrows rising.

"Oh, are you saving this for someone else?" He pointed down at the bench his obnoxiously perfect rear end was gracing. "I can move over there and sit by you."

"I was thinking you could move over there." I jerked my head toward the other side of the café.

"But what would your sister or Kevin think if they saw us eating on opposite ends of the room? That would be hard to explain. They might think it's weird."

"Weird is having to sit across from you while I try to choke down my oatmeal."

"If you hate oatmeal so much, you should have ordered something else."

I fought a laugh, keeping my face perfectly plain. "It's not the oatmeal making me sick to my stomach."

A waitress delivered our breakfasts. "Can I get you anything else?"

"I'm okay for now," I said, smiling at her.

Jack nodded in agreement, and we were left alone again. He scooted his glass of juice closer to himself and ran his finger along the rim, looking down at the orange liquid. His hands were large, his knuckles sprinkled with dark hair. They were lightly tanned, just like the rest of his skin. He was probably one of those people who went outside for an hour and achieved a perfectly golden hue. I hated those people. I went outside for an hour and my skin resembled a fire hydrant.

He looked up at me. "Today is really going to be a challenge for you, isn't it?"

"You mean making sure everything is perfect for my only sister's wedding cruise or having to pretend I tolerate you?"

Something flashed in Jack's eyes. "Your little spreadsheet doesn't guarantee perfection for you?"

"It gets pretty close." Spreadsheets have never steered me wrong. There was something comforting about the neat, orderly cells holding all the information I could possibly need in one space. "There are worse things than being ultra prepared," I defended.

"Not everything needs preparation. You probably miss out on some great experiences because they aren't neatly organized for you."

I shook my head. "They're a tool given to us by the computer gods to improve our lives."

His eyebrows shot up. "Lives? Don't tell me you have a ten-year plan somewhere in Excel?"

Then I wouldn't say it out loud. "What's wrong with that?"

Jack scoffed. "Seriously? Live a little." He lifted his orange juice and downed the entire thing at once.

"Whoa, *savor* it a little," I muttered.

He put the glass on the table and wiped his mouth. "Why do you care how I drink my juice?"

Why did he care how I organized my life? "That's freshly squeezed. Do you know what kind of effort goes into getting you that tiny cup? It's meant to be enjoyed."

He smirked. "I did enjoy it."

"It was gone too fast for you to enjoy much of anything."

"Maybe that's the experience I was going after. A quick rush. None of this slow burn, make sure it fits in the schedule stuff for me."

"Then you're missing out. You could enjoy it longer if you'd savor it."

His gaze flicked down to my lips. "I can think of a few things I like to savor."

My stomach dropped to the dirty tile floor, taking my breath with it. If he was trying to unsteady me—ugh, it was working.

Jack leaned closer and lowered his voice. "Orange juice isn't one of them."

Goodbye rational thought. Jack's husky voice chased it away. My veins were buzzing, and I was pretty sure my juice wasn't spiked.

I was saved from needing to respond by the approach of my little sister. "Good morning, love birds!" she squealed, pulling Kevin by the hand. I glanced at the time on my computer. 7:36. *How* had the time gone so fast? Maybe Jack made the clock speed up alongside my heart rate. Like, from boiling in anger and no other reason.

A quick glance behind Amelia proved they'd come alone. Thank heavens. I could only handle so much sorority in the morning.

"Can we join you?" Kevin asked, his voice raspy as if he'd recently woken up.

"Of course!" I beamed, sliding my computer over on the table to make room for Amelia.

She pulled Kevin away. "We need to order first."

I moved my oatmeal and orange juice over with me, and a plate of pancakes with a side of bacon immediately took the vacated spot. Jack moved around the table to slide in beside me before I had even finished settling my things. He brought a cloud of muted cologne that smelled even better than the bacon.

"What are you doing?" I whisper-hissed.

He leaned close, matching my whisper. "Sitting beside my girlfriend."

"My sister could have sat there."

"She would much rather sit beside her fiancé, don't you think?"

I moved to argue, but the way Amelia was wrapped in Kevin's arms at the counter proved Jack's point. I huffed. "Fine. But don't get any funny ideas."

His green eyes danced. "Like what?"

"I don't know. Trying to hold my hand."

He tucked his chin a little. "You don't let your boyfriends hold your hand?"

"You're not actually my boyf—"

"Today I am."

Amelia and Kevin returned, and I pasted a smile on my face. Jack elbowed me softly in the side. "Tone it down, Sunshine, or you'll give yourself away."

He had a point. I took a sip of juice to give myself a chance to reset.

"So," Amelia said, settling into her seat with a little shimmy. "I want to hear *everything*."

I spit my juice back into the cup. Jack started patting me on the back. "Silly Lauren. Always swallowing her gum."

I put the cup down and shot him a warning look. "Wrong pipe."

"Mmhmm."

Kevin laughed. "It's so weird to see y'all flirting."

If that qualified as flirting in Kevin's opinion, then I felt bad for my sister. Amelia tucked some of her light brown hair behind her ear and leaned into Kevin's side as his arm came around her shoulders. She waited expectantly.

"We ran into each other," I blurted.

Jack laughed, snaking his arm over my shoulders to mirror Kevin and Amelia. "Literally."

Amelia's eyes popped. "Like a car accident?"

"No, just a bump in the shoulder." Jack squeezed mine as he said it, and I tried to fight the warmth bleeding through my skin from his touch.

I was getting all sorts of feelings this morning, and they needed to stop. I knew they weren't coming from any chemistry specific to Jack. They were a result of the man-famine that had spanned the last six months of my life.

I was so desperate to be touched that even someone who thoroughly repulsed me was sending a flock of sparrows through my abdomen. I mean, I didn't typically despise people as a general rule, but you couldn't listen to a five-minute voice-mail identifying all the reasons you're uptight and un-dateable without harboring some resentment.

His thumb ran over the top of my shoulder, sending obnoxious goosebumps down my arm. "Lauren wasn't easy to win over, but I managed in the end."

Definitely not foreshadowing our actual situation.

Amelia laughed. "I believe that. She was so angry with you after that date."

"Can you blame me?" I said, a grin splitting my face.

"Not really," Amelia agreed. "I'm so glad you've worked things out. You are a literal enemies-to-lovers story in real life. This is romance."

I had never been so happy to have a waitress interrupt a conversation. She put Kevin and Amelia's breakfasts in front of them and left again.

Kevin shoveled a bite into his mouth and leveled his gaze at Jack. "How did work take your last-minute absence?"

"Well enough." He shrugged.

Last minute. That was right. Jack wasn't supposed to make it on the cruise, which I'd been happy about, of course, but it had disappointed Amelia. For Kevin's sake, I was assuming. I didn't know if she had a particular fondness for Jack or not. I also didn't know what had kept him from joining us originally, only that it had something to do with work.

"The board isn't planning to demote you now?" Amelia asked, taking me by surprise. I didn't know she was familiar enough with Jack to know what he was working on.

"They can't." He cut a bite of pancakes with his fork. "I've planned most of the event. Job security."

"If you've already planned it—"

"They can't execute it without me." He ate the bite of pancakes and cut another. "Trust me, my job and that stupid conference will both be waiting for me when I return."

Amelia pulled out her phone and started scrolling, satisfied.

I'd perked up, though. The word *conference* was like a shot of espresso to my veins. "What do you do again?"

Jack hesitated a beat. "Marketing."

I flipped through my mental rolodex for marketing conferences coming up. Nope, nothing. "What kind of conference?"

"Medical. I'm just on their marketing team, so I'm on the conference board."

My world stuttered to a stop. He couldn't possibly be in charge of planning one of the biggest conferences in Dallas, could he? "The MediCorp conference at the Event Center downtown?"

His fork hovered over the plate. "Yeahhh . . ."

"How do you not know what he does?" Amelia asked, narrowing her gaze.

This was it. The moment of truth. I'd said I wouldn't lie, so here goes—

"You don't know everything about Kevin, I bet," Jack said smoothly.

"No," she agreed, "but I probably know most things."

"Did you in the beginning of your relationship?"

She didn't seem convinced, but lowered her attention to her breakfast. I hovered on a swinging rope bridge between her and Jack, searching for the right words in the rocky chasm beneath my feet. *We're not actually dating. Last night was a weird thing, and I don't really know how it all happened because it happened so fast, but now apparently we're pretending to date to keep Sydney off Jack's back, so can you play along with it and please don't be mad?*

That was better than nothing.

I cleared my throat and straightened in my seat. "Listen, Ames. We're not—"

"Good morning!" Sydney hollered, evidently unaware of the other people eating breakfast who were probably enjoying the general peacefulness before she'd arrived. Cara was right behind her, and she waved as they went to the counter to order.

Well, I couldn't give my confession now. I shoved my last few bites of oatmeal in my mouth and didn't bother finishing my backwash juice.

"So much for savoring," Jack said, leaning close.

I pressed my shoulder against his, though there wasn't as much give there as I'd expected. "More like an opportunity has arisen for an empty hotel room. I'm going to take it."

"Should I come?"

"Not necessary." I put my computer away and started edging toward him on the bench seat, bumping into him in the universal language that stated *let me out*.

Jack wasn't budging. "I don't mind. I've finished eating anyway."

I looked into his green eyes and told myself they weren't mesmerizing. The fact was, I couldn't get Jack's job out of my head. It was spinning like a kid's twirly top and made it hard to think of anything else. His company was putting on one of the largest events this spring in Dallas. He was on the board. The potential here was so alluring I could kiss it.

"Fine. Yes, please, come with me."

His gaze snapped to mine, flashing. Was his playfulness engaging? He made me nervous when he looked at me that intently, so I turned my attention to collecting my things, which were already gathered in my laptop bag.

Now I just looked silly.

Jack finally had pity on me and scooted off the bench, offering me his hand when I gracefully exited as well. "The seat's all yours," he said to Sydney and Cara, gesturing to our vacated places at the table, our breakfast dishes waiting to be cleared.

"Thanks!" Cara didn't seem to care. She took a seat.

Sydney pouted. "You don't want to stay a little longer?" Her eyes roamed him. I wanted to wave a hand in her face, like *hello, I'm standing right here. It's me, his (fake) girlfriend.*

Jack squeezed my fingers, pulling me closer. Safety blanket, that was me. "We're good. It's almost time to head over to the ship, right? I'm sure we'll see you soon."

He all but dragged me away. When we reached the elevator and the door closed, he still didn't release my hand. I pulled it lightly from his grip, and he looked at me, surprised. He'd probably forgotten he'd been holding it.

"You really sure you don't want to be my girlfriend for the week?"

"That depends."

He perked up.

I sucked in a breath and faced him. This was it. Or this *could* be it. Fate had given me a chance to secure my promotion. "How would you feel about moving your MediCorp conference to the Hunnam Hotel?"

CHAPTER SEVEN

LAUREN

JACK WAS the kind of attractive that usually reserved itself for the ultra-cocky or untouchable. When Amelia and Kevin had set up our blind date, I hadn't needed any convincing. I'd seen pictures, and he was delicious. But I quickly learned that he was more likely to give me cavities—no, a root canal—than satisfy my metaphorical sweet tooth.

But that didn't make it any easier to pretend I wasn't attracted to him. The way he stood now, too close to me in this elevator, the concentration on his brow, I was almost considering how good he smelled.

It was taking major effort, but I was doing my best not to breathe too deeply.

"Are you holding your breath?"

I let it out in a whoosh. "What? No."

He didn't believe me.

"So, what do you say?" I asked.

The elevator doors opened, and we stepped into the hallway. Jack ran a hand over his forehead. "I think that's a big ask."

Shoot. So, he wasn't sold yet. But . . . he also hadn't said *no* either. "So is pretending to like you for a week."

His eyes flashed. "Not just *like*, Lauren."

"I didn't realize our fake relationship had hit any other milestone."

"If I'm bringing my career into this, the stakes are definitely changing."

My heart pumped faster, the potential for furthering my own career giving me a shot of adrenaline or dopamine or whatever it was that made you excited and happy. Giddy? Was I giddy? That wasn't normal for me. I supposed dangling a shiny new conference in front of me was enough to get me drooling.

He turned down the hall, and I fell in step beside him. "We would have to keep the contract essentially the same as the one we have with the Event Center for my board to roll with this."

"Done."

He side-eyed me. "And you would have to provide a future discount for returning."

I hesitated only slightly. "Done."

"And I want suites set aside for all my execs during the conference so we can stay in the hotel."

"Done." His requirements weren't bad at all. If this meant bringing such an enormous conference to the Hunnam Group, I would drop grapes in his mouth poolside while fanning him with an enormous leaf. He did not realize the lengths I was willing to go.

We stopped before Jack's door. His green eyes pierced me, and I fought the temptation to take a step back. I held my ground, waiting for him to speak. He might have been waiting for the same thing, the way he was staring at me, his eyes unmoving, slightly narrowing, honing in.

"You'll have to pretend, for the duration of the cruise, that you actually like me, Lauren."

The word *done* caught in my throat. He was right. I couldn't be fake dating him and trying to steer clear of him at the same time. When we were together, we would be *together*.

"Not as easy to promise?" he asked.

"Of course not. That's an entire week of pretending." And I didn't lie to my sister.

Well, I hadn't lied to her before this weekend. If I did this, that would be fully breaking my promise to myself. But it would also mean reducing her stress during her wedding and getting the promotion I'd worked so hard for. Without this conference, Jerry had the promotion in the bag. I needed my own event, and it needed to be on a large scale.

"You'll set up the contract before we start this whole façade, right?" I asked.

Jack rubbed a hand over his chin, more serious than I knew he was capable of being. "I can't. If you don't hold up your side of things, I'm not going to the effort of moving our conference. So you have to do yours first."

That was fair. "How do I know you have that kind of power?"

"I pretty much run the conference board. I don't have that kind of power on my own, but I can win them over." He flashed me a smile.

Yeah, I had zero doubts about his ability to win anyone over. It was a steady mental stream of him making out with the waitress on our date and that awful voicemail that kept me from falling victim to his charm. His flirting wasn't real. It was a means to an end. Like everything else in life, it wouldn't last anyway.

I played with the zipper of my laptop bag. "Do we have a deal?"

He lowered his voice, his eyes flicking back and forth between mine. "I have stipulations for the relationship."

I swallowed. He was standing so close it was almost time to stop breathing again. "What are they?"

"You have to sit by me."

"Well, yeah." Wasn't that a given?

"You have to spend time with me."

I nodded. I was essentially his Sydney-repellent, so this came with the territory.

"And you can't work on the ship."

There it was. The record scratching. "What? Why?"

"I will help you with whatever's going on at your job that's making you willing to date me for a week, but you have to put the computer away when we reach that ship and devote your attention to your sister."

It was an oddly selfless parameter from him, and it made my defenses rise. "I already planned on not working." Or at least, not working *too much*.

"Then it won't be hard to agree. It's part of the deal, Lauren. You work on that cruise and the bet is off."

Could I sever myself from the office for an entire week? I mean, they expected it, of course, but I had still planned on staying mildly in touch so I wasn't too out of the loop when I returned, or so buried in emails it would take days to dig myself out. It would be a sacrifice, but it was worth bringing the Medi-Corp conference to the Hunnam Group. It would be worth earning my promotion.

"Fine."

"We have a deal?" Jack stuck out his hand.

I slid mine into it. "We have a deal."

He tightened his grip and pulled me in, sliding his hands around my waist and anchoring me close. My body went into fright mode, completely still, clocking the motion and the location of his large hands on my back as he pulled me in for a hug.

"What are you doing?" I asked.

"If we're going to date, you have to get used to being touched, Lauren."

"Eww."

"It's just a hug," he said in exasperation, like he was tired of explaining the globe to a group of flat-earthers.

He was right, though. I agreed to do this, so touching was part of the territory. I relaxed a little, trying not to breathe in his delicious scent.

"Usually, during a hug," he whispered into my ear, "both people put their arms around the other person."

I rolled my eyes but gave in. It wouldn't hurt to get the first real hug over with. I mean, not *real*, but also not forced upon me in a fit of panic in front of Sydney or my sister like they were last night. I put my arms lightly around Jack's waist and he readjusted so he was still holding me just as tightly. He pressed into my back, and I turned my head away from his neck, resting it against the hollow from his collarbone. I stopped trying to hold my breath and relaxed.

I hated to admit this, even to myself, but it felt nice to be hugged. Even if it was by the devil's spawn himself.

When *was* the last time I'd hugged someone beyond a quick greeting or a farewell? Probably Derek, the last guy I had dated. But that hadn't lasted long.

Jack inhaled deeply, his chest pressing against mine, then exhaled and relaxed into me. It was like we were doing a yoga move. Warmth seeped into my chest, thawing my ice-cold heart.

"This isn't so bad, is it?" Jack's voice in my ear was like a shot of heat through my body.

Nope. This was not good. We could fake date for a week so my sister could relax during her wedding and my career's trajectory would be secured, but I would *not* develop feelings for this guy. I'd end up like every other girl who was victim to his green eyes and smooth talking—disappointed.

I pulled back, averting my gaze. My cheeks were warm, and I didn't want him thinking my blush was because I enjoyed whatever that was. It was a hug. Studies had been done to prove that eight second hugs literally released oxytocin and boosted your immune system, so really, it was science. They were impossible *not* to enjoy.

Pulling my bag strap higher on my shoulder again, I fished in my pocket for my room key, then turned toward my door.

"Where are you going?"

Away. To breathe. To remind myself why those feelings were just a biological reaction. In no way could I allow myself to fall victim to Jack's ridiculous charm. "To cram some work in."

"Hey, we agreed—"

"No working *on the ship*. Yep, I remember." I flashed him a smile before unlocking my door and slipping inside to the refuge of a dark room. I slumped on the desk chair and exhaled. What had I gotten myself into?

CHAPTER EIGHT

LAUREN

HOW DID we end up in this mess? How did I manage to find myself in line at the guest services desk on the ship with Jack and Amelia, the tinkling of slot machines and laughter from enthusiastic players in the casino behind us only further grating my nerves? I was a block of hard parmesan, and all of these things were slowly chipping away at me.

"I don't think it will come to anything," I said for the fiftieth time. "There is no way they'll be able to accommodate us so last-minute. Cruise ships have crazy rules."

Jack shot me a warning look. "Amelia's right, though. We might as well try."

Might as well *try* to give up our own personal space and the safety of our separate rooms every night? Make an attempt to sacrifice those valuable, sacred spaces where we can recharge each night for another day of fake liking each other?

"Isn't it their job to be accommodating?" Amelia asked. "You're in the hospitality business. You should know."

"Which is why I don't want to make extra work for them right now. They probably have requests falling out of their ears."

Jack's eyebrows lifted. "I think the expression is *coming* out of their ears."

I wrinkled my nose. "Either way, there's too much stuff leaving orifices."

Amelia looked mildly disturbed at this exchange. She pulled her vibrating phone out of her pocket and put it to her ear. "Hang on guys, it's Kev. Hi, baby."

She walked toward the tall windows on the other side of the room to get away from the casino noise. Blue ocean sparkled through those windows, and I inhaled patience.

"I'm sorry," Jack said.

"You're talking like it's a done deal already." I smoothed a loose lock of hair back into my knot and patted it down to ensure it was all in order. "They might not be able to move us."

His eyebrows bent together, disbelieving. "You know they will."

"Well, as long as Amelia stays on the phone over there, we only have to pretend to try."

Jack was still for a minute. "You think she'll believe it if we say they couldn't help us?"

No. "It's worth a shot."

Jack stepped a little closer, making his cologne fly up my nose against my will. It had a weird effect of calming me and grating at me at the same time. Stupid, hot, nice-smelling man who wanted to share my room and my personal space.

Why was he being so nice anyway? I had the experience and the voicemail to prove how much he wasn't into me. Maybe a normal person would have deleted it long ago, but now I was glad I couldn't ever bring myself to hit that trash icon. I might need to be reminded of why Jack was bad news.

"If you're worried how my presence will affect your game with the men on board, I'm sure we can work around it," he said.

I cringed. "Gross. Are you serious? I'm not here for hookups. I'm here for my sister's wedding."

"I think those things go together for a lot of people."

"I'm not one of them." I tipped my head back to hold his sparkling, green eyes. He was too close, trying to read me too much. Then it hit me that maybe *he* was the one worried about his "on-board game" with the ladies. "But if *you* are concerned about your ability—"

"I'm not." He didn't move. I could actually feel his breath on my nose, but it wasn't in my nature to back down, so I stood my ground. Jack's voice was low. "If I wanted that, I wouldn't have asked you to shield me from Sydney."

Good point. "So you're really here to focus on the wedding?"

"I'd be offended by your obvious distrust, but I brought it up first."

"History has given me enough reason to doubt you, so don't be too hard on yourself. My opinion of you was pretty cemented before today."

His jaw flexed. "You can't spend the whole cruise bringing up our date. Amelia will catch on that we aren't the happy couple we're pretending to be."

"Amelia's not here."

"Can I help you?" the middle-aged woman behind the counter asked, her smile wide and strained. I felt for her on a molecular level.

Jack slipped his arm around my back and guided me up to the counter. He was so smooth. At some point I was going to need to stop being surprised every time he touched me. But it wasn't just the actual, physical touching that threw me off—it was also the way it made me feel.

I was a strong, brave, independent woman, and I should not be so *comforted* by a man throwing his arm around me. It went against everything I believed in and everything I had stood for the last few years. I hadn't practically raised my sister, then lost my grandma—who had actually raised us—and found a way to survive, only to melt at the touch of Jack's hand to the small of my back.

Except this was me, a total puddle on the carpet in front of the help desk.

"Ma'am?" she asked. She was about as old as my mother would've been, her highlights grown out a few inches too many and an overbright smile revealing straight, white teeth.

What was that? *Focus*, Lauren.

"We booked our rooms separately," Jack said, painting a smile over his handsome face. "We were hoping you could move me from the room I'm in to share with this lovely lady?"

She paused, staring at Jack as if struck by something he said. That was the moment where she decided whether to help us or send us away, and thanks to Jack's smooth smile, she had clearly made her decision in his favor. "Let me see what I can do."

"Thank you, Cheryl. You don't know what this would mean to us."

"Laying it on a little thick there?" I muttered, elbowing him slightly, but he only slid his hand further on my waist and pulled me tighter against him.

She asked for our cards and information, her nails clacking away at the keyboard. "Unfortunately, because you weren't booked under the same card, I can't move you from one room to the other."

Phew. Sweet relief.

"But," she said, stretching out the word and lowering her voice a little, "if you're willing to pay for an upgrade, I can move both of you to a balcony room."

"You have an opening?" I said, more surprised than accepting of this potential change.

"We sail at capacity, so none of the rooms are open."

Huh?

"How does that work?" Jack asked. "It's my first cruise, so I don't know how any of this works."

"It's better if I don't explain," she said, sending him a wink before working away at the keyboard again. "But if these guests change their mind and join us, you'll be back in your original rooms."

She was a finagler. I understood. I was one of those too. There were always loopholes for jumping when you really wanted to help a customer.

Jack and I stood in silence for a few more minutes before she looked up again. "If you can wait until we set sail, see me here and I'll re-key your cards. I can't do it until we've left the port. That way we're guaranteed the other guests aren't joining us."

"Understood," Jack said, pulling me flush against his rock-hard side.

Wait, re-key our cards? I hadn't actually agreed to anything yet.

"The change in room fees will be charged to your account when this goes through. As of right now, everything is ready to go, but you'll have to sign the form before anything can be processed."

Again, we didn't agree to anything. I looked for my sister. She had put her phone away and was looking out the windows on the opposite side of the room still, out of earshot. "I don't—"

"Thank you, Cheryl," Jack said. "You have made one man very happy."

She beamed at Jack. I wanted to punch him in the stomach. His fingers were playing my waist like a piano now. When we reached our room—whenever that was—I was going to lay down some ground rules. All this touching was further clouding my brain, and we couldn't have that. Not when I was supposed to be executing a wedding this week.

"It's the least I can do," Cheryl said. "You look like my son, so I couldn't resist pulling a string."

Jack beamed. "I've never been so glad to resemble someone else. Thank you, ma'am. You have a blessed day."

He led me away from the desk.

"What the heck?" I whisper-yelled. "Not only do we have to share a room, but now we have to pay for it? We never actually agreed to pay for an upgrade anyway."

"We'd do that if we were together," he said quietly. "Don't worry about the extra expense. I'll cover it."

I was an extremist when it came to being cheap, and I was the first to admit so. But when you grew up as poor as I had, it was hard parting with money unnecessarily. Especially for something like this. The way he'd thrown that offer out there, so blasé, made me want to be contradictory just for the sake of it.

"No. I'm benefitting from this arrangement too. We're partners, and we'll split the cost." Besides, if he started paying for things, that would only feel even more like we were a real couple. I wanted to avoid that as much as possible.

"Suit yourself."

"Good idea!" Kevin yelled, startling us both. He had come out of nowhere, Amelia right behind him, flashing his perfect teeth. "Grab your suits and meet us at the pool? The girls want to tan."

Which was my perfect segue out of that activity. "I can't. I'll just burn."

"Sunscreen?" Kevin offered, as if I'd never heard of the invention before.

"I'll still burn."

"It's true," Amelia said, corroborating my claim. "She has the palest skin."

Thanks, sis. "But you should all go! I'll just get my book and find a quiet place to read."

Kevin looked at me like I was a monkey behind a glass wall. I would bet half my life savings he hadn't read a book since middle school.

Half, because it would be reckless to bet the whole thing, no matter how sure the outcome.

Amelia looked torn. "I can come hang out with you—"

"No, don't worry about it. I haven't had time to read a book in ages. I won't feel left out." I tried to smile, but she still looked worried. The last thing I wanted was to make her feel like the wedding party was divided, but sunbathing just wasn't something I could do. "Thank your genes you don't have to sit out with me."

She gave me a nose-wrinkling smile, but I knew she was relieved. Her olive skin tanned as quickly as mine burned.

"Don't stress about it," Jack said, slipping his hand around mine. His fingers interlocked with mine perfectly, and he gave me a gentle squeeze. "Lauren won't be alone. I'd rather be with her anyway."

Relief washed over Amelia's face. "Great. So we'll meet up afterward?"

"For sure," I said through somewhat clenched teeth.

"What did they say about the rooms?" she asked, looking between us.

"We have to come back after we set sail, but they think they can help us."

"Great." Amelia beamed.

I let Jack pull me in the opposite direction, toward the bank of elevators that would take us to my old room to get my book from my bag.

"What floor?" he asked.

"One." I'm cheap, remember? I wasn't going to pay more than I had to. This wasn't a pencil skirt that would last me years and years. It was a place to sleep for a week.

He looked at me quickly. "Really?"

"I don't get seasick, so I don't really have a reason to need a window."

"The view?"

"Like I'll have time for that." I'd planned on sneaking in some work before our agreement. Now I had more time than I would know what to do with. "Well, I guess I will now, but my plan before . . ." I trailed off when the doors opened to let out two bikini-clad women showing more confidence than I possessed in my entire body.

"Jack!" Sydney said, ignoring me.

"I thought Amelia texted to meet y'all at the service desk?" Cara said, twisting her curls back into a clip.

"Kevin and Amelia went to change for the pool," Jack said. "We'll see you later."

Sydney pouted. I was fairly sure she pushed her shoulders together to accentuate more than just her disappointment. "Why? You should come hang out with us now!"

"Maybe later." Jack stepped past them to stop the elevator doors from closing, then pulled me inside with him. "See you at dinner."

Sydney frowned.

The doors shut, and Jack expelled a breath. "She's freaking relentless."

"Honestly. Did you notice how she didn't look at me once?" I stepped away, pulling my hand from his as he hit the button to reach my floor. "Oh, *Jack*. How good to see you, *Jack*. Come watch me swim, *Jack*," I said, affecting a high voice.

A smile played on his lips. "Can you see now why I was a little desperate?"

I chuckled. "Maybe."

"Good."

"If I was your real girlfriend, I'd probably expect you to tell her to back off."

"If you were my real girlfriend, you could do that yourself."

"But I'm not."

"No, but you're supposed to pretend you are. So maybe later tonight we can make it clear that she can stop trying so hard."

If it was up to Jack, that would probably include making out in the hot tub while everyone else watched. If I wanted this to remain as non-romantic as possible, I needed to put my thinking cap on. "I'll come up with something."

"Great." Jack watched me curiously. "I can't wait."

CHAPTER NINE

JACK

"THEY WANT TO PLAY MINI GOLF," I said, sitting up and looking over at Lauren. She was lounging in the chair next to mine, out on the lido deck beneath a shaded overhang. The pool was visible a few decks below us with people rimming the outer perimeter and kids splashing each other in the center. A DJ stood on the deck just above the pool, right across the open expanse from us, playing pop music and pretending he enjoyed it.

Lauren's book rested over her stomach, keeping the place, her head leaned back and eyes closed. "How are you texting them?" she asked. "Didn't we already leave the port?"

I opened the cruise app and showed her my phone. "We can message each other using the ship's Wi-Fi if we're in their app."

Lauren lifted her head. "Okay, good, because I didn't plan on paying for Wi-Fi after you revoked my work privileges." She stretched, then started to get up. "Mini golf it is. I just need to run down to the room and put my book away first. Want me to take anything of yours?"

"I'll go with you."

She lifted a shoulder. "No need. It will only take a second."

I could tell when I wasn't wanted. Which, around Lauren, was always. As a man who had never struggled with making friends, this was unnatural for me. I couldn't tell why she didn't like me, or what I'd done to give her such a sour expression every time she looked at me. I didn't really understand where it all had gone wrong on our date, either, if I was being honest. All I knew was that she seemed to think we were in agreement about how awful it had been.

If anything, *I* had ample reason not to like *her*. She was the rude one who ditched me in the middle of dinner with no note or text to explain. I had to hear that she'd left from our waitress. But if I could forgive and move on, so could she.

"Do you know how to pull up the map on the app?" I asked.

"I can figure it out."

My phone buzzed, so I guess we weren't *that* far from port. I'd sent a message to my boss earlier about the possibility of moving the conference to another venue, and he'd just responded. "Wait, Lauren."

She hovered above me. I turned my phone so she could read the text, which she did aloud. "Certainly worth discussing. You know I love a good discount." She looked at me, confused. "Who's Brad?"

"My boss. I told him I had a lead on a great venue with substantial discounts for the conference. I wanted you to know I'm taking this seriously."

She nodded, giving me a strange look. "Okay. Consider it noted."

"Now you can act like my girlfriend with confidence."

Lauren rolled her eyes, but I sensed a bit of ease in her posture. "I'll see you at mini golf."

I was hesitant to leave her, but she didn't give me a choice. She started walking away before I could say anything more. The sun beat down on us and sparkled over the ocean. Florida was disappearing into the distance, and the growing ratio of shimmery water around us compared to our ship made me feel small.

The mini golf place was up a few decks, hanging out near the ropes course. The girls hadn't changed out of their swimsuits, but—thankfully—had shorts on. I wasn't sure I could handle Sydney much longer if she was going to keep trying to entice me. It wasn't working. I didn't know how to convey that without being rude, but I hoped Lauren was coming up with a plan.

Judging by the determination in my ex's eyes, we were going to need it.

Sydney pulled a second golf club from the rack and brought it to me. "Ready to lose?"

"Yes." Best not to engage in banter, right? With the way the ship rocked, albeit slowly, none of us were likely to do very well anyway.

Lucas brought his club over and pretended to knock me from behind. "Are we making this interesting?"

Kevin perked up. "Loser has to . . ." He looked away in thought.

"Loser has to kiss the winner," Sydney said.

"Since some of us are about to get married," Amelia said. "I'm vetoing that."

Sydney raised her dark eyebrow. "You're pretty confident you'll win?"

"No. But more than half of us are in relationships."

"Let's stop trying to kiss other people's boyfriends," Lauren said, coming up behind me and sliding her hand down my forearm. She interlocked our fingers and I wondered if my entire body was going to overheat or if that was just the sun. Lauren leaned against me. "I don't think Kevin wants to kiss any of us anyway."

Sydney could have been shooting fire from her eyes.

"I got it," Lucas said, snapping. "Loser has to jump in the pool naked."

"It's a family cruise," Cara said, right as a kid ran by with a basketball. "Maybe keep it PG."

"Winner picks what we do tonight after dinner?" Amelia asked like it was a question. "There are a lot of options."

There were varying degrees of assent, and everyone got their golf clubs to begin. Lauren moved to leave when I tugged her back. "Thanks for that," I whispered.

She looked up at me and her sunglasses slipped down her nose a little. Her hazel eyes were a golden green in this light, her hair looking more honey than brown. "It was nothing. I told you I'd handle it."

"You *hand*led it, all right."

A laugh tore from her chest that was more surprise than humor as she pushed her glasses back up. "Punny, are we?"

I grinned. To get one of those laughs again, I could sacrifice my pride for puns.

Lauren immediately looked away, tempering her smile as if she'd realized who she was laughing with and had to remind herself not to find me funny. But that bit of light had shown through her otherwise austere façade, and now I knew I had the power to crack into the Lauren underneath. If she didn't want me trying too hard to win her over, she shouldn't have made herself such a challenge.

"Bride and groom go first," Cara said, leading the way to the start of the course.

We followed them over and stood at the back of the line, me behind Lauren, waiting for our turn. Hovering would more accurately describe my efforts here. Getting as close to her as possible without touching. If it was a game, I'd be going pro.

Only, I'd underestimated Lauren's competitive nature. We were on our sixth hole—of nine—and our scores were neck and neck. She lined up her ball and squared her shoulders, swinging to hit just as the deck shifted and the ball rolled away. But she'd nicked it.

"One."

She looked up. "That didn't count."

"Yes it did. It was a swing and you hit the ball."

Her mouth hung open. "The ship moved and the ball rolled. Boat rules. Doesn't count."

I looked up at the sky. It was too bright, even with my sunglasses on, but I'd committed to this pose and I was seeing it through. "Boat rules? Hmmm. Sounds like Miss Foley wants to cheat."

She scoffed. "It isn't cheating, it's *fair*."

I took a step closer to her. "All is fair in love and war, Sunshine."

"You don't want to declare war against me, Fletcher. I've won our office scavenger hunt three years in a row, and it's not from any aptitude for finding things."

"Actually, war seems like fun." My blood was pumping, my heart clipping along at a faster beat. Just holding her undivided attention was heady in a way I hadn't experienced lately. Was it a false sense of accomplishment hitting my veins? My body believing it was winning because she wasn't ignoring me?

I didn't really care what the cause was. Lauren's eyes were sparking and I was here for it.

She wasn't backing down, either. "Blood was spilled at our last event."

"You *hurt* someone to win a scavenger hunt?"

"She hurt herself trying so hard to beat me, but it couldn't be done."

I stepped up next to her, chest to chest, one inch of gloriously tense space between us. Her eyes were visible through the lenses of her sunglasses, but still I wanted to remove them. "Be careful challenging me."

I wanted to sound deep and foreboding, but my whisper

lacked the gravitas I was going for. The way I wanted her was pretty evident.

Her eyes flickered, something passing over her face. Was she feeling this, too? This weird, pulling sensation, like she was a fridge and I was a magnet. Or maybe we could both be magnets —I didn't think she'd like me comparing her to a kitchen appliance.

"What's taking so long?" Sydney called.

Lauren's eyes flicked to the group over my shoulder and back to my face. She bent to put her ball back on the starting dot and swung again. It rolled forward, moving a little with the ship until it dropped into the hole. She lifted both of her arms. "Hole in one!"

"Two," I insisted.

Lauren turned slack-jawed surprise on me. "One. I hit it *once* and it made it into the hole."

It was impressive for a cruise ship mini golf game, but I kept my expression passive. "Twice. You hit the ball twice for that hole."

Her little nose lifted in the air. "You're impossible."

"I won," Cara announced, skipping up to us.

It was too soon to know that, surely. "You don't know how many points—"

"My score is twelve."

I reached down to pick up my ball. "Yep, you've won."

Lauren scowled, but she didn't bother continuing to play either. The rocking ship made it harder, which was a fun challenge, but Sydney's eyes were boring into me like a laser pointer. Banter with Lauren was much less fun when there was an unhappy audience paying close attention to our every move.

Cara grinned, her white teeth glowing in the sun. "Which means I get to choose what we do tonight. So, get ready for dinner, because we're eating at seven and then it's 90s night at the club!"

Oh, joy.

"Are we dressing up?" Lauren asked. "I don't really have anything for it."

"Not in 90s clothes," Cara said, pushing a dark curl out of her face. "I think the music will just be themed." She leaned closer to Lauren, giving her a quick once-over. "Did you bring anything nice?"

Lauren's cheeks pinked under her sunglasses. "Amelia told me the dress code. I have . . . things . . . to wear."

Cara looked skeptical. I wanted to turn her by the shoulders and set her off in a different direction.

If Lauren didn't already feel out of place around Amelia and her friends, she probably did now. I reached for her golf club and ball, taking them from her hands, my fingers swiping over her palms. "I'll put these away. We need to go see our friend at the help desk anyway now that we've left the port."

"Oh, right," she said, sounding distracted. "Thanks."

I put our things away and went back for her. Cara was still talking, telling Lauren what to wear to dinner—I guess it wasn't Cara's first cruise—and I slid in between them, slipping my hand into Lauren's. Her fingers interlocked with mine easily, closing over my hand probably more on impulse than anything else.

"We'll see you at dinner," I said, giving the group a little wave and pulling Lauren away.

"You could have let her finish." She pulled her hand from mine to hold onto the stairs railing as we descended to the deck below. Totally unnecessary, if you asked me. I was a good enough stabilizer on my own.

"I didn't realize you wanted her fashion advice," I said.

"It wasn't fashion advice. It was a dress code."

"A condescending one."

Her attention wavered. "You noticed it, too? They all see me as the grandma in the group."

"You're my age, I think," I said carefully. "No one thinks you're old."

"To the girls, twenty-eight is ancient. I'm too close to thirty." She gave a dramatic shiver.

But I stopped listening. Standing in the center of the lobby, waiting for the elevators, was my cousin's husband, my one-time nemesis, Levi Watson, wearing a tall white cowboy hat. He was, after Sydney and a few other questionable dates I'd had recently, the last person in the world I wanted to see—let alone on a boat where we would be traveling without escape for the next week.

I took Lauren by the shoulders and pivoted her in the other direction, pulling her down a hallway. I did not stay long enough to see if my cousin was with him.

Lauren made a surprised sound. "What the—"

"As I live and breathe!" I heard the thickest Texan accent this side of the Mississippi. "The one and only Jackson Fletcher."

My shoulders bunched.

"I told you I saw him, sugar, and I was right."

I turned around to find Levi walking toward us, his Hawaiian shirt flapping open and his arm around my cousin Annie. She was short and blonde, a little package with a lot of fire. *Her* I didn't mind. Her husband? I just might need restraints by the end of this cruise.

"I didn't know y'all were going on a cruise," I said. Let alone *my* exact same cruise. Which of the gods had I made unhappy in order to be strapped to this karma?

"How could you?" Annie asked, her bright smile so familiar it caused a pain in my gut. She was the image of her mom, who just so happened to be the image of mine. *Literally.* Our moms were identical twins. "You'd have to come home once in a while in order to know anything about us."

I pulled Annie into a hug.

"Five years," Levi bragged, pulling his wife back under his

arm. "This one here has been saddled to me for five years now, so we're fixin' to celebrate."

"Who's your friend?" Annie asked.

Friend? Oh, gosh. "This is Lauren Foley."

"Hi," Lauren said, putting out her hand to shake.

Annie pulled her right in for a hug, Arcadia Creek style. Small town Texans didn't do anything halfway. "Any *friend* of Jack's is a friend of mine." The way she embellished the word friend made it obvious she assumed we were much more than that.

For the sake of the cruise and everything we'd planned, she would need to believe it. At least for a week. Could I count on her being too cheap for Wi-Fi or international data packages? If we could get to the end of the week, then I could tell her the truth and she wouldn't go home and inform my entire extended family that I had a girlfriend—the very last thing I needed. My mom and her sisters became the Spanish freaking Inquisition when it came to relationships. No one meddled like a Southern Momma, and I had four of them.

"My cousin Annie and her husband, Levi," I explained.

"It's nice to meet you," Lauren said, a little flustered—probably from the strength of Annie's hug. "And happy anniversary. We're just here for my sister's wedding."

Shoot. That was another thing that couldn't really slip until we got home. Maybe if I steered Lauren out of here quickly, Annie wouldn't catch Kevin's name or make any comments to anyone who knew someone who might know his parents. What was the point of eloping if your secret wasn't safe?

"We're meeting up with the wedding party for dinner, so—"

"Go on, then," Annie said, squeezing my arm. "Don't be a stranger, Jack."

"See you around, Jackson," Levi called.

Why did that feel like a threat? "Still not my name," I said.

We walked down the corridor where I'd tried to escape originally for no other reason than to leave the space they were in. It meant taking the long way around to the help desk, but I needed the time to think. Lauren's gaze on me was hot and thick, and I waited until we were totally clear before I peeked her way.

She wore the widest grin I'd ever seen on her. "You have some explaining to do, *sugar*."

CHAPTER TEN

LAUREN

JACK WAS quiet all through dinner. He turned on the charm while Cheryl helped us move our rooms and change our key cards, but when it came to getting ready in our newly shared room or eating dinner at the large round table with the group, he was silent. It wasn't until we were searching out the club that had listed 90s night on the program that he completely disappeared, though.

He'd been tight lipped about why running into a member of his extended family had bothered him. Then again, I didn't have cousins, so I didn't really understand.

"Did Jack leave?" Lucas asked, sidling up to sit beside me at the bar while the girls and Kevin danced in the center of the room to *Baby One More Time*. He'd shed his dinner coat, his brown neck glistening from sweat. He'd been out there with them before Britney Spears took over the speakers.

"Maybe? I haven't seen him in a while."

He shot me a confused glance. "Aren't y'all dating?"

"I'm not his mother." I took a drink. If I was really dating Jack, I would have followed him from the room and asked if he was all right, but as it stood, it was probably better if we didn't cross personal boundaries.

Also, when I'd joked earlier about wanting to know why he'd been all weird around Annie and Levi, he shut me down. I wasn't eager to try and earn his confidence again.

"You're not a dancer?" Lucas asked.

I grimaced. "It's not really my scene."

He leaned against the bar to watch the women. "It's definitely Amelia's scene." He let out a sigh and started mouthing along with Britney Spears, bobbing his head.

"Why aren't you out there anymore?"

"Oh, I . . ." Lucas looked from me to our friends. He flashed me a guilty look.

Hold up. My stomach tingled uncomfortably. "Did you come over here because *you felt sorry for me?*"

"No," Lucas promised, in what was most certainly a lie. The poor guy looked between me and my sister, panic edging in.

I stood up. "I'm sitting here by *choice.*"

"I know." He did not sound confident.

I stared at him until he stood from his stool, all six-foot-five of him towering over me. His efforts to make me feel less like a grandma were sweet, really, in a totally mortifying way. It wasn't an aversion to dancing or 90s music that kept my butt on that barstool—it was my inability to dance in front of other people and look good doing it. Amelia had gotten all those genes. I was stuck with a lack of rhythm.

Lucas slinked back to the group, which was growing more difficult to see as the crowd expanded with each passing song. How long did I need to sit and watch the throng of people yelling out the lyrics to *Bye Bye Bye* from NSYNC before I could fake a couple yawns and make my exit? It had been a long day. Pretending I enjoyed being around my archnemesis was fatiguing work.

The music changed to a Nelly song, and the lights overhead

got my attention when they shifted to blue. It reminded me of the mature wedding we hosted a few weeks ago. Conferences weren't the only events that brought money into the hotel. Receptions that looked much like what I was forced to watch right now contributed a huge portion of our revenue. Maybe by hyperfocusing on the largest conferences, I was missing an opportunity to prove my competence.

My mind buzzed with the wispy edges of an idea, but I couldn't focus enough to identify it. That was fine. There was a process to brainstorming that was sure to yield results with the proper steps. It began with my favorite thing of all time: list-making.

I pulled out my phone and started a list of events that used our hotel on a smaller scale. Weddings, anniversary parties, bat mitzvahs, retirement celebrations, work parties. It was endless. If I could find a way to capitalize on those events *and* bring Jack's MediCorp conference to our venue, I had to be a shoe-in for the promoti—

"Work?" Jack's voice in my ear was closer and silkier than it had any right to be. He *tsked*, plopping down on the empty seat beside me. "That's breaking the rules, Sunshine."

I turned my phone off and put it in my pocket. "I wasn't working. I was thinking."

"About work? Still breaking the rules."

"We never said anything about work-related thoughts. Now that you've brought it up, I think we do need to go over a few things."

He leaned his elbows back on the bar, relaxed. "Like?"

I still felt the goosebumps from his lips near my ear. "No unnecessary touching."

Jack surveyed me with sizzling blue eyes and the ghost of a smirk. "What constitutes necessary?"

"Whatever we need to sell our story is fine, but when the

others aren't around or watching us, we don't need to be touching. In any way."

Could he tell how much he'd affected me at mini golf? Or holding my hand after? All those skinful moments seemed over the top, confusing me. I set my gaze on my sister to avoid his eye.

The last thing I could do was allow myself to soften around him. These moments made me feel things, and that was dangerous. Especially when none of it was real.

Jack pushed away from leaning on the bar and swiveled on his stool to face me. I felt the pressure of my seat change when he rested his foot against it, his knee brushing my leg. "What about this?"

"Unnecessary." I swallowed. "No one is even looking."

"But my body language is couple-y. Isn't that what we want in case they do look this way?"

"It's what *you* want, maybe. I just need to survive this week." I wrinkled my nose. "And please don't say couple-y about us."

He pressed his knee harder into my thigh. "What other rules do you have?"

Deep breath, Lauren. My only job right now was to resist feeling anything for him. But his little touches and the way he looked into my eyes only reminded me why I liked being in a relationship. The attention. The touching. The whole *not feeling alone* part. It was tempting to lean into the situation a little, enjoy the perks of having someone devote his attention to me so fully. But that meant lowering my defenses, and Jack had done nothing to earn that, even on a fake-boyfriend level.

Really, all I could feel now was his knee pressing into my leg. What had he asked me? Right. Rules. "No random hookups. Fake relationships are one thing, but I won't be fake cheated on too."

"That's fair and it goes both ways." He nodded. "Anything else?"

"I get the first shower."

"Tonight?"

"Always."

"I'm guessing the hot water here is unlimited, like everything else."

"It's a matter of how long my hair takes to dry."

His eyes flicked to my hair. "You can't twist it to death into that knot thing while it's wet? What difference would it make?"

Knot thing? Twist it *to death*? My style was perfectly sleek and presentable. "There's nothing wrong with my hair."

"Not if you're trying to channel the Trunchbull."

Literally the image used in any meme to demonstrate a bun done wrong. "Thank you, Mr. Charmer."

"You don't look *bad*—"

I slid from the stool. "I'll stop you there before you say something even worse. I'm going back to the room to shower. Give me an hour at least."

He recovered from his surprise and looked at the time on his phone. "I have to stay here for another hour?"

I leaned in—too close, because now I could smell his delicious cologne—and whispered. "Maybe you should have considered that when you disappeared for the last hour."

His face tightened. "I just needed a minute."

"And now I'm giving you sixty more. You're welcome." I started to walk away when Jack took my hand and spun me back toward him, sliding his other hand around my waist and pulling me close. He still sat on the stool, and I was nestled right between his knees. My hands went up and pressed against his shirt on impulse, feeling the hard planes of his stomach. "What the—"

"Sydney's coming this way. Can your shower wait five minutes?"

At this point, it needed to. I couldn't move. Jack's hands were tight on my waist and clouding my thoughts. It had been so long since anyone held me like this, the pressure soft but sure, like he was gently laying claim to me. "Since she's the whole point of *this*, do I really have a choice?"

He smiled victoriously. "Nope." His smile wavered. "For the record, I consider this necessary touching."

Sydney barreled up to the bar. She leaned against it and giggled. "You guys coming to dance?"

She asked both of us, but her eyes were on Jack.

"We're not really feeling it tonight," I said.

Sydney pouted, sticking out her bottom lip.

"We can do one dance," Jack said, his hands moving subtly to my back.

Panic tightened my gut. "I can't dance, though. I really don't think—"

"Just one, snookums? For me?" His puppy eyes were vastly effective.

I fought the allure, but it just wasn't in me to deny puppy eyes. Or break our agreement. "Just one. But then I need to go to sleep. I'm exhausted."

Jack's hand dragged down my waist, finding my fingers. He pulled me through the throng of unsteady cruisers to the center of the room where the lights flashed and my sister and her friends were grouped, Sydney following close behind us. She joined them seamlessly, dancing close enough that there was no way she wasn't pressing herself against Jack, though the darkness made it hard to see. All around me, people danced with abandon.

I didn't know how to exercise abandon. I was pure spreadsheets and sharpened pencils and clear, concise order. Chaos made me dizzy and uncomfortable.

Amelia looked surprised to see me but tried to cover it.

I tugged on Jack's hand. "This is a bad idea."

"Let your hair down!" he called, yelling because the music was so loud. The DJ had imposed a techno beat behind the classic 90s songs, making them easier to dance to for today's clubbers.

"I literally do not know how," I yelled, right as the song changed. The background beat disappeared, launching us smoothly into the slow cadence of Savage Garden's *Truly, Madly, Deeply*. "You've got to be kidding me."

Jack didn't look amused. He wanted to slow dance with me about as much as a gazelle wants to hang out with a lion.

I stepped closer. "Let's just go."

"One dance, remember?" He leaned forward, his lips brushing my ear. "Can't give them reason to doubt us now."

He was right. For the sake of my sister's trust—and the MediCorp conference—I had to see this through. I let Jack slip his arms around me while I held on to his shoulders.

"Loosen up," he said, moving his arms a little. "You're like a robot."

"I tried to warn you." I inhaled slowly, turning my head to let the breath out while I tried to relax my muscles and sway to the music with him. I caught Amelia's face beside me while she swayed in Kevin's arms. She grinned, shooting me a quick thumbs up.

Jack's warm breath tickled my ear, driving goosebumps down my neck. "The trick to dancing is relaxing," he murmured. "You can't move with the beat if you're tense. You have to breathe, relax, feel it in your body, then move accordingly. Not what you think you should do, just how you feel."

Right now I was feeling Jack everywhere. His hand on my waist, his other moving over my back, his stomach pressed to mine, his breath in my ear. I couldn't relax, or I'd be even closer to him. It was hard to remember he was Enemy Number One when it felt so good to be held—even to *this* song.

"You're doing a terrible job of relaxing," he said.

"It's not easy when the devil himself is trying to coerce me."

"Okay, fine. Think of someone you like. Got a guy back home?"

"No."

"Just think of one. Anyone. The last really good date you went on."

I searched my brain but came up short.

Jack peeked down at me, pulling back a little and giving me some breathing room. "Don't say you haven't gone on a date—"

"If I'd had a really good date recently, don't you think I'd still be with that guy?"

"Not always," he muttered, looking away.

Amelia was watching us sway like stiff cardboard. My eyelids fluttered closed. I tried to loosen up, let the beat flow through me, slow as it was. I let Jack lead, tried to be putty in his arms.

"It's not working." I stopped in the middle of the dance floor.

Jack nudged me along gently, watching me, a groove between his dark eyebrows. "You really can't dance."

"Never tried to pretend otherwise."

"Huh." He gave an understanding, enlightening nod.

His acceptance was annoying. I knew I was rhythmless, but he didn't have to look at me like I was some foreign alien specimen. "It's not that crazy. Lots of people can't dance."

"But they can at least follow a lead." His hands moved on my waist a little, but he didn't let go. Didn't pull away. "It's weird," he muttered, his gaze like floodlights searching me. There was no escaping it.

"What?"

"You have a fault, Lauren. That means you're human."

To that, I had no response.

"I figured you were half cyborg or something with all the rigidity and the lists and the schedules . . . you know what? That theory still stands." He nudged me. "You're still about as stiff as a cyborg would be."

My lips pulled into the smallest hint of a smile, and I shook my head. His words were unkind, but his eyes weren't. It almost felt like he was playing my game now. Giving me what he thought I wanted to hear.

The song came to a close. I pulled away from him. "Give me an hour," I reminded him.

Jack nodded before I walked from the room. I was glad we'd already had that plan in place, because it was going to take at least that long for my body to calm down from the effects of being in his arms, from his whispers raising goosebumps on my neck, from his laughter slipping through my veins like lava. I was not unaffected by Jack, and I needed to find a way to reverse that *very* quickly. Starting with an icy, cold shower.

CHAPTER ELEVEN

JACK

"THIS MEETING IS CALLED TO ORDER," Kevin said, hitting his empty orange juice cup on the table. The wide windows behind him framed sparkling blue ocean as far as the eye could see. We were all gathered around the breakfast table while the groom waited for conversation to die down so he could address us. "My lady," he said, giving his fiancée a flourishing gesture.

They were so sweet it made my teeth hurt.

Amelia rolled her eyes, but she was fighting a smile. "We have two days until the wedding. Since tomorrow is mostly snorkeling, today is prep work. Y'all have the morning free while Kevin and I get our couple's massage, then the ladies are booked for facials and mani-pedis at two. Dinner together, then the hot tub tonight. Questions?"

No one had any. I peeked at Lauren, but she hadn't paid me much attention since the dance we'd shared last night. I'd gotten back to our room to find her asleep—or faking it—with pillows halfway down the king-sized bed making a line of demarcation. A feather-filled wall. A *Do Not Cross* border.

She didn't need to worry. The boundary was fine with me.

But now we were at breakfast and her hair *was no longer in a tight knot.* It had graduated to a low ponytail, running between her shoulder blades in smooth, honey-brown locks. She was so close to letting it loose. I was tempted to just hook the elastic in my finger and help her along.

Lauren turned toward me suddenly. "Oh, I don't think we need to."

Could she read minds? I'd been daydreaming about running my fingers through her silky ponytail, but her wide eyes were more aversion than disgust. I had no idea what she was trying to get us out of.

"Jack wouldn't care, anyway," she said. "We don't have to do that."

She spoke for me. That most assuredly meant I *would* care and we *should* do that, whatever that was. "Hold on, now. Don't be hasty."

Lauren's eyes widened a smidge. "Really, Ames." She turned toward her sister again. "We don't want to take away from yours and Kevin's special time."

Amelia's smile brightened. "Nonsense, Sissy. We want you there."

Was I the only one who noticed Lauren's cringe?

Amelia stood, looking from her sister to me. "See y'all in half an hour?"

"Yep," Lauren said with resignation.

We all got up from the breakfast table and filed from the dining room.

"Thanks for nothing," Lauren hissed when she reached my side.

"What did we sign up for?"

She shot me a glare. "*You* signed us up for a couple's massage with the bride and groom."

Oh.

"Lunch at that taco place by the pool?" Cara asked before we separated.

"Sounds good to me," I called, waving.

She, Sydney, and Lucas took off—my guess was to spend the morning in the casino or poolside. Probably both. Which sounded so much better than being rubbed down by a stranger.

"I don't really do massages," I said, smoothing a hand over my chin while we went down the steps to the lido deck.

Lauren's eyebrows shot up, and she tucked her chin. "Really? Because you seemed pretty eager back there."

"I hadn't been paying attention."

She started walking toward the side of the boat, where the water shone against the sun so brightly it was impossible to keep looking at it. "This is what you get for being contrary, then. A nice, oily rub down."

"Could you make it sound worse?"

Challenge lit her eyes. "Naked. With your—"

"Worst enemy?"

"Your best friend and his fiancée *and* an incredible woman who doesn't enjoy being in the same room as you."

"Yet."

"Never," she said, looking out over the water.

Why was banter with her so enlivening? It was rapid and smart, pulsing through me, sparking the air between us. "Don't give me a challenge if you don't want me to achieve it."

Lauren spun on the deck so her back was to the railing and put her finger up. "Not a challenge. A fact."

"You find me charming."

"As charming as a third-degree sunburn."

That wasn't the way it had felt last night when she was struggling to breathe on the dance floor—*during a slow song*. It wasn't how that dance felt for me, either. I didn't enjoy admitting to myself that despite Lauren's rigidity and her severe dislike of me, there was something extremely satisfying when she melted against me. Her beauty had never been in question, and the more I watched her sacrifice her pride for her sister, *care* about her sister, the more layers of hostility seem to wear off.

There was a human somewhere underneath that persnickety cyborg exterior, and I was going to find it, one destroyed robotic panel at a time.

Lauren straightened. "Why are you looking at me like that?"

"Like what?"

"Like I'm one of your ugly T-shirts or a slice of pizza."

I looked down at my shirt. It wasn't ugly. It was just bright.

She narrowed her eyes. "If this is an attempt at charming me, it's a failure."

Consider the gauntlet thrown down.

I took a step toward her, reaching for the railing on either side until she was boxed in. This close, she smelled of sunshine and spreadsheets—so fresh, probably her laundry detergent, and so pinned up. Lauren took a quick inhale and watched me carefully.

There was space. I had long arms. While I was keeping her from leaving, I wasn't touching her except for small brushes here or there. "You can't tell me you would prefer to spend the morning being oiled and rubbed down."

"Which is why I tried to get us out of it." Her voice sounded tight. "But my sister added us to their appointment for *bonding* time, which you appeared to want."

"I'm not opposed to bonding as a general rule." I tried to make the moment more intimate by lowering my voice.

Lauren raised hers. "What? I can't hear you. Crashing of the waves and all that."

Was the little minx trying to ruin the mood? Change the tone of the conversation? I fought a smile, because she would only do that if my efforts were working.

I stepped closer, gripping the railing a little harder to keep myself from actually touching her. "I don't believe you."

"When have you ever?" she scoffed, trying to appear unaffected. She crossed her arms.

But I was the Sherlock of women's feelings, and I deduced her to be completely affected. I leaned toward her, bumping into her crossed arms with my chest. Bypassing her pink lips, I brought my mouth to her ear, brushing my cheek softly against hers. "Your poker face isn't as good as you think it is, Sunshine."

"Don't call me that," she said breathlessly. Her tone did something to my chest, tightening and heating it simultaneously.

I couldn't lean back and look at her now or she might see through me. I kept my mouth close to her ear, but that only had the effect of making her talk into my ear as well. I was not all right with this. But I couldn't back down, not when there was a challenge I had to win. "It's nicer than the other nickname I have for you."

"Irony is never nice."

That surprised me. She thought I was calling her Sunshine sarcastically?

"What's the other nickname?" she asked.

I brought my lips closer to her ear, so close I could feel the shell of it as I spoke. "Wouldn't you like to know?"

Lauren gave a shudder. *Yes.* I was the champion of this round. But she'd gotten a few hits in, too.

I pulled back enough to see her hazel eyes and froze; the way they watched me so bright and clear in the sunlight was arresting.

"I would, actually."

Would what? I was lost. It was annoying that this was happening with Lauren, of all people, but I had actually, legitimately gotten lost in her eyes. I stepped away. She couldn't know how much she'd shaken me. This relationship was fake. It was getting to my head a little, making me feel things for Lauren she would never allow.

It was important to remember that she did not like me in any way. "Where's the spa?"

"This way." Lauren stepped past me. I watched her walk for a minute before she glanced at me over her shoulder, her expression asking if I was going to follow her.

I was. But right now, I was wondering if it was a good idea, and if all this was still worth keeping Sydney off my back.

THE ROBES WERE PLUSH, the room was quiet except for soft music playing from speakers I couldn't see, and Lauren was silent. Maybe I had gone too far with my little experiment next to the railing. Maybe I pushed her too much.

"Come back here," Amelia said, peeking from the next room over. "They have four beds so we can be together."

"Oh, great!" Lauren's enthusiasm was ridiculously fake. Amelia didn't seem to notice, though.

"We can do anything if we do it together," I said quietly with mock solemnity.

Lauren's lips quirked. The woman was fighting a smile! She pulled the large white bathrobe tighter and followed her sister into the next room. It was awkward getting beneath the sheets with Amelia and Kevin in the room, but we all managed to do it while staying modestly covered. It helped that we'd been told we could keep our underwear on, too. Our massage therapists entered the room and the soothing music was turned up a little.

My massage therapist started by rubbing oil into the skin on my back. Oh man, that felt good.

"If you relax, madam, you will feel better," someone said beside me. I lifted my head, unsurprised to see it was the woman engaged to help Lauren.

"I'm relaxed," she lied. Her voice had gone tense. On a scale of one to panic, she sounded like she had just been asked to meet a client without any prep notes.

The woman got back to work, rubbing lotion into Lauren's back.

"Return your face to the center, please," my guy asked me. I did as he bid.

"I'm so glad y'all are getting along," Amelia said a few beds down, her voice muffled by the towel and the chair. "Now there are so many things we can do together. This is like the best-case scenario."

"Yeah," Kevin added. "You're so much better than the last guy. No more putting up with that—"

"Watch it," Amelia said. "That was months ago."

"Derek?" Lauren asked, breathless. Why was she still breathless? "I thought y'all liked Derek."

My stomach clenched. Who was this guy?

"I like my hammer, but that doesn't mean I want to hang out with it."

Was that Kevin's way of calling Derek a tool? "Who's Derek?"

"No one," Lauren said loudly.

"A guy Lauren dated," Amelia said. "He was really into himself."

"You would be too if you had such a successful law firm," she muttered.

"A lawyer?" I gave a low whistle. "I bet the man could really appreciate a good list."

"He could," Lauren said, her voice still high and breathy. She pushed up. "You know what, I think I'm done. I'll Venmo you, Ames. I just—I can't."

I lifted my head to see Lauren slipping back into the waiting area where the changing rooms were located. She'd pulled the entire sheet from the bed, wrapped around to cover herself, and left her massage therapist standing at the table with wide eyes.

Amelia sighed, pushing herself up.

"I'll go." I shot my massage therapist an apologetic smile, sliding from the table in my boxer briefs and into my robe.

Amelia shook her head. "She's my sister, I should talk to her."

It was time to play the card I really didn't have the right to use. "She's my girlfriend. Stay, finish your time together, and don't worry about Lauren. She'll be fine." I gave Amelia my most reassuring smile, and she relaxed. At least my charm worked on one of the Foley girls.

Now to find the other one.

CHAPTER TWELVE

LAUREN

IT HAD BEEN SO LONG since I'd had an anxiety attack, I hadn't seen the signs until it was too late to stop them. Maybe it was Kevin bringing up my ex-boyfriend or feeling trapped in the room with Jack and my sister. I felt vulnerable with no escape. In the waiting room, I was alone, with space, and I could breathe. My heart rate was already starting to regulate, which was proof that I'd done the right thing leaving that massage. I inhaled deeply, letting it out slowly. Then inhaled again—

"Lauren?"

I sputtered, spitting my exhale without dignity. I pulled the sheet around me tighter and peeked over my shoulder at Jack in a bathrobe slipping out of the massage room. I was covered by a thin white sheet. He kept his gaze on my face, like a gentleman.

That was unexpected.

"You okay?" he asked gently.

"Totally." My heart hammered again, and I worked on slowing my breathing. "It's normal to freak out in the middle of an activity that's specifically designed to bring you relaxation."

He squinted. "There were no spreadsheets involved, so could we really call that peaceful? The least they could do would be to provide you with a PowerPoint presenting the different benefits of the massage in real time."

I chuckled, turning away from him and sliding into the changing room. He was ribbing me, but it didn't feel malicious. In fact, I could feel the way my body was relaxing on its own again. "You can go back and finish. I'm not imploding anymore."

"I don't think it's quite the same without the fourth wheel."

Yikes. He was right. Third-wheeling the bride and groom would feel awkward, even if neither of them cared. I pulled my tank over my head and slid into my shorts. Using the mirror, I smoothed my low ponytail again. When I stepped out of the changing room, Jack was standing there, waiting for me, fully dressed. He wore the same tan shorts and bright blue casual T-shirt he'd had on earlier, only now the combination seemed to make his eyes stand out. His hands were slung in his pockets, and he watched me.

"I'm not fragile," I said, walking past him and heading for the door.

He was right behind me. "Didn't think it for a minute."

"Then you don't have to babysit me."

"Didn't really think of it that way, either."

I stopped halfway down the walkway that led to the stairs. We were on one of the highest decks for the spa, so the view was incredible, but I tore my gaze away from the brilliant ocean, landing squarely on Jack's worried eyes. "You're not my boyfriend. This isn't real. So you don't have to follow me and make sure I'm okay."

Especially because I wasn't okay. I had almost had a mild anxiety attack in front of my sister and her fiancé and a guy that already thought really terribly of me.

Audience aside, the annoying thing was that I didn't know why it had happened in the first place. I didn't know what triggered the anxiety running through my body like an explosion of fire ants. I'd had massages before, and they were fine. If I hadn't gotten out of there when I did, maybe it would've been worse, but I had stepped away before anything could escalate. While my heart was still galloping and my nerves were a little frayed, I could feel I was coming down from whatever that had been.

It wasn't a big deal. It wasn't even a thing. And I certainly didn't need Jack Fletcher thinking I was fragile.

He dipped his head. "Am I allowed to check on you as a friend?"

"You don't really qualify for that, either."

Hurt splashed over his face, but it was gone as quickly as it came. I questioned whether I'd seen it at all. He gave me a lazy, cocky smile. "Either way, you're saddled with me, Sunshine. Let's make the most of it and get ourselves some soft serve."

"Ice cream?"

He shrugged.

It was late morning, but the sun was beating down on us. That actually sounded really good. "I could go for a cone."

Jack dipped his head in a quick nod and turned toward the stairs again, one of his hands slung in his pocket. He was so perfectly casual. So unaffected.

"You must've had a really nasty breakup," I mused.

He lifted one dark eyebrow. "What makes you say that?"

"Because you're desperate to keep me around at all times in case you run into Sydney. What did she do? Key your car or hide out in your garage to collect clippings of your hair?"

"I actually had a garage at my old apartment, but not anymore." He sounded distant, lost in dreams. "But no, she didn't stalk me. You'd think we dated for years based on the number of voicemails she left after I ended things, though. It wasn't pretty."

Yikes. "Did you ever try calling her back and reasoning with her?"

Jack nodded. "Multiple times. She just begged and begged. It wasn't her most dignified moment."

I appraised him, trying to see what it was that Sydney couldn't seem to let go of. Yeah, he was really attractive, if you were into the whole cut jawline and muscles thing. But he wasn't the only hot businessman in Dallas.

"I know, I don't get it either," he said, holding the door for me to exit the Adults Only section of the ship.

"That's not what I was thinking." It was *exactly* what I was thinking. I caught a whiff of his cologne as I walked past him and tried to school my expression not to show how much I liked those hints of sage and citrus. "Begging? That's a bit much."

"I would put money on the fact that you've never begged anyone for anything in your entire life," he said.

"That's a weird observation to make."

A smirk played over his lips, drawing my attention there. "I'm right, aren't I?"

"I won't feel ashamed of having self-respect." When Derek broke up with me, I'd packed all the things he'd left in my car and apartment and quietly left them on his front porch. It was raining then, and a few of those items were entirely constructed of paper—namely, the books he'd borrowed from his boss—but I didn't make a big deal out of the breakup and never once asked him to reconsider. Why would I want to date a man who didn't want me?

Jack pretended to shoot a basketball in the air and made a *swish* sound. "Point for me."

We reached the soft-serve machine and each pulled out a styrofoam-flavored cone. He gestured for me to go first, and I twirled vanilla soft serve twice as high as I should have. I was licking the peak off the top when Annie popped through the door that led to the buffet. Her blonde hair was in two braids and she sported a light pink cowboy hat that went with her pink shorts.

She threw her arms in the air. "My fourth favorite cousin! And his *friend*!"

Jack swore under his breath. He finished topping off his ice cream and turned to face Annie. "Fourth? I thought I was at least number two."

Annie gave him a sassy grin. "Colt helped Levi remove a dead tree from our property a few weeks back. Had to bump him right on up to number one."

"That won't last," Jack said, offering her his unadulterated ice cream cone. "Gracie won't stand for it."

She took it, licking the top. "Mmm. Thanks."

"There's more where that came from. Literally. It's all-you-can-eat."

The door swung open again to reveal her husband, Levi, in another Hawaiin shirt and cowboy boots. Jack swore again, and Annie shot him a look that clearly said *play nice*. Well, this was a fun development.

"I thought we'd see you around more," Levi said, taking his wife's cone and licking the top before giving it back to her. She didn't seem to mind.

Jack looked slightly disgusted. "It's only been a day."

"Where are y'all headed?" I asked. "Anywhere fun?"

"Bingo!" Annie gave a little shimmy. "My friend Sharlene won two thousand dollars on her cruise a few weeks ago. It happens to ordinary people."

"Impressive."

Annie's little hand wrapped around my arm. "Join us! It'll be such a hoot."

"A hoot!" I echoed, raising my eyebrows at Jack. His expression clearly said to reject his cousin immediately. I turned my attention back on Annie. "We'd love to!"

BINGO WAS MORE fun than I expected it to be. I'd always pictured older women with neon visors, and while that demographic certainly made up a large portion of the audience, there were so many others. Families, young couples, a whole section of college kids who probably weren't coherent enough to accurately read the cards and thus posed little threat to us.

We bought our cards and daubers. I slid onto a bench seat beside Annie. Levi and Jack made up the bookends.

Erin, the cruise director, was giving her sales spiel on the bonus cards in the center of the stage.

"Have you done this before?" I asked.

"Never!" Annie said. "Hoping for beginner's luck."

Jack's arm spread out over the top of the long bench seat, coming dangerously close to resting on me. It felt natural to lean into his side, which was surprising. That should feel anything but appropriate, and the more I reminded myself we were not a real couple and we had already established a rule of only necessary touching, the more I wanted to break that rule.

Annie's attention moved over the top of my head to rest on Jack. "So how long has this been a thing?"

"It's really new," he said.

"But you've already reached cruising together status?"

"Just because of my sister's wedding," I said quickly. Didn't need to give them the wrong idea of the depth of our relationship. "We are *very* much in the baby stage of dating."

"Practically *just* got together," Jack added.

Annie's eyes sparkled. "Methinks the man doth protest way too much."

She wasn't exact on that reference, but it was close enough. She was definitely correct in assuming Jack was lying about something. I hurried to change the subject. "Are y'all from Texas, too?"

"Arcadia Creek," Annie said proudly, like she expected me to know the town.

"Where is that?"

Levi whistled. "We'll try not to take it personally that you haven't shared anything about your hometown with your girl-friend, Jackson."

Whoa. Okay, first off, no one ever actually told these guys I was his girlfriend. Second, hometown? That sounded so quaint. So *Friday Night Lights* or Hallmark Channel.

Jack leaned over a little, his arm pulling me tightly to his side. Was he trying to make up for our mistake by looking more couple-y or just using me as a shield? "Like Lauren said, we haven't been together long."

Annie still looked hurt. You'd think he refused to claim his family or something, not just the place they lived.

Erin the cruise director got louder. "Who's ready to win a thousand dollars?"

The audience went wild, Annie included.

"Great! Come back tonight for the thousand-dollar game. Right now, $750 is up for grabs! But we're going to start out with a $100 game. Pay attention to that orange card. Winner walks away with $100. Okay, first ball . . . I-17."

"Tricky lady," Annie mumbled.

"You're going down, Fletcher," Levi said, looking at his board. His attention was on the balls being called, but he didn't seem to want to drop the matter of the town. "You coming home for Tucker's party?"

Jack's hand tightened on my arm.

"Who's Tucker?" I asked.

Annie's head whipped toward me so fast her blonde hair swung. "Jack's brother. You mean he's told you nothing of his family, either?"

"New relationship?" I claimed. "We haven't gotten that far yet."

"But y'all can travel to Florida and board a ship already. You feel safe enough to do that with a man you hardly know?"

"We don't *hardly know* one another," Jack said, a bite to his voice that made me sit up a little taller. "You know Kevin Dougherty?"

"Your friend from college?" Annie asked.

"Right. He's marrying Lauren's sister. We've known each other for years. Just not well."

"Doesn't he come from old Texas money?" Annie asked, marking off another Bingo number while Erin continued to call them out. "Why are they getting married on a cruise?"

"It's more of an elopement."

Annie lifted her face, her eyes sparkling.

"It's top secret," Jack said in a distinctly warning tone.

"My lips are as sealed as a new puppy's eyes."

Great imagery.

"B-6," Erin called. "Who has B-6?"

"Me!" Annie screamed, marking it off. "If she says G-52, I'll win."

"You still working for that doctor in Dallas, Jackson?" Levi asked.

Jack shifted. "Medical equipment company, yeah. You still drilling teeth in Arcadia?"

"Only when the cows don't need me," he said.

That was something I hadn't heard of before. "You're an animal dentist?"

Levi looked at me like I painted spots on my face and moo'd.

"He has cows on his farm," Jack explained. "And he's a dentist for humans on the side."

"G-56," Erin called. "Who is taking that hundred dollars? Anyone close?"

Screams went up around the room.

Annie frowned. "That one was close for me."

My board was anything but. It was randomly spotted with nothing resembling a Bingo at all. Jack pulled his arm out from behind me, coloring in the last circle that had been called.

My back felt a chill where his arm had been. It wanted him

there still. Purely for the sake of warmth in this highly air conditioned room and for no other reason at all. Not how comfortable it was to be wrapped up by him. After my minor anxiety attack earlier, it felt nice to be held together, even if it was only for the sake of his cousin.

"You need to bring her out to Arcadia," Annie said, clearly talking to Jack. "Come to Tucker's journeyman party. You know everyone will love to see yo—Ah!" She screamed, daubing a square after Erin announced it. "BINGO!!!" Annie jumped up and down, screaming her win. She ran to the stage as the cruise director beckoned her forward to check her card.

I clapped, then turned to find Jack frowning. I bumped his shoulder with mine. "Disappointed? There are two more games on this sheet. You still have a chance of winning one of them."

His mouth flickered in a halfhearted smile. His green eyes were sad, tugging at my heartstrings. "No, it's not that."

Jack was quiet. Brooding. The male embodiment of a tiny little sloth you just wanted to lift into your arms and cuddle. "Is it all that hometown stuff?" I lowered my voice, leaning close so Levi didn't overhear. "I don't think anyone really cares about how little you've told me. We haven't given ourselves up."

"No, it's my brother's party." He looked down at the Bingo board, his dauber marking an X over the finished game card. "He didn't invite me."

CHAPTER THIRTEEN

JACK

MY SWIM TRUNKS WERE ON, and I sat on the edge of my bed—
no, *our* bed—waiting for Lauren to finish getting into her swimsuit for the hot tub. I flipped through the movies available on
the TV, but without HGTV nothing really caught my eye, so I
powered it off and tossed the remote onto the desk. I'd spent
the afternoon with Kevin and Lucas losing too much money at
blackjack, and dinner had been overly loud. Lauren had been
watching me all night with the glint of pity, and I didn't want
that from anyone, let alone *her*. She had no family except for
Amelia, and I was over here crying because my brother didn't
invite me to his party.

Yes, I was ashamed of myself, thanks for asking.

I leaned back on the huge bed until my head hit the towel-
pig our room cleaner had folded for us and closed my eyes to
rest. Lauren had been in the bathroom for twenty minutes
already, but if I knew women, I predicted it would be at least
that long again until she was ready to hit the hot tub.

I, on the other hand, was wisely using this time away from
Lauren's watchful eye to wallow in my own sadness without an
audience. Why hadn't Tucker invited me to his journeyman

party? And the same with Wyatt's birthday party last week. My phone number hadn't changed. My email address was the same. They all knew where I lived.

Did no one want me there? Had I offended them all with my city preferences?

Or, worse . . . was it an oversight and everyone was starting to forget about me?

The door to the bathroom opened, but I still stared at the ceiling. Impressive. Lauren was much faster than I'd expected.

She cleared her throat. "Um, Jack?"

I sat up. That tone didn't sound good. "Yeah?"

"You can go on without me. I'll meet you there."

I peered at her as she poked her head out of the bathroom but kept her body hidden. "What's wrong?" I asked.

"Nothing."

"Liar."

"I just need a minute."

"I can wait."

"*Jack.*"

"Yeah?"

She made a frustrated sound. "My suit is torn."

"Torn?" I covered a laugh with a cough. Judging by her wry expression, I wasn't very successful. "How so?"

"In the seam—actually does it matter? I can't go out like this. I need you to leave so I can get my other suit."

"You brought two?" It was no surprise the woman had a backup. She probably had a backup for that backup too.

"It's a cruise. That's not weird."

My lips curled in amusement. "And now you're stranded."

Lauren narrowed her eyes. "Don't ruin this, Jack. I was just starting to warm up to you."

I crossed the room to the closet. "Where's your other suit? I can grab it for you."

"I don't need your help, just your absence."

This wreaked heavily of fishiness. "Why?"

"I just don't. Please leave. I'll change and meet you at the hot tub."

"What if Sydney is the only one there? I can't arrive by myself."

"Then wait outside the door," she said through clenched teeth.

"Or tell me where your suit is so I can help you."

"I don't need your help," she repeated with exasperation. Her hazel eyes rounded widely. Her hair was pulled back in a clip, but her bare shoulder poked through the doorway and she looked like a heavy mix of obstinate and tired.

Something in her gaze tugged at my chest. She was so busy being independent she was missing out on one of the finer things in life: having people to rely on. "You know it doesn't make you weak to accept help, right? There's nothing wrong with letting someone do something for you."

Her eyes tightened. "That's not what this is about."

"You just don't want me to see your crabby pajamas? I got a good look at those this morning."

"No." She closed her eyes and drew in a breath. "Fine. Whatever. It's in the second drawer down. Mint green."

The drawers were inside the closet. I opened the one she indicated and pulled out her bathing suit—the only item in the drawer. Proof, I guessed, that she just didn't want to have to ask me for help. Was I that unapproachable? I knew our original blind date—and this trip—didn't have an auspicious beginning, but I'd started to feel like we were warming up to each other a little.

I tossed her the suit, and she disappeared into the bathroom again. Our balcony door was on the other end of the room, so I let myself out there while I waited and leaned over the railing, looking out at the vast black ocean. The sun had set, making the dark water appear fathomless and deep. Stars shone overhead, twinkling above the glittering water.

Familiar cackling laughter caught my attention and I looked down, finding three adults-only hot tubs lined up a few decks below us, but perfectly visible. A woman sat in one of them across from a guy, and while he was a complete stranger, she was not.

The balcony door slid open. "I'm ready—"

"Shhh!" I said quickly, putting my finger to Lauren's lips. I nodded toward the hot tubs. "Sydney is down there, as predicted. She probably hurried just in case she could catch me alone."

Lauren stepped out, peeking over the edge of our balcony. She wore a high waisted two-piece with ruffles lining the straps and neckline and a pair of shorts. The swimsuit was sleek and elegant, just like her. She might have been wearing a one-piece for how well she was covered, but it was still one of the most appealing things I'd ever seen.

Cool wind whipped over us, and Lauren gave a little shiver to the sound of Sydney's laughter. "I guess you would have been the third wheel if you'd gone on ahead like I asked."

"Thank you for saving me from such a fate."

She stepped back into the room and pulled on a crew neck sweatshirt with a row of watercolor cactuses across the front. "Coercion is more accurate."

I followed her. "I like to call it persistence."

"Is that what they claimed on your last restraining order?"

"That's confidential information," I deadpanned, earning a small laugh. I closed the balcony door behind me and faced Lauren, but she didn't move. I nodded to her sweatshirt. "Just like you. Prickly but cute."

She didn't react. "What happened at Bingo?"

My stomach tightened. "Annie won. We both lost. The cruise ship is eighty bucks richer for our participation."

"That's not what I mean."

I knew that. "Why the sudden interest, Spreadsheets?"

Lauren did a double take, holding my gaze. "That nickname is not sticking."

Anything to change the subject. "I like it. There's a nice ring to it . . . might it be precision? Authenticity?"

She rolled her eyes. "Yes, I'm a nerd. You're so funny for pointing it out. Why did Tucker's party make you sad?"

Man, *she* was persistent. "Sad?" I guffawed like a tropical bird.

Lauren took a slight step toward me, making my throat close up. She rested her hands on my shoulders, and a small part of me wished I'd already taken my T-shirt off for this moment so I could feel her fingers on my skin. This might be the first time Lauren had touched me of her own volition without anyone around to prove something to, and judging by my increased pulse, I liked it.

Raising her chin just slightly, she looked me in the eyes. "I'm a safe person, Jack. My internal secret-holder is a Gringotts vault, and I won't even be in your life once this ship docks in Miami again."

Why did that thought sour my stomach? I cleared my throat. "It's nothing, really."

Disappointment flashed over her face. She dropped her hands, to my great regret.

I wanted them back on me. "It's just a celebration for Tucker becoming a journeyman at work. He's an electrical lineman, and they have to apprentice for years before reaching this level. It's a pretty big deal."

"He didn't tell you about it?"

"The journeyman thing? Yeah. I knew. The party? Nope." Familiar hurt slashed through me again. "Arcadia Creek is about an hour away from my apartment. It's not an unreasonable drive, and I'm willing to do it. I'm guessing he just didn't want to put me out."

"But it would be nice to be asked," she said gently.

I held her eyes, the green and browns swimming together in compassion. "I would go if he asked. If I was wanted there, I'd definitely go."

"Then go," she said simply.

"I wasn't invited."

"Surprise him. He's your brother, you can do that. Are you close?"

"Yeah. I'm pretty close with both of my brothers. And the handful of cousins my age. There are a lot of Fletchers and Fletcher-adjacents in Arcadia."

"It must be hard living so far from them."

I shrugged. "It was my choice."

She nodded, slipping her feet into her sandals. "You want to grab an ice cream cone on our way to the hot tub? Give our friends more time so we aren't there alone with Sydney and the guy she's with?"

We could peek over our balcony railing and see if anyone else had arrived, but I didn't want to shortcut anything. A few more minutes with Lauren sounded really good to me. "Lead the way, Spreadsheets."

LAUREN LICKED her cone as we walked across the empty walkway, lights coming up from the floor periodically to show the way. She looked so cozy in her oversized sweater and shorts, like I could pull her onto my lap and feel like I was snuggling a person-sized teddy bear. I didn't know when I started to see her as more than an obnoxious woman who hated me. Now she was just cheeky and apprehensive, like a puzzle box that needed a bit more prodding before it would open up.

But I *would* get her to open up. I was determined now. There didn't seem to be enough joy in her life, but I thought maybe I could show her how to find some. How to put the spreadsheets aside and enjoy the moment. She'd said herself that our relationship ended when we reached Miami again. What did I have to lose?

We walked slowly, Lauren dragging her hand along the railing that went from the lido deck to the adults-only hot tubs on the side of the boat.

"You eat slower than a tractor on the highway."

She eyed me. "You mean, I savor?"

"Ice cream melts. You can only savor it for so long."

She stopped walking and poked her tongue out, running it slowly over the side of her ice cream, then closed her eyes and sighed.

I swallowed hard. Was she *trying* to make me want to kiss her? No, she wouldn't do that. Lauren wasn't Sydney. She didn't resort to tricks.

She didn't need to.

Either way, she was making me hungry, and it wasn't for ice cream. "Hurry up before I take a bite to help you along."

"You had an entire cone."

"And I *was* satisfied. But now you're making it look good again."

She met my eyes. "Poor Jack. Always rushing through things and regretting it later." Putting the ice cream to her mouth, she licked it again, even slower.

My gut clenched. I hadn't wanted a woman the way I wanted to pull her toward me in a long time. *No unnecessary touching.* Where was a party full of people who believed us to be in a relationship and a sprig of mistletoe when you needed it, Hallmark?

When she went for another lick, I grew desperate. Taking her by the wrist, I pulled her arm like a lever until her ice cream cone was in front of my face, then bit off the entirety of the peaked soft serve in one desperate mouthful.

Lauren's mouth dropped open. "Thief!"

"Want it back?" I asked, my mouth full, my hand still circling her wrist.

Her nose wrinkled adorably. She tugged, taking a bite from the top of the cone. "Keep it."

"Y'all coming?" Lucas called behind us. I tensed, not ready to join the others, but we had little choice. At least their presence was good for something. It was no longer *unnecessary* touching. I released her arm and took her free hand, pulling her toward me and lacing my fingers between hers.

"Next time you steal my ice cream, I'm breaking up with you."

"Don't entice me," I joked, leading her around the partitions. The hot tubs all looked full now. Lucas led us to the one on the far end. Lauren crunched away at her cone while we took off our layers in the chilly evening.

Lucas stripped to his swim trunks and kicked off his shoes, hurrying to get in the water. Lauren took another bite, then leaned down to pick up his discarded flip flops from the middle of the floor, moving them to the side of the walkway.

When she straightened, she found me watching her. "It's dark. I don't want anyone to trip."

I nodded. Taking my T-shirt from the hem, I pulled it over my shoulders and tossed it onto a free deck chair. I slid my shoes beneath the chair and turned to find Lauren, the last bit of her cone suspended before her mouth, her eyes on my torso. Should I flex now? How obvious would that be on a scale from Subtle to Clearly I Want To Make This Girl Want Me? Probably land me somewhere in the Fishing For Attention zone.

I flexed anyway.

Lauren popped the rest of her cone in her mouth and turned away from me to slip off her sweatshirt and shorts. For the sake of my own sanity, I climbed up the steps into the hot tub while she did that.

"Jackhammer!" Kevin called, lifting both arms in the air in triumph. Amelia was nestled against his side, Cara and Lucas on either side of them. Sydney sat across, taking up the middle of the remaining space, and the guy she'd been with earlier was gone.

I hovered at the entrance, waiting for her to move one way or the other so Lauren could sit between us.

She didn't move.

"Freezing," Lauren said behind me, the wind whipping around us while the ship moved. The sun wasn't there to warm us.

She peeked around me, and I could practically feel her realizing our situation. She gently pushed me to the side and stepped past me, down into the water with a gentle sigh as she submerged herself, taking the seat nearest the stairs. She reached for my hand and pulled me down, scooting gently toward Sydney until she had to be totally pressed against her.

But Sydney still wouldn't move. "There's space over here," she said, indicating I could fill it on her opposite side.

"So scoot then," Lauren said.

Sydney stared at her for another minute before giving up and moving over.

Bless Lauren. She made room for me to squeeze in beside her, and my arm went around her back, pulling her up close to my side. Not unnecessary. Claim-staking. She reached for the hand I dangled over her shoulder and held it like we were a real couple. My body was warming, and I didn't think it was entirely due to the bubbly, heated water.

Amelia gave an awkward laugh, looking from Sydney to me.

"Never have I ever?" Lucas asked, wearing an evil grin.

"No!" Cara splashed him. "I hate that game."

"Because you always lose."

She glared playfully.

"I'm down," Kevin said, eyeing Amelia, who shrugged.

"Fine." I nudged Lauren, and she looked up at me. She was way too close right now, nestled into my side so perfectly. All it would take was a little leaning for my lips to meet hers.

"I've never played," she admitted.

"Everyone puts up a hand," Cara said, demonstrating like she was about to give a high-five. "We go around the circle saying things we've never done, and you lower a finger if you've done that thing. First person to put down all five fingers loses."

"Girls love this game," Kevin complained.

"So does Lucas," Cara quipped.

"I'll start." Sydney put her hand up and everyone else followed suit. She looked at Lauren, then me. "Never have I ever kissed Amelia."

Anger pooled in my belly like a spilled drink. I could have thrown her from the hot tub. I glanced at Kevin, then the water, and lowered one finger.

CHAPTER FOURTEEN

LAUREN

IT WAS SO quiet I could hear the bubbles in the hot tub. Kevin stared at Jack in confusion, so I followed his line of sight to Jack's hand to find his pointer finger bending down.

What? Jack had kissed my sister?

"When was this?" Kevin asked, his voice carefully calm.

Amelia gave an uncomfortable laugh. "You knew about this, babe. It was before we started dating. That Alpha Phi party."

"That's where we met," Kevin said.

"Right, but you were with that other girl from your master's program." She put her hand on his cheek. "It was so long ago."

Kevin chuckled awkwardly, giving his head a shake. "Yeah, you're right. Years."

"I told you when you asked me out that I'd kissed your friend."

He nodded. "I guess I didn't realize it was Jack." Then he shook himself. "Weird. But okay. This is okay."

"It wasn't even good," Amelia added, sending Jack a saucy smile.

"The worst," Jack agreed tensely.

Sydney didn't seem satisfied by the way no one was exploding. "Maybe Lauren needs to kiss Kevin now so we can really compare."

I caught my soon-to-be brother-in-law's eye and wrinkled my nose. "Weird. No thanks."

The feeling was mutual. Obviously. It was a weird thing to suggest.

"Which sister is the better kisser?" Sydney asked archly, leaning forward a little in the water.

I looked at Jack on impulse. He didn't know the answer. He'd only kissed one of us, but no one else knew that.

Jack's gaze lowered to my lips. Something flashed in his eyes that looked more like irritation than attraction. Why was Sydney so obnoxious? He met her gaze. "A gentleman never tells."

"Oh, wrong answer. No girlfriend wants to hear that," Sydney crowed.

Jack stood, and water fell from his sculpted chest in rivulets. "Anyone want a drink? I'm buying."

He gathered orders to take back to the bar with him, and Lucas joined him to help carry everything back. When he left, Amelia swam to his seat and sat beside me. "I haven't seen you much today."

"We spent two hours getting our nails and facials done this afternoon."

"But I didn't *see* you."

She was fishing about my weird exit during the massages this morning, but a hot tub full of her friends wasn't the place to have this conversation, even if Cara was trying to make up for the awkwardness by asking Kevin about work. "I'm fine, really."

Amelia didn't look convinced. "I don't want you to do anything you don't want to do, Lo."

"I've had a really good time so far." Which was true. I thought being saddled with Jack for the week was going to make it completely miserable. He was turning out to be nothing like the man I'd made him in my mind.

Sure, he kissed waitresses in the middle of dates and left mean voicemails about how stuck up a lady could be, but on this trip he'd been funny and thoughtful and full of layers I didn't realize he'd had.

He also had kissed my sister and never told his best friend, and it felt weird. Not for Kevin and Amelia; their five-year relationship was going to be fine. Sydney was only trying to drive a wedge between me and Jack, and it wouldn't work. But also, it was weird that he'd kissed her already and not me. I didn't really want to think about how Jack thought of me. Amelia was the younger, prettier, perkier Foley. She was none of the things he'd complained about me being after that date, which was a lowering thought.

"I just want you to enjoy yourself," Amelia said.

"I am."

"So don't feel like you *have* to stick around if you'd rather not."

My discomfort grew. Was this her polite way of saying that it might just be better if I called it a night? Honestly, at this point, I didn't want to be out here, but that didn't make it sting less when she made it clear she didn't want me out here either.

I tried for a bright smile. "If you're sure, then I think I'll go."

"Are we okay?"

"Of course we are. I'll see you in the morning. We have to head out at eight, right?"

"Yeah," she confirmed. "We need to meet our ride on the dock at eight-thirty."

I stood, the cold air hitting me fast. "Then goodnight, everyone. I'll see you all on the beach tomorrow."

Cara whistled a catcall, and Kevin wished me a good night. I hurried from the hot tub and pulled a towel around me, slipping my feet into my sandals. It was suddenly important that I get back to the room before Jack noticed me missing. I wanted a hot shower and my snuggly crab pajamas before he reached our room, and I was afraid he would ditch his friends the moment he realized his shield was gone.

Why did it feel so icky to imagine Jack with Amelia? I didn't like it, and I *really* didn't like how much I didn't like it.

My feelings for him were undoubtedly becoming complicated.

I made it to the room and opened the balcony door, cocking my ear to the side to listen to the people in the hot tubs below. I wanted to know if Jack was back yet.

The voices blended together, mixing with the other two hot tubs. I closed the door before I could be caught spying and pulled my bag into the bathroom with me to shower.

But over the next thirty minutes while I cleansed and readied for bed, I couldn't help playing Amelia's words over in my head. *Don't feel like you have to stick around if you'd rather not.* Was I really the grandma harshing their vibe? Did people even have a vibe anymore, or was that term outdated? Something I wouldn't know since I was old.

I was more lost than Alice among the Wonderland mushrooms.

By the time I got out of the shower and brushed my teeth and hair, it was only nine-thirty. Maybe I could find *Fixer Upper* on the TV and lose myself in Chip and Joanna's adorable relationship and impeccable taste. I grabbed the remote, nestled in bed, and turned on the TV when I heard the beep of a keycard at the door.

Without thinking, I hit power, tossed the remote on Jack's side of the bed, and closed my eyes, pretending I was asleep. Was that childish? Maybe. Did it mean I wouldn't have to talk about what happened in the hot tub? Most definitely.

Worth it.

Jack moved about quietly for a minute before he went into the bathroom, and I heard the shower come on. I nestled further into the bed, wishing I'd also turned the lights out before faking sleep. They burned bright orange behind my eyelids and made actual sleep difficult to manage.

Which could also be due to my racing heart.

Jack was out of the shower and brushing his teeth pretty quickly, and before I knew it, he was walking around the room turning out the lights. Ah, sweet relief.

The mattress compressed on his side, my blankets tugging tightly when he climbed into bed.

The silence sat around us so fully it was loud, despite the people below our balcony still partying in the hot tubs.

"I know you're awake," he said quietly.

My eyes shot open. "How?"

"You're not breathing deeply or steadily. It's pretty obvious."

"So much for avoiding you. I could have been watching *Fixer Upper* this whole time."

"You found a home renovation channel?" he asked, sounding hopeful.

"No, but I was trying to." I lifted up on my elbow to see his face over the wall of pillows I'd made. "You like HGTV?"

He shot me a sheepish look. "Love it. But don't tell anyone. This is privileged information."

How privileged was he talking? "Like only your friends know?"

"Only my girlfriend. It's not something I advertise."

Girlfriend. The word wrapped around me like a weighted blanket. Jack's eyes were dark, glittering in the dim room. We could close the drapes completely and block out the deck lights outside, but it was also nice being able to see his expression.

I lifted one shoulder in an awkward shrug. "There's nothing wrong with a man who likes design shows."

"I love *renovations*," he clarified.

"Same point." I dropped back down to lay flat, staring at the dark ceiling.

He was silent for a minute. "You left."

"Us grandmas and our early bedtimes. Don't want to mess with the routine."

"Did you clean your dentures?"

"And put my hair in curlers."

"Now *that* I would love to see."

The weird thing was, he sounded like he meant it. "You have a thing for old ladies?"

"No." I could hear him turn on the bed to face me. "I just want to see you with your hair down again. It would have to be in order to roll into curlers, I'm guessing."

My heart hammered. The room was dark, the sounds from outside muffled by the walls and glass door to the balcony. I could hear Jack breathing, and it wasn't deep or steady either, so he was clearly as awake as I felt. "My hair is down now," I said.

Jack sat up. "I didn't notice since it's hard to see in here. Will you show me?"

This felt a little like the time Tommy asked me to kiss him in first grade. "What do I get out of it?"

"The joy in your heart of knowing you cheered up a friend."

"Hmm. Not good enough."

He looked down at me. "I can see you, you know. My eyes have adjusted now."

"Then stop looking." I took one of the pillows from the makeshift wall that ran between us and put it over my face.

Jack leaned over. "Due to the danger of suffocation, I cannot allow you to hide this way." He tugged at the pillow, but I held fast.

"A gentleman doesn't take a lady's pillow."

"I never pretended to be a gentleman."

"You did," I said, sitting up but still holding the pillow in front of me. "In the hot tub. *A gentleman never tells!*"

"That was obviously an avoidance tactic," he said somewhere behind the pillow shield I was holding. After a minute of silence, he asked, "Are you ticklish?"

"What?"

His hands snaked under the pillow and went for my sides, moving quickly and making me squeal. I chucked the pillow at him, falling over in high-pitched laughter I could not control for the life of me.

"STOP!" I called between giggles, his fingers dancing over my sensitive abdomen.

Jack immediately retreated, his grin so wide his teeth were gleaming in the dark room. "Careful or you'll make the neighbors send someone to check on you."

"It would only serve you right if they did make assumptions." My chest heaved while I tried to regain normal breathing. I'd been spun around, so twisted in the blankets that our bed was no longer neat and orderly with perfectly divided sections. Pillows were strewn everywhere, the sheets twisted around one of my legs, and I was on my hands and knees, prepared to fight off any further tickling attempts.

"That was extremely satisfying," Jack said.

I sat back on my heels at the foot of the bed, opposite him. "Making me squeal like a terrified pig?"

"No, watching you lose control. Your laugh was just the cherry on top."

He'd pinpointed exactly why I hated being tickled. I was *so* ticklish, like beyond normal, and I hated it. I hated losing control and not being able to quiet my volume or keep myself from kicking out involuntarily. It was a full body reflex—vocal chords included—and totally out of my hands. There was nothing in the world I hated more than not having things well in hand.

So, why did I have the slightest temptation to entice him to do it again?

"If you tickle me again," I warned, "you're sleeping outside."

"Good thing it's warm," he said, reaching toward me slowly.

I picked up a pillow and hit his hands down. "No."

Jack immediately stopped. "Okay."

Okay? Really? It was that easy? I mean, it always should be that easy, but I hadn't expected him to back down so quickly. "Thank you."

"I'm just trying to keep myself from being thrown in cruise ship jail."

I chuckled, shaking my head. I was sitting back on my heels, hugging a pillow to me, my half-wet hair falling in frizzy strands around my face.

"Huh," he said, tilting his head to the side. "You should leave it down more often."

I picked up a chunk of hair and dropped it against my shoulder with a splat. "Don't be ridiculous."

Jack put up both hands as if to say that he was nothing but genuine. He climbed from the bed and reached for me. "Here. We won't be able to fix this mess unless we get off."

I took his hand, untangling my foot and climbing down. He straightened the sheets and blankets, then reassembled my pillow wall. He moved to my side of the bed and folded back the blanket in a triangle, then gestured to it like Vanna White. "Your bed awaits."

This was weird. Jack was so large but quiet, waiting for me to climb into bed. "It looks like you're waiting to tuck me in," I joked.

"I am," he said quietly.

My heart leapt to my throat. No one had ever done that for me before. Literally. My mom must have done it when I was a toddler and she was still alive, but I couldn't remember those years.

I slid under the blankets and Jack pulled them over me, tucking the edges underneath my sides. He stood above me, looking down for a minute. "Yep. Just as good as I imagined."

I couldn't breathe as I waited for him to round the bed and

climb in on his side. He pulled the blanket over himself and let out a sigh that went straight into my heart.

"Jack?" I whispered, reaching over the pillow wall to find his hand. He let me take it, and I pressed it with all the warmth I had. "Thank you. No one has ever done that for me before."

"Tickled you? I can see why. You're terrifyingly loud."

"No." I swallowed. "Tucked me in."

He was really quiet. "Your parents just weren't bedtime routine people?" he asked gently.

"My parents died when Amelia was a baby. I was only four when my grandma took us in, but she worked two jobs just to make ends meet, so she was perpetually exhausted."

"And that meant sacrificing your childhood," he whispered.

I hesitated, drawing in a breath. "My grandma loved us, and she worked hard. I never lacked feeling like someone was watching out for me. But that someone was constantly working to provide for *us*, and I helped how I could."

I shrugged off the overwhelming sadness that crushed me anytime I'd thought of my grandmother. We'd lost her a few years ago to lung cancer, and I missed her with every part of me. Since I had turned seven, I'd been Amelia's overseer and caretaker in many ways, but losing Grandma meant Amelia and I were all we had.

"You had no other family to step in or help?"

"Both of my parents were only children and my dad lost his parents to heart disease and age. They were older when they had him. My grandma's husband was out of the picture long before we entered it. We just didn't have anyone else."

Silence fell over us. "Not to sound like a creep, but I'm happy to tuck you in whenever you want."

I laughed lightly, my body warming, my heart thudding.

Jack seemed to sense that I was done talking. He pulled my hand up and pressed a kiss to the underside of my wrist. "Good night, Lo."

My throat clogged with emotion. I squeezed his fingers and let him hold my hand, resting both of ours together on his chest. We lay like that until my arm went numb and tingly. I pulled my hand from his grip and rolled over before falling asleep.

CHAPTER FIFTEEN

JACK

THE IMAGE of Lauren in a bathing suit last night had been everything I could hope for and more—elegant and beautiful despite being somewhat modestly covered. She'd had good taste last night. But somewhere in the night, her sense of fashion took a nosedive. The image of Lauren prepared for a day snorkeling in the Caribbean was going too far. Her outfit resembled a nun's habit more than swimwear. Black with long sleeves, she was covered from her neck to her wrists in a rash guard with long, dark board shorts that reached her knees.

Yet still she managed to look sleek. Maybe that was due in part to the return of the low, conservative ponytail.

"I thought you only brought two swimsuits," I said when she stepped from the bathroom.

Lauren approached the vanity mirror and looked at me through the reflection before taking out her ponytail and dividing her hair into two sections. "This isn't a swimsuit."

"I agree," I said with conviction.

"It's insurance."

"Against men?"

She started to twist the hair at the front of her hairline in an intricate pattern. Oh, she was French braiding it. "First off, I don't dress for men."

"Nope. You dress for the job you want."

The way her eyes flicked to me again made me wonder if I was correct. "Second off, this is one of those times when function trumps fashion. I burn really easily."

Now I felt bad for giving her a hard time. She *did* have super pale skin.

Lauren applied sunscreen to her face and adjusted the straps at her shoulder beneath the rash guard. "I was supposed to wear the other suit underneath my rash guard. This one doesn't really work well." She pulled a face, trying to move the straps again. "Gosh, this is *so* tight. It didn't feel this bad when I tried it on at home."

"Why can't you just wear the other suit beneath it then?" I asked.

"It's ripped in a sensitive location."

"But it'll be under that," I said, swirling my hands to indicate her outfit. "It'll be hidden."

She shook her head. "I won't risk it. What if I tear these shorts on a rock or something? Then I'm not covered."

"You can take a vacation from constant risk analysis, you know."

She finished sunscreening the visible parts of her skin and shot me a look over her shoulder. "But I'm happier with it. Safer. More settled and less anxious."

I threw my hands in the air. "Fine. Just trying to help you lighten up."

Well, that had certainly been the wrong thing to say. Lauren's eyes narrowed, her mouth pinching. It had entirely the opposite effect of what I'd been trying to do, instead making her more tense. She grabbed her small bag, slid her feet into her sandals, and went for the door without another word.

I hurried to follow her, nabbing my room key, phone, and

shoes, and hustling down the hallway to catch up to her. "I didn't mean it—"

"Yes, you did," she snapped.

"Whoa."

She didn't slow down.

I'd hit a nerve, and it bit at me. "I'm sorry, Lauren. I'm not trying to be rude—"

She rounded on me fast, her eyes sparking, her finger jabbing into my chest. "Just because I like to be prepared, it doesn't mean I don't know how to enjoy myself. You can make smart choices and protect yourself against terrible pain and *still* be fun."

I leaned forward, forcing her finger to press into my chest harder. "Yeah, you can. But you can also keep yourself from relaxing when you worry too much about things." Her admission last night about no one ever having tucked her in—that had wrecked me. It had taken every ounce of self-control I possessed not to push aside the stupid pillow wall and pull her into my arms, to provide her comfort. No one needed to grow up and take on such responsibility as early as she had.

Her life had been hijacked from a young age, and I kind of wondered if she was never going to heal from that if no one showed her how.

Lauren shook her head, dropping her hand.

I scooped it up, tugging her closer until her face was only a few inches from mine, our chests so close they almost touched, but not quite. "Let me show you how to let go."

Her hazel eyes locked on mine. "That sounds like an icky pick-up line."

"I don't have to pick you up. You're already my girlfriend."

"But I'm not," she said. "Not really. I'm here for Amelia. She's my focus for the week."

So, basically, she wouldn't let anything distract her. Not feelings or the chemistry that was buzzing between us or the possibility that I just might know what I was talking about.

Our chests were both rising and falling in quick tandem. My blood pumped hard, roaring in my ears. I had the sudden overwhelming desire to pull her another three inches closer and crash my lips against hers. I imagined it, the way she would feel against me, the satisfaction it would provide. I stared into her glinting hazel eyes with intense focus. Her attention dropped to my lips, building my longing until it was a roaring river crashing against a dam wall.

But I couldn't let it break. We had an agreement that benefited me: keeping Sydney at a distance. Kissing Lauren would only be taking advantage of the position I'd put her in and muddying the waters, right?

I'm here for Amelia. She wasn't here for me.

After learning about her family last night in more detail and her relationship with Amelia, it occurred to me that this wedding cruise had to be super hard on both Foley women. One of them was getting married and they had *no one else.* No parents, not the grandmother who raised them, no extended family —nothing.

Kissing Lauren would only make me the unprincipled player she thought I was, preying on her in a time of vulnerability. But seeing her eyes on my lips, I felt like she wanted this as much as I did.

Which meant I had to back off.

I dropped her hand, taking a step back. "We're going to be late."

Lauren's hazel eyes closed briefly before she turned to keep walking down the hallway, and I fell in step beside her. "No more talking," she said. "We are in a relationship in front of the others, but only for the sake of the MediCorp conference—"

"And keeping Sydney away."

"—and nothing else. No unnecessary touching. No deep

conversations." She wouldn't look at me as she talked. "We are not friends, Jack."

That stung, but I didn't argue.

I also didn't take her hand when we reached the dock and found our friends waiting. I didn't slide my arm around her waist when we sat in the mid-sized boat with other tourists to take us out snorkeling in the crystal teal water. I didn't pull her close to my side to make room for the young family who climbed on after us, or respond when Sydney asked for help putting her sunscreen on.

And I certainly didn't watch Lauren's every single movement, yearning with every particle of my being to hold her.

Okay, that last one was a lie.

"IT'S TOO TIGHT. I can't lift my arms."

Lauren's voice reached me above the sound of water moving in and out of my ears. The snorkeling boat was anchored, the majority of the tourists in the water a few yards away with their snorkels down, admiring the reef and the fish. But I was treading water, eavesdropping on my fake girlfriend's conversation with her sister. They faced away from me near the end of the boat, treading water.

"Then take it off," Amelia said.

Lauren shook her head. "I didn't apply any sunscreen underneath it. My shoulders are unprotected."

"Just stay under the water and the sun can't get to you."

"Is that true?"

Amelia dipped her head side to side as if she was thinking about it. "Probably. We only have an hour before we have to be back on the boat anyway."

"An hour is long enough to burn, Ames."

"Is it though? Or will you just get a little pink that will turn into a bit of a tan?" She sounded hopeful.

"Burn. I'll definitely burn."

"Some color would look good with your maid of honor dress."

"Some color will make me *match* my dress." Lauren gave a frustrated sigh and lightened the tone of her voice. "Go find Kevin. I'll figure this out."

"I'm not leaving you—"

That was my entrance. I swam toward them. "I'm here," I said, making them both turn in the water to face me.

Amelia looked relieved. Lauren looked mad.

"Problem solved! Boyfriend to the rescue. I'll leave you to it." Amelia grinned at me. "You don't even need to swim, Lo. Jack can tow you around!"

Lauren's face pinched even further, but she said nothing as her sister swam away.

"You can't swim?" I asked. The water was clear enough that I could see her legs moving beneath it.

"I can't lift my arms."

"And part of your pre-snorkeling ultra preparation to-do list wasn't to put sunscreen on beneath your rash guard in case you couldn't swim in it?" I tsked. "I'm ashamed of you."

"I'm ashamed of myself." She kicked her legs in overtime to keep herself up, but her arms weren't really moving much under the water. That would make it hard to swim around the reef.

"You really can't lift your arms?"

"I really can't. The shoulders are so tight they won't let me lift my arms high enough. It's not something I thought to test at home."

"Guess you can't prepare for everything."

She glared at me. I threw the rest of my preparation jokes into the vault for another day.

The rest of the group was getting further away, and I could

see how frustrated Lauren was becoming. Amelia's suggestion didn't sound half bad to me, anyway. "Want to climb on my back? I'm happy to swim for both of us."

"Definitely not."

"Yeah, it would be hard to resist me after I let you hold on like that," I joked, to lessen the sting of rejection.

She let her head fall back and tried to lift her arms again, but I could see where the shirt grew tight at the seam near her armpits and she was straining.

"Let's get back into the boat and I'll help you sunscreen your back."

Lauren groaned. "It won't work. My skin is already wet."

"It's better than nothing. If you want to snorkel, I'll help you. It's your call."

She seemed to consider this for a moment before delivering a world-weary sigh. "Fine. Thanks."

We climbed up the unsteady metal ladder into the boat, water dripping from us like tiny waterfalls and pooling at our feet. I grabbed some sunscreen from the bench that someone left behind and tried to avert my eyes when Lauren peeled the black rash guard off and set it down on the bench seat. She wore the same mint green swimsuit from last night, and it was hard not to stare while she toweled down her skin and dried it as best as she could.

"Need help?"

"Just on my back." She faced away from me. I used my towel to dry her skin better, but water dripped from her braids, fighting me. Squeezing out twice as much sunscreen as I thought I needed, I started rubbing it in circles on her back while she took care of her chest and arms. It took about five minutes to rub the lotion into her damp skin, but I did my best, running my fingers beneath her straps just to be extra safe.

"Ready?" I asked, when she picked up her snorkel again.

"Go ahead, Jack. I'll meet you in the water. I want to give it a minute to soak in."

Man, she *really* did not take this whole sunburning thing lightly.

I jumped into the water, then fitted my snorkel on and swam away from the boat toward the reef. The water grew a little more shallow there, but all I had to do was look down and an entire aquatic ecosystem was eight feet below me. Orange coral spread out like spongy fingers while teal and yellow striped fish swam below me in a glittering school.

Cara and Lucas were just ahead of me, and I joined them, searching where Cara pointed to find an enormous orange starfish blending into the coral. Communication was more difficult beneath the water, but it was quiet and peaceful, watching the marine life without anything to distract me.

Until Lauren swam up. Her eyes were unreadable, but she came up to my side and I reached for her hand, pointing out the starfish. She thumbs-upped me when she saw it, then she pointed out an orange and yellow fish that swam just below our stomachs. I had to release her hand in order to swim, but I gestured to Cara and Lucas ahead of us, and we followed them through the reef, pointing out cool fish and weird rocks while the water eased us back and forth gently on the waves, like the reef itself was breathing.

This would have been impossible without arm mobility. I was glad she had thrown caution to the wind and joined us. We found the rest of our friends. Sydney moved to position herself near me, her arm brushing my stomach and my chest while she swam a little too close. The woman was relentless. At some point she needed to see that her tactics weren't going to entice me and give up, right? This whole situation was my own stupid fault for going out with her in the first place. But I'd been lonely, and she was beautiful. At the time, I hadn't seen the monster of a situation I was creating.

Lauren noticed it now, though. She took my hand, tugging me closer to her side. Even after our disagreement this morning, she was still holding up her part of the arrangement.

I kicked up until my head was free of the water and pulled the snorkel from my mouth for a breather. Sunlight beamed overhead, forcing me to squint and rub water from my face.

Lauren followed me, pulling her gear up on her forehead, the mouthpiece dangling down. "You okay?"

The skin around her eyes was red from the imprint of the goggles, her lips plump from the breathing tube, and I couldn't help but smile. "Yeah. Just giving them a second to move on. Sydney kept touching my chest," I said with a shudder.

"You can't find it that repulsive if you dated her," Lauren said.

"I never said Sydney was repulsive. She's beautiful. But being touched without asking for it feels gross, regardless of who it is."

Lauren looked like she gave this consideration, watching the tops of our friends' snorkels move away from us. Probably so they wouldn't get kicked from our treading. "Noted."

"You're different," I hurried to say. "You can touch me anytime you want. Consider this my full consent."

"But you just said it was gross whenever it's unasked for."

"The difference is that I want you to," I said, not even a hint of a smile on my face. And the thing was, I meant it.

CHAPTER SIXTEEN

LAUREN

THE WARM SUN glared overhead despite the fact that it was still winter back at home. I treaded water across from Jack, and aside from the boat with our captain in my peripheral vision, I didn't see anything around him except for gently waving teal water and the occasional tourist.

It was all blending into nothing, because his words ran on a loop in my head.

You can touch me anytime you want. I want you to.

The trouble was, I wanted me to, also. I wanted to slide my hands over his strong shoulders and pull him close and feel what it would be like to have someone else help carry my problems for a minute. His back was broad. He could probably hold quite a few of them and not even feel it.

But wanting this and succumbing to the temptation of his cocky smile and glittering green eyes were two different things. He wasn't a Forever guy. He was a Just For Fun guy.

I couldn't do Just For Fun. It wasn't in my nature.

"Should we find our friends?" I asked, pulling my goggles down to cover my eyes again. It made Jack all blurry, which was probably a good thing. He looked too attractive with his bare shoulders dipping out of the ocean, his muscles rippling while he moved his arms to keep afloat. Distance and the buffer of other people would be good.

Jack didn't move. But I didn't either.

"They're probably wondering what we're doing," I said lamely.

"They think we're dating." Jack swam a little closer. "I guarantee none of them are wondering what we're doing. It stops being interesting gossip once two people are together."

He had a point. "I'm not sure Sydney got the memo, though."

"Maybe she doesn't believe us." Jack reached over and lifted my goggles back onto my forehead, then looked down at my lips. "We might need to try something else to convince her I'm not on the market."

"Now *that* definitely sounded like a line."

"Is it working?"

Yes. "Maybe if we had an audience, it would. Everyone's underwater now."

Jack swam up until he was almost touching me. Our arms were both out to the sides, keeping us up and making our breathing heavy from the effort. He slipped one arm around my waist, pulling me close. "Good point. They can all see everything underwater." His fingers skimmed my waist, driving goosebumps over my skin. "I would file this under totally necessary touching."

My pulse raced. His hand was strong and warm, the pressure dropping lava along my waist. "I'm sure Sydney's attention is on the fish, not us."

"Doubt it. She has a sixth sense for where I'm at. Guaranteed she's watching us right now."

"You think highly of yourself."

He lifted an eyebrow. "No, I've just had to fend her off for a while. It's exhausting."

"Why is she so obsessed with you?"

"Because she had a taste, I guess." He didn't sound cocky about it, though. "She wants a relationship with me, and we had a bit of it, but then I cut her off. She didn't get enough, maybe? Or she's just super competitive? I don't know. None of my other ex-girlfriends have been this crazy after we broke up." He tilted his head a little, the water dripping from his hair into the ocean. "What about you? Your last boyfriend was . . ."

"Derek. We didn't date long, and then he was over it. I let him go without making a scene because I didn't really have time to devote to a relationship anyway." Breakups were also easier to manage if you decided you were better off without the other person. Even if it was only a lie you told yourself. It definitely helped me get over him faster.

"Right. The guy Kevin didn't like."

"I'm not gauging who I date based on Kevin's approval."

"He has solid taste."

"In women." I shrugged. "He's marrying my sister, so I can't really argue that point."

"Kevin really likes me," Jack said quietly. "I'm pretty sure I have his full approval."

My smile widened, but I shook my head. It was impossible to tell whether this was just flirty Jack, who wanted a kiss because he was a guy, or if he *meant it*. I wanted to believe he was being authentic, but my mind flashed back to our first date and the voicemail he left me.

"You and I had our chance," I said. "Didn't work out."

"Yeah, and you never really told me why." His second arm came around my waist now, and it was impossible to tread water without kicking him. "Just let me hold you up."

I succumbed, letting him hold me in the water, relaxing while the ocean waves lulled us. It was suddenly overwhelmingly peaceful. How the heck was he treading enough for the both of us?

"So. Why did you bail on our date?" he pushed, his breathing coming faster. Clearly the man was exerting extra energy keeping us both above water.

"You know." I closed my eyes, letting the sun wash over me, my arms around his shoulders. One of his arms held me tight, but the other was working to keep us afloat, and I pressed my hand to his deltoid, feeling the muscle move.

"No, I really don't."

I peeled my eyes open. He looked serious. "Does making out with a waitress in the hallway of the restaurant mean anything to you?"

He went quiet, his mouth dropping open. Ocean water went inside and he turned his head to spit it out. "What?"

"You know what. I don't date guys who cheat mid-date."

He cringed. "Is it cheating if we weren't together yet?"

So he wasn't denying it. Part of me hoped, the longer I'd spent time with him on this ship, that maybe he would have some reason to explain it all away. He'd been drunk and didn't realize the waitress wasn't me. It hadn't been him, but someone with the exact same shirt, haircut, and jawline. He had a secret twin no one knew about. But his guilty face was taking owner-ship and it soured my stomach.

His expression morphed into confusion. "Wait, it wasn't cheating at all," he said, holding me tighter, like he was going to keep me from running away. "You left before I kissed her."

"I left *because* you kissed her," I corrected.

Jack narrowed his eyes, shaking his head softly. "She was waiting for me when I came out of the bathroom to tell me you'd left. We talked for a minute, and she kissed me, which wasn't expected. It took me a while to stop her."

"I saw you guys, Jack. It took a *long* while." I considered what he said, though.

He didn't seem satisfied. "Why would she lie about you leaving?"

"I took a phone call." It hit me that she'd probably seen me walk outside, but she must have known I was going to return. I was only talking on the phone.

"So she assumed . . . and then you came back and saw us." Jack's eyes turned pleading. "I'm not proud. But I didn't seek her out. I knew her already—her cousin worked in my office and we'd hung out before. It wasn't like she was a total stranger. I don't kiss every attractive woman I speak to."

My insides turned to sludge. "You were on a date with someone else, though."

"I didn't know that. I thought the date had ended."

That I'd ended it. Could I really be mad he'd moved on so quickly? It stung, for sure.

"It doesn't matter," I said. "It's the past, and it's why we don't have a future."

He looked at me long and hard. "That's why you left the restaurant and didn't return any of my texts."

"Part of it." I didn't want to go into the voicemail bit. Not here. It was too embarrassing. I pushed away from his chest, kicking my legs to keep me afloat. Cold rushed over where his skin had been pressed to mine, keeping me warm. "I think our hour is almost up. I want to see more fish before they call us back."

"Lauren, wait. We should discuss this." To his credit, he looked sincere.

"In the middle of the ocean?"

"Back on the ship, then?" he asked. "Please?"

"There's no point," I called, swimming further away. "We're here for Amelia and Kevin. Let's try to remember that." I put my goggles on and shoved the mouthpiece in before dunking my head underneath the water, where it became silent immediately.

139

I SHOULD HAVE LISTENED to my gut. It knew things my brain didn't. It had a sense all its own, and thus far in my life it had yet to steer me wrong.

It knew fake-dating Jack was a bad idea. Check.

It knew I would start falling for him and end up disappointed. Check.

And it knew an hour without a rashguard in the sun would give me severely burned shoulders. *Check.*

I stood with my back to the mirror, pushing my finger lightly against my shoulder blade and watching the skin turn white where I pressed, only to contrast the increasingly pink skin around it. Maybe it would only be a little sore. It wasn't bad yet, and I *did* layer on sunscreen before getting in the water.

A girl could cross her fingers and hope.

The shower turned off. I made a split-second decision to avoid Jack and slid my feet into my sandals. Knocking lightly at the bathroom door, I leaned close. "Meet you at dinner! Bye!"

"Wait," came his muffled reply. "Lauren—"

But I was already out in the hallway, the door swinging shut behind me. We needed a little space and distance, because my heart wanted to listen when he was telling me he wanted to put our past behind us, but this entire arrangement wasn't real. I knew he was just fooling himself. He was caught up in the cruise and all the time we'd spent together; it wasn't a lasting situation.

Besides, I wouldn't have time for a relationship once we were back on land. The only reason I was free to spend so much time with him now was because he'd made it illegal for me to check in with work. I dreaded the sheer amount of emails piling up in my inbox right now.

My body itched to find a quiet corner and my laptop and see what kind of mess was waiting for me back home in the office, but it wasn't worth sacrificing the MediCorp conference over.

Jerry would just have to limp along this week until I was back to set everything to rights again.

My champagne-colored dress was a little *Marilyn Monroe above the subway grate* in shape, but a little longer, and it swung with each step I took.

"Hey fancy lady," a woman called behind me. I turned just to see who she was talking to and found Annie coming toward me, her black dress made of lace with a slip beneath it and bell sleeves that flared at the wrists. She was, of course, wearing bright teal cowboy boots.

A laugh bubbled from my chest when I realized she was talking to me. Fancy? "I'm really not."

"That's a killer dress." She ran her fingers over the fabric at the hem.

"We're supposed to dress up a little tonight for dinner."

Annie gave a shimmy. "Which is why I dusted off this gem."

"You look great." I glanced down the hall behind her. "Where's Levi?"

Annie pulled a face. "Sick. He thinks he had bad shrimp at the port today. I'm going to dinner on my own because he doesn't want me sitting around the room while he empties his stomach."

That took so much more confidence than I possessed in my pinky finger. "To the dining room?"

Annie put up her hands and shook out her blonde curls. "I'm all dressed for it, aren't I?"

"You should join us."

She started walking beside me but blew a raspberry through her lips. "Not necessary. I don't mind sitting alone, and I don't want to intrude on your wedding week."

"We'd love to have you. It's more of an elopement, so the group is really small. Honestly. You should just have dinner with us. Jack would love it."

Annie shook her head. "Don't know about that, sugar."

An alarm went off in my head, reminding me that this woman had known Jack since they were babies. "Why not? Because he's distanced himself from your family lately?"

"He's always been distant. That boy was jumping to leave Arcadia Creek before he could walk." She shot me a smile. "Not really. I mean, he just never wanted to stick around. It's no surprise to any of us that he loves his fancy Dallas job."

"Then why—"

"I'm a reminder of home, I think," she said gently. "He probably doesn't want me around his big city friends."

That didn't really sound like Jack, but Annie would know better than I would. I threaded my arm through hers. "I want you around. So come as my guest."

"I don't know."

"Just come," I said. "I'm an old lady to my sister and her friends. If anyone knows how it feels for your family to put up with your presence, it's me. Trust me."

Annie threaded her arm through mine, grinning. She fairly bounced with every step. "All right, Lauren. I'll be a Golden Girl with you."

CHAPTER SEVENTEEN

LAUREN

JACK WAS UNCHARACTERISTICALLY quiet at dinner, but his cousin was the opposite. She commanded the room smoothly, a perfect blend of funny and exuberant without being too loud or sloppy. It hadn't taken long for everyone to agree to karaoke tonight at her behest, and we found ourselves in a dark bar well after dinner, seated around a large table against the wall.

"You have to do a love ballad together!" Annie said. "It's almost your wedding!"

Amelia laughed, leaning back on her bench seat against the wall. "No one wants to hear that. Trust me."

"You can hold a tune," I said.

She took a sip from her drink. "A normal song, maybe. Not all those oooo's that come with long, slow love songs."

"We can't sing together, anyway," Kevin said, sliding his arm around her waist to pull her closer to his side. "I signed up to do my own thing."

Amelia's mouth dropped open, turning her neck to try and see her fiancé over her shoulder. "What song?"

"It's a surprise." Kevin grinned, raising his glass in a toast to

Jack and Lucas, who both just shook their heads. The guys had planned something.

Jack sat on a chair beside mine. He pulled it closer and leaned his elbows against the table, dipping his head so it rested near my ear. "Why are you avoiding me?"

"I'm not."

He gave a pointed look to where his cousin sat on my other side.

"I told you," I whispered. "We ran into each other on the way to dinner. Her husband is sick."

His lifted eyebrows said enough. That's not what he'd meant. And he was totally right about me avoiding him, so I couldn't really defend myself. Not that I could tell him the truth either: that I was scared. That his explanation about the waitress kiss had taken the wind out of my sails. That the way he looked at me made me feel like the only person on the whole ship. That he was making me feel things I'd never felt with anyone else before. That I saw *potential*.

"What?" he asked, probably reading my mind like the vampire from Twilight. It would explain a lot, for sure.

I shook my head, turning to face the stage, when Jack's arm went around my shoulders. Pain shot through my skin, making me pull away and gasp.

"I hurt you?" he asked, retreating at once.

"No, it's nothing. Just a little burned." It was *not* nothing, and I was most certainly turning into a firetruck as we sat here in this dark bar.

He clearly wasn't buying it, anyway. "That sounded like a lot more than nothing."

"Next we have Kevin and the Groomsmen!" the announcer called from his seat at the DJ station.

Jack looked up.

"Is that your band name?" Annie called, while Cara whistled and the rest of the table clapped.

Jack held my gaze, looking like he didn't want to move.

"Go sing!" I said, clapping along with everyone else.

He got up, following Kevin and Lucas to the stage. Kevin took the center and both groomsmen stood behind him in a V formation. The song began, and I recognized it at once.

"This one goes out to my bride," Kevin said, looking at our table. The colored lights overhead made his blond hair look red. "I can't wait to become your husband tomorrow, baby."

The room erupted in cheers and whistles. I snuck a look at my sister and found her emotional eyes glued to the stage. Kevin and I might not totally mesh, but his love for Amelia was undoubtable. Even if Amelia seemed young to me, they were the real deal. I needed to let go of my frustration at how much Amelia had veered from the five-year plan I'd designed for her. She was happy, and she was totally and completely loved.

A fact that Kevin continued to shout to the whole room in an off-key rendition of *I Do (Cherish You)* by 98° that had seen better microphones. Jack and Lucas were fabulous backup singers, performing silly, exaggerated dance moves that had the room laughing.

When their song came to a close, Annie leaned in. "Okay, girls, we have to show them up now. Who knows *Wannabe*?"

"Um, everyone," Sydney said.

"Shouldn't we do a love song?" Cara asked.

Amelia laughed. "I'm always down for Spice Girls if I get to be Ginger."

"Dibs on Posh," Sydney said. Then she eyed me. "Too bad there's no Stuck-Up Spice."

"Be nice," Amelia said, moving aside while Kevin slid into the space beside her. She kissed her fiancé. "Y'all did an amazing job."

"I make a pretty good backup singer," Lucas said, popping a pretend collar.

"I'll go sign us up." Annie jumped from her seat and crossed to the DJ.

"What song are you doing?" Jack asked.

Amelia clapped. "It's a surprise! Your cousin is *fun*, Jack. Why haven't you brought her around before?"

"She doesn't come up to Dallas much."

I shot him a look, but he avoided catching my eye. The issues were so much deeper than he made them sound. Whether or not Jack liked his hometown, his cousin had made it sound like he didn't want anything to do with it. Did his family feel the same, wondering if he wanted to avoid them, too, by extension?

Annie slid back into her seat, having overheard the end of the conversation. "Well, you make it impossible anyway, with how busy you are." She leaned in and lowered her voice. "The real reason he doesn't invite us up has nothing to do with me. Jack and Levi had a bit of a thing in high school, but he's too polite to mention it now."

"A thing?" Lucas asked, lifting his eyebrows.

"Rivalry," Jack explained quickly. "Levi was constantly trying to one-up me. It was petty and exhausting and we've grown out of it."

"Don't act like you weren't just as petty," Annie said, laughing. "I remember when you facilitated a whole party in the school gym just so you could dump fruit punch on Levi when he got there. We'd just seen the movie *Carrie*," she added in explanation.

"Fine. I played into it just as much as he did. He should be glad I didn't use real pig's blood."

Cara scrunched up her face. "Gross."

Jack laughed. "But that's small-town Texas for you. We had to find *something* to pass the time."

Annie flinched. I reached back and put my hand on Jack's knee to stop him from saying more.

A few more songs went by before it was the ladies' turn to hit the stage. We stood in a line, sharing microphones, and despite the words popping up on the TV, I remembered most of them. Cara took a microphone to the center stage and rapped Scary Spice's monologue perfectly and the crowd erupted. When we finished the song, we all bowed. Amelia threw her arms around me in a hug and I hissed, pushing her off.

"What?" she asked with concern.

"Sunburn." I cringed. "I think I need to check the shop for aloe before they close."

"No." Her forehead creased in concern. "Seriously?"

I'd told her this would happen. I'd also spent my entire life being this easily burned, so it wasn't a crazy surprise. She tanned, I turned into Sebastian from *The Little Mermaid*.

"Then go," she said, walking back toward the tables by my side. "I'm so sorry, Lo."

"It's not your fault." I'd made my choice, and now I was heartily regretting it. "Is there anything else on the agenda for tonight?"

"No. You're coming to my room in the morning to get ready, right?"

"Yes, ma'am. I'll be there at seven."

Amelia looked like she was about to go in for another hug but stopped herself.

I stood behind my seat while someone took the stage to start *My Heart Will Go On*. I was pretty sure it was standard practice— a karaoke night could not be complete until *Titanic* made an appearance in some form. Still, a little insensitive for a cruise, right?

"I'll see y'all in the morning."

"You're leaving?" Annie asked, sounding actually disappointed. Bless her. That made me feel good. "I was hoping to get more dirt on my good-for-nothing cousin. Or give *you* some dirt. Y'all know I have plenty."

"That'll have to wait," Jack said in good humor, rising. He faced me. "I'll come with you."

"You don't have to—"

He gave me a look that cut off my words at the pass. It was intense, the lights from the stage reflecting in his eyes and making them glow. He gently put a hand on my lower back and led me from the room.

"I'm searching out some aloe first," I explained.

"I've got nothing but time."

The shop was closing when we got there, but the guy let me buy a bottle of neon blue aloe to take back to the room.

Jack walked behind me. "Okay, ouch."

I tried to look over my shoulder at my back. "That bad?"

"How bad does it feel?"

"Like fire anytime someone touches me."

"It looks about as bad," he said, catching up to walk at my side.

"So I am now a hands-off situation."

"Darn."

I chuckled. "Annie fits in well with everyone."

"She's always been a bit of a chameleon . . . with a big mouth. But that's just the Texan in her."

"I'm Texan too," I said, opening the door to our room.

"But you're from the Metroplex. It's different."

That was fair. Annie's accent was definitely a lot thicker than mine. I tossed my key on the desk and walked to the vanity mirror, turning to look at my back. "Oh, no." My skin was already an angry red over my shoulders and back, except for the stark white stripes where my swimsuit straps had been.

Jack hovered behind me. "It's pretty bad."

"And it's only going to get worse."

He cringed. "It might not."

"It probably will."

He reached for the aloe in my hand and started peeling off the sanitation cover. "Not if this stuff works its magic."

"I can do it myself," I said stubbornly, not making a move to take the aloe from him. I turned away from the mirror to face Jack.

He looked down at me, feeling far closer than he'd been a moment ago. "Do you want to change so you don't get aloe on your dress?"

"Yes. Good idea." I pulled pajama shorts and a tank from my drawer and slipped into the bathroom to change. The color was even worse in that light, or maybe it was just more obvious against the stark white of the rest of my body. I looked like the Marvel logo. All white and red in nonsensical stripes and slashes.

I put on a tank and shorts and went back into the room. Jack was sitting on the edge of the bed, his dress shirt unbuttoned at the neck. He hit the bottle against his hands a few times. "Do you want to lay on your stomach? Then I can slather it on and you don't have to move."

That was surprisingly thoughtful. Accepting help from him was not as easy though. It required me to be vulnerable in a way I wasn't used to, which was uncomfortable. "I can probably manage," I said, more out of reflex than anything else. I was actively regretting the words as they formed and left my mouth. "I do it at home all the time."

"Well, you aren't home now and you have my hands at your disposal, so you might as well take advantage of them."

"Don't feel like you have to—"

"It's just aloe, Lauren."

Not to me, it wasn't. It was neon blue vulnerability. "Okay, you're right. Thanks." I laid down on my stomach and pulled the straps down on my tank to make my back totally open for aloe, then folded my arms over the pillow. When Jack didn't move, I looked at him over my shoulder. "Is everything okay?"

"Yeah, sorry." He shook his head as if he was shaking off a thought. "I was debating forcing you to outright ask for my help."

Why not? I'd already sunk this far. "Will you please help me, Jack."

He grinned. "Was that so hard?"

"Utterly painful."

"Like this is about to be," he muttered. He sat on the edge of the mattress, making it dip from his weight.

I closed my eyes while he gently smoothed a thick layer of aloe over my taut, hot skin. I sucked in a breath, feeling the heat radiate while little needles drove into my back from his touch.

"When you said you burned easily, you weren't kidding."

I shut my eyes, waiting for the torture to end. "Some of us were cursed with ultra sensitive, impossible-to-tan skin. It's just life. I have to be extra careful in the sun."

"I feel bad for making fun of your rashguard, now."

"When did you make fun of my rashguard?"

"In my head. But I'd wear a full body cover up if I burned this fast."

I grinned, smug. "You're paying penance now."

"How? Oh—helping you?" He laughed, his fingers gliding slowly down my back. "This is no punishment."

My cheeks went hot.

"It looks painful," he muttered.

"It is painful."

"I can kiss it better, if you want."

"That'll only make it hurt worse."

"I wasn't thinking of kissing the burns."

My heart spiked.

"But," he continued, "we probably need to finish our conversation from earlier."

"It's not really necessary." I was glad I could bury my face in the pillow, that I didn't have to look at him when I said this.

"We're just helping each other out. We don't have to pretend like this is something more than it is."

Jack was really quiet. I could feel his hands moving gently down my back, then over my shoulders and around my neck, slowly rubbing the gel into my burn.

Quick. I needed a subject change. "Have you written your best man speech?"

His hand froze. "They want speeches?"

"So I guess you probably haven't."

"No, of course not. Who are we giving them to? There are like seven of us, including the bride and groom."

"Amelia has a bit of a thing planned after the wedding with lunch at a local restaurant. It'll be then."

Jack swore.

"I can help you write it," I offered.

"No, it's okay. It probably needs to come from my heart," he said begrudgingly.

"If you want to practice any ideas on me, I'll be your audience."

"What, so you can make sure it passes muster?"

Obviously. "No, of course not. Just trying to help."

"All finished." He got up from the bed, his voice trailing away while he moved about the room, rifling through a drawer and probably pulling out pajamas. "Now don't move and let that soak in."

"Yes, sir."

"And Lauren?"

"Yeah?"

"I'm not pretending."

The door shut, and he disappeared into the bathroom before I could respond, which was just as well, because I had no idea what to say.

CHAPTER EIGHTEEN

LAUREN

KEEPING the groom from setting eyes on the bride before the wedding was next to impossible when you planned a beach elopement in the middle of the Caribbean. Kevin and Amelia decided not to worry about it, but the guys planned to be waiting on the dock for us so there would still be something of a bridal reveal. I intended to film it for posterity's sake. And also Instagram.

But first, the bride had to stop fretting over her hair.

"Is it beachy enough?" Amelia sat in front of the mirror in her stateroom, looking at Cara through the mirror with wide eyes. "I wanted beach waves, but I'm afraid I just look like a hippie."

Was that not the look she was going for?

Cara leaned down, serious eyes. "You look boho, babe. Don't worry."

I was so out of my depth here. I sat rigidly on the edge of the bed while Cara helped style her hair at the vanity mirror. Sydney was in the bathroom getting ready, but aside from that, we were almost ready to go.

Cara and I wore matching shimmery pink dresses that

looked better on me than I expected—and *fantastic* on her—and I'd let her curl my hair so it would fall over my shoulders and cover most of my bold red sunburn. I had to admit the look wasn't bad. The dresses were similar to Amelia's gown—bias cut that reached the floor, with a slit to the knee and thin straps over the shoulders. But our pinks set us aside as the bridesmaids.

I consulted the time on my phone. "The guys are probably down there waiting. Are you ready?"

Amelia drew in a shaky breath. "I can't believe it's my wedding day. I've been waiting years for this and it's just . . . it's *here*."

A warning bell rang in my head. "Are you getting cold feet?"

"Gosh, no!" Amelia looked offended. "Kevin is the one. I have no doubt about that. But these *pictures* are forever."

Okay, that was valid. I stood next to Cara, looking down at my sister through the mirror. "You look incredible. No one is going to think 1970s or Woodstock when they see you."

"Nope," Cara said. "They're going to think Boho Chic Insta Influencer."

Not sure that's what she was going for either.

Amelia tilted her head back. "That's so sweet, Cara," she said with genuine affection.

I stand corrected. Apparently, it was exactly what she was going for.

Sydney came out of the bathroom. "I'm ready!"

We all stopped what we were doing and stared. She wore a white dress that went down to her ankles, a long slit up the side. It was simple and chic and looked *exactly* like a wedding dress . . . no, exactly like *Amelia's* wedding dress.

That girl had always been drama, but this time she'd gone too far.

"Are you kidding?" Cara said.

Sydney pushed her dark hair behind her shoulders. "What?"

Okay, time to step in. Sydney had spent the first half of the cruise trying to steal my boyfriend, cause drama, and now she was trying to upstage the bride? I knew she'd been friends with Amelia almost their entire lives, the type of friendship that made Amelia put up with her for the sake of longevity, but my sister was too nice for her own good sometimes. I'd kept my mouth civil until now, but she'd crossed the line. "You need to change your dress."

"Um, no."

"Change it now," I said. "Or you aren't coming."

Sydney's eyes flashed to Amelia. "It's not your wedding, Lauren."

"No, but it's *someone's* wedding. Why would you wear a long white gown to a wedding?"

"It's at the beach," she said flippantly, but I could see her confidence slipping. She fiddled with her hair again, looking at Amelia.

What had she expected? That because Amelia was kind of a pushover when it came to Sydney, she could get away with trying to upstage the bride? It was true that Amelia didn't step in often where her friend was concerned, which meant Sydney got away with a lot, but this was low, even for her.

Sydney was right, though. It wasn't my wedding. I looked at Amelia, handing her the microphone so to speak. "Your call."

Amelia looked between us, stress flashing in her eyes.

Cara shook her head. "Don't act innocent, Syd. This isn't okay."

Something like anger sparked on Sydney's evil face. "If you'd gotten me a bridesmaid dress, I wouldn't have had to pull something from my closet."

So that's what this was about? Her irritation at being an afterthought? There was a reason Amelia hadn't invited her initially. I wished she hadn't caved to the guilt, or felt like she needed to spare other people's feelings, and just stayed strong. But we couldn't change that. We could only act now.

I nudged my sister. "It's your wedding, Ames. You should stand up for yourself."

Amelia drew in a breath and let it out. "I don't want you to come to my wedding in a wedding dress, Syd."

Sydney scoffed. "This is just a normal dress."

"It looks a lot like mine. Do you have anything else to wear? I can lend you something if you—"

"Whatever." She turned away, walking from the room.

"Wait!" Amelia called, running after her. "Should we wait for you to change?"

"Don't bother," Sydney called from the hallway.

Was the woman seriously skipping her friend's wedding because of a dress? Amelia came back into the room, her eyes suspiciously wet. At least her eyelash extensions wouldn't run.

"Don't cry over her." Cara moved to rub circles on Amelia's back. "She was basically asking for that. You know she spent like a year in love with Kevin, so maybe this is residual resentment. She's never satisfied unless she's causing drama for someone else."

Amelia let out a frustrated sound. "That was so long ago."

"Sydney doesn't know how to do anything without causing trouble," I said, the proof in all the shenanigans Amelia had put up with over the last fifteen years, let alone the last few days. "Don't let her ruin your day."

"I won't." Amelia lifted her chin. "I knew I shouldn't have invited her. She's been nothing but drama since we got to Florida. But I felt bad not inviting her when she's been in my life for so long, you know?"

Because there were very few people we could claim such longevity with. I got it. I really did. But at some point, it was okay to recognize the toxicity in a relationship and let it go.

"You're too nice for your own good." Cara walked toward the door. "Now, let's shake that off and go find your groom."

She drew in a breath and nodded resolutely. "Sounds good to me."

IF I'D HAD any residual doubts about Kevin's love for my sister, his face when we stepped onto the dock put them all to rest, six feet under with a granite gravestone on top. He lit up, and I caught it on camera for Amelia to watch over and over again. She walked up to him slowly, holding the tropical bouquet we'd preordered from the cruise ship. Her grin split her face, and he picked her up right in the center of the dock and spun her slowly, kissing her like someone had just pronounced them husband and wife.

A little premature, but the moment was magic. When he set her down, he put a fist in the air and yelled. "I'm getting married today!"

People walking along the shops lining the water shouted their support. Weddings were universally happy events. I was thrilled to have gotten the whole thing on camera.

My gaze slid behind the couple, where Jack was standing, his attention squarely on me. The weight of his stare settled, leaving my chest humming. The guys wore tan pants and white dress shirts open at the collar, and I was here for it.

Amelia had wanted a barefoot-on-the-beach wedding, and thus far, everyone looked perfect. Relaxed but nice, which was pretty much Amelia in a nutshell. Her long white gown was elegant and simple, her hair wavy and falling down her back. *Oh, tears, please hold off.* I was too cheap for eyelash extensions, and I couldn't afford to have my mascara run before the pictures.

Jack walked up to my side. "Where's Sydney?"

"Somewhere on deck wearing a long white dress."

He raised his brown eyebrows. "Yikes."

Even a man knew that was a big fat no-no.

"Amelia told her to take a hike?" he asked.

"She asked Sydney to change, and Sydney stormed off." I leaned closer and lowered my voice, inhaling his aftershave. "I'm kind of relieved. She never should have been here. She's too selfish and she always has been."

"But you're worried?"

"How did you know?" I started down the dock after Cara, Lucas, and the happy couple. We resembled a wedding march already, in a way. "I'm afraid the guilt is going to ruin Amelia's day."

Jack took my hand, sending butterflies to my stomach. "We won't let it."

I looked down. "Is this necessary touching?"

"Completely. I don't want to trip on this uneven dock. I need your stability."

"Probably in more ways than one."

Jack drew in a fake-dramatic gasp. "Are you offering to make a spreadsheet for me?"

"Don't tempt me."

He smiled, the lazy curve of his lips reaching through my chest.

Ugh. Why did I have to feel things for him? For Jack Fletcher of all people.

He bumped his shoulder lightly into mine. "I love your hair, by the way."

"It was Cara's idea."

"Remind me to thank her later."

A blush stole up my neck, but I pretended not to be affected by his praise. I didn't know if I was doing a very good job of it, though. Probably in part because my feelings toward Jack had changed, regardless of how hard I'd tried not to let myself fall for him. He was charming and kind, and if it wasn't for the voicemail on my phone that made me feel low and ridiculous, we could have really given this whole dating thing a shot the first time around. It stood to reason that when there was chemistry during a fake relationship, it would cross over into the real world a little, right?

Or maybe that was the problem. It *wouldn't* cross over into our real lives, and I was just fooling myself. That was much more likely.

"What's wrong?" he asked, somehow sensing my mood shift.

"Nothing." My smile could rival stuffed crust when it came to cheesy content. It was also just as artificial.

"Are you sure—"

"It's my sister's wedding." I hoped those words spoke for themselves. This wasn't the time or place for this conversation. If anything, it would need to be avoided at all costs until we reached Miami and went our separate ways. I couldn't afford to allow myself feelings that would only end up hurting me later. My brain was too full to add anything else to worry about. Like a man. Or, more specifically, like a broken heart.

CHAPTER NINETEEN

LAUREN

THE WEDDING WAS PERFECT, as expected. A wooden pergola with white gauzy fabric framed white sand, clear teal water, and the happy couple. The moment they were pronounced husband and wife, we all threw our flowers in the air and hollered while Kevin dipped Amelia and kissed her. The photographer on scene captured the entire event, and despite my stern self-lecture earlier, my eyes sought Jack immediately.

He was already watching me.

Oh, goodbye heart. You're so far gone.

When the couple eventually broke apart and the initial cheering had passed, we hugged them. I squeezed Kevin a little extra. "Welcome to the family," I said.

He looked down at me. "Glad to be here."

He meant it. Okay, fine. So maybe they weren't too young for this. Maybe I'd like having a brother too.

When it was my turn for Amelia, she started crying. "I love you, Sissy."

"Love you too. This wedding was absolute perfection."

"And it isn't over yet," Kevin said, grinning like he was about to announce the winners of the on-board belly flop competition we'd tragically witnessed yesterday. "I have lunch planned."

"We booked a table, Kev," Amelia said, freezing.

"I canceled it. Don't worry, wife. You'll like this," he promised, taking her hand and pulling her close. "We just have to hurry so we don't miss it."

Amelia looked unsure. As the person who'd researched restaurants and went to the trouble of calling ahead to book us a table for lunch, I was feeling a little like the waves getting close to our bare toes: salty.

"You'll *all* like it," Kevin reiterated, giving me a look that meant he was probably reading my mind now. "Let's go."

We followed him back up the shore after Kevin tipped the photographer and thanked the officiator.

Once we reached the surprise he'd booked, my mouth dropped clear open. Kevin's family had money. We all knew this. It was part of the reason for this whole elopement, since his parents believed my kind, guileless sister to be a fortune-hunter. But when I saw the yacht he'd scheduled for half a day to cart us around the Bahamas for a sea-faring wedding reception, I was still swept away.

Maybe I hadn't previously registered just how wealthy Kevin was, especially if he could drop this kind of money on an experience that would only last a few hours.

We all got on board and were shown to the front of the boat, where food was set out around deck furniture and music blasted through the speakers. It was elegant and fancy, and even if Amelia only wanted a beach wedding followed by lunch with her friends, I could tell she was impressed.

It was hard not to be, even if I felt the expense was probably ridiculous. My penny-pinching vein throbbed, but I suppressed it. This was Amelia's day. Who cared if the cost of this excursion could probably go into mutual funds for thirty years and yield a return big enough to fund an entire fleet of yachts?

Oh, gosh. Maybe Kevin could already afford a fleet of yachts. You had to in order to spend like this, right?

Enough, Lauren. This was Amelia's day.

And it was really, really nice. They drove us away from the island and anchored, leaving us floating in the middle of the ocean. The sun glared down, so I stayed in the shade of the overhang and munched on steak kabobs, goat cheese dip, and some sort of incredible crab pastry thing while everyone else lounged on the deck just a few steps below me.

Jack filled a plate and carried it to where I was sitting. "May I?"

The little bench seat wasn't very big. "Sydney isn't here, you know. I don't need to be your shield right now."

"Maybe I just want to sit by you."

That wasn't part of the agreement.

Jack settled beside me, our arms pressed together. "Is your eye twitching over the last-minute change in plans?"

I nudged his knee with mine. "I'm not psychotic. I can be happy for Amelia."

"And simultaneously bugged that we haven't followed the schedule?"

"I was more annoyed before I had one of these crab things. Kevin can hijack our plans anytime he wants if he's going to provide more of these."

"Noted."

The music was bumping and Cara walked out to the center of the deck to dance. She was trying to entice us all to join her, but everyone else was eating.

I swiped another bite of goat cheese dip. "As if that piece of information will ever be useful to you. We part ways in Miami, remember?"

Jack lowered the steak kabob back to his plate. "You know we don't have to do that, right?"

"I thought about that," I agreed. "If our flight here was any indication, it's possible we'll be on the same one going home, too."

Jack laughed. "Not what I meant. Are you willfully being ignorant? You can't really fail to see that I'm falling for you, right?"

My heart kicked up a notch. Fall*ing*? As in already en route? They were the words I wanted to hear, but I was too scared to believe them. I picked up Jack's crab pastry and popped it into my mouth so I wouldn't A: have to speak right away, and B: be tempted to kiss him.

Crab breath would save me from making a fool out of myself.

Jack took my plate and set it on the table beside our little bench. He put his next to it. "I'm sorry, Lauren. I'm sorry for what happened on our date. I regret it, and I don't know what I was thinking—well, I *wasn't* thinking, obviously. I should have looked for you. Can you find it in you to forgive me? To give me a real chance?"

"You're going to be overheard," I whispered.

"Not over the music," he countered. Swinging out one of his arms, he gestured to the sparkling ocean beneath us. "There's nowhere to run this time, so just hear me out. I'm serious, Lauren. We're good together. We both live in Dallas. Why not see where this goes?"

Jack wanted to date me? Like *for real* date me? It was such a surprise that he could conceivably want this. Did he not see the lack of wisdom in it? Knowing all the reasons it was a bad idea didn't settle the anticipation bubbling in my stomach, either. His green eyes were earnest. I couldn't hold them any longer or I would combust.

"It's not a good idea." I picked up my water and took a few long swallows, but his attention didn't waver from my face. My shoulders lifted. "It isn't wise."

"How?"

"If we break up now, we can be chill when we see each

other in the future. A real break up would give us real feelings. Kevin and Amelia will have baby showers and birthday parties and all sorts of things we'll both be attending. Do we really want to ruin all those experiences by getting feelings involved?"

He sat back. "You think breaking up is inevitable?"

He didn't? "I mean, the chance is super high that we wouldn't last forever."

"Why?"

I pointed to my chest. "Spreadsheets." Then I tapped his chest. "Sunshine."

"So your argument is that we're too different?"

And that most relationships failed, but I wasn't going to say that part out loud. Did I want it to? No. But I was realistic. "Statistically speaking, we wouldn't last a year."

"How about we just try to last the cruise instead?" He studied me for a moment, his eyes serious. "Then we can get home and try to last another week. Then maybe a month. *Then* we can worry about all this year stuff."

"What are you saying?"

"I'm saying we don't have to plan our wedding today, Lauren. We can decide to give *us* a shot and worry about the rest as it comes."

I nodded toward the happy newlywed couple. "And if we have a messy breakup and have to face each other at their Christmas party this year, what then?"

"For someone who's dead set on our inevitable doom, you seem pretty confident that Kev and Amelia will last forever."

"Of course they will." I watched Kevin dance circles around my laughing sister. "They've been together for years, anyway."

They seemed to notice us watching them. "Come dance!" Kevin shouted.

I stood, running my hands down my dress.

"Now you're willing to dance?" Jack scoffed playfully. "Have you always run from clever, handsome men who are super into you?"

My heart hammered. "No, I only run from the ugly ones."

I started walking away but Jack laughed, taking me around the waist to pull me into his arms. "Ugly, huh? That explains why you can't stand the thought of being my girlfriend."

"Yep, sorry to be blunt." His arms went tighter, pulling me close, looking down in my eyes with a challenge. I swallowed, pasting a smile on my face. "I just think you're hideous. I can't imagine having to look at you longer than necessary."

"This must be really painful for you, then," he murmured, his face just inches from mine.

"Agonizing."

"Then close your eyes."

What? That sounded like a bad idea. Also, it sounded like a really, really good one.

"You can trust me."

Could I, though? Wasn't that the reason for my hesitation? I started to pull back.

"Lauren," he said, his tone making me freeze. "Just give me a chance. You can't predict *everything*, you know. Sometimes you just have to give it a shot and see how the chips fall."

Was he right? Was I the one standing in the way of what could possibly be a great relationship? It was true that he wasn't as awful as I'd initially believed. In the days we'd fake-dated on the ship, he hadn't so much as looked at another woman. Maybe our first impressions of each other were wrong—or maybe the past two years had given each of us a little time to grow.

The truth was I liked Jack . . . *a lot*. My entire body buzzed in his arms. I ran from him every time he grew serious because I was scared to believe he could be sincere—which I wasn't hiding very well. It wasn't a big secret.

But here he was, just asking me to *try*.

I could do that, right? Just for a few days, at least, to see what happened. Worst case scenario, we would get off the ship in Miami and end things there. I wouldn't fall irrevocably in love with him that soon, anyway.

Probably.

But the way I felt now in his arms . . . maybe I was being reckless, but I wasn't quite ready to give that up yet, either.

"Okay."

He grew still. "What?"

"Okay. We can watch the chips fall and cross our fingers they don't land in a fire pit."

"Not the enthusiasm I was hoping for, but it'll do." He grinned, his fingers splaying widely on my back. Sunlight shone in his green eyes, highlighting his perfect smile.

I sucked in a breath through my teeth. Fire tore over my skin, half burn, half Jack. "Gentler, please."

He immediately loosened his hold. "Sorry. I forgot about the sunburn." He dropped his hand to my lower back and slid the other one around my neck. "Better?"

"Mmhmm."

A grin split his face. "Lost the ability to speak?"

"No, just enjoying this." *While I have it.*

Jack looked down into my eyes, his own turning dark and deep as the ocean.

"We have an audience," I whispered.

"No one's paying attention to us. Besides, they already think we're dating. Let's prove it to them."

"What a *line*, Jack."

"But did it work?"

I leaned in, nodding gently. "Yeah."

His lips pressed gently to mine, his fingers getting lost in the hair at the nape of my neck. He amped up the emotion slowly, pulling me closer, making me cling to him until I couldn't breathe. Jack kissed me like he was starving, warming me from the inside, like I didn't just feel the heat from the sun, but had become it instead. His lips moved over mine, speaking their own language that I fully understood. He broke away, drawing in a breath. Then he looked at me. "You've been hiding *that* all this time?"

"Pace yourself," I said.

"I have been. This is a long con, Lauren."

I laughed, but he cut the sound off with another kiss, and I didn't mind.

Someone—probably Kevin—made a catcall sound, and we broke apart. I pressed my forehead into his collarbone, but I felt his arm lift in the air. "Yeah, we're coming."

Jack took my hand to pull me down the steps toward the dancers, interlacing our fingers. He pressed a kiss to the back of my knuckles and whispered. "Best. Day. Ever."

Honestly, I had to agree.

CHAPTER TWENTY

JACK

WE RETURNED to the ship just in time to make it before the doors closed and headed down the long, narrow corridor toward the elevators.

"Dinner tonight?" Lucas called from the back of our group.

I took Lauren's hand, interlacing our fingers. "I'm stuffed."

"Me, too," Cara said, groaning. She shoved Lucas playfully. "How can you even think of food right now?"

He grinned, flashing his white teeth. "When am I not thinking of food?"

"Hot tub instead?" Cara asked.

Kevin whistled, pulling Amelia into his side. "Count us out."

"Come up to the buffet before you disappear," Lucas said. "We need to throw rice."

"Shut up," Kevin said, but he was grinning. They got in an elevator and disappeared to the sound of whooping and cheers.

When the door closed, Cara clapped her hands together. "Okay. Afterparty?"

"I'm not really feeling the hot tub," Lauren said, scrunching her nose. I bet she wanted to avoid hot water on her burn. I didn't blame her at all.

Cara leaned over, bumping Lauren's hip. "Should we go dancing? Might as well show off these dresses."

I happened to know clubbing wasn't anywhere on Lauren's radar for a fun time. I looked down at her sparkling hazel eyes. Her red burn peeked out from behind golden brown waves. Did she need more aloe?

"There's a movie by the pool, I think," Lucas said.

"Oh, yeah." Cara started buzzing, hopping up on her toes. "I think it was *Moana*."

"A kid movie?"

"A *great* movie," Cara argued. She turned to face us. "Meet y'all there in like twenty minutes?"

I looked down at Lauren, hoping for some sign that she wasn't into the movie idea, either. Anything that would give us an excuse to go off and do our own thing. She shrugged, her gaze flicking from me to Cara. "I like *Moana*. But I probably need a sweatshirt."

I squeezed her fingers. "We'll see y'all out on the lido deck, then."

We all filed into the elevator and got off on our respective floors. Lauren had let go of my hand to stand beside Cara, and I found myself itching to lean close to her. Somehow I'd gone from wondering why her hair was so tight to needing to touch her at all times.

Was I obsessed with Lauren Foley? Yeah, it seemed like I was.

It took longer than twenty minutes to change into shorts and sweaters for the windy lido deck and make a pit stop at the ice cream machine, but we still beat Lucas and Cara there. We claimed four chairs and I sent a message to the chat to tell them where we were.

Moana was already singing about the ocean when we sat down. Our seats weren't great, clear in the back and partially blocked by the edge of the deck above us, but I didn't really care. I wasn't here for the movie.

Lauren leaned back, stretching her legs out along the chair. I flung my leg over the side of my chair and rested it so it grazed her calf.

She licked her ice cream, shooting me a suspicious side-eye. "Clingy, much?"

"Is my leg repulsing you? I can move—"

She reached out and pulled on my calf, putting it right back on her chair. It was a pretty huge statement from her. I had the sense that Lauren didn't take anything lightly, that claiming me like this was a huge step for her.

It heightened my need to make sure I didn't do anything to mess up whatever was growing between us. She watched me for a long moment before licking her ice cream to keep it from dripping.

"You're such a slow eater," I complained.

"You mean I'm great at savoring?"

I rolled my eyes dramatically but didn't fight the grin stretching my cheeks. "If eating was a sport, I'd win. Just call me cruise champion."

"As someone who got both a great conference and a . . . date out of this cruise, I think I'm the winner."

A date? That was how she defined me? It was too soon for 'boyfriend' in our real lives, I agreed, but I wanted to think we were more advanced than that casual representation.

Also, I didn't know how much I liked being put after the conference when it came to her list of accomplishments for the week. I'd rather be the top prize.

"So I'm your trophy boy?"

She grinned, taking a bite of ice cream. "Don't be offended. You have no idea how much I needed that conference."

A niggle of unease weaved through my gut. What if Brad didn't pull through for me? It would crush Lauren, obviously, but would it ruin her career too? No, I couldn't think like that. He'd told me it was worth discussing. I just had to make sure my argument was good enough, and that—on top of the discount Lauren prepared to offer—put this deal in the bag.

I swung both of my legs over the side of my lounge chair so I was sitting up, facing Lauren.

"What's going on?" She took the last bite of her cone.

I waited for her to finish chewing it. Having her full attention, without the computer Amelia thought she was grafted to, was probably not going to last long after we docked in Miami, so I intended to take advantage of every minute on this boat. "Turns out I'm hungry."

"The buffet place is open," she said, sitting up and facing me so our knees were staggered between our chairs. "I think they have pizza all night, too."

"What even is this life?" I grinned, leaning forward, my elbows resting on my knees.

Lauren leaned forward too. "A vacation from your health goals and reasonable eating schedule, obviously."

"Who says I have any health goals?"

She cocked an eyebrow. "Um, your abs do."

She had me there. My grin was so wide it was almost embarrassing, and I was flushed with the overwhelming need to show her exactly how much I enjoyed spending time with her.

I closed the distance between our lips, kissing her while our arms both leaned casually in front of us and our knees pressed together. She lit me up from the inside, giving me the desire to share more than I'd ever wanted to share before. I was actually tempted to tell her about the project waiting for me in Arcadia Creek. The one I was supposed to spend my weekends on, but instead had neglected for the last few years.

She made me want to schedule my time better so I *could* devote the time to it that I'd originally intended. She made me want to pull her onto my lounge chair and ignore the hundred other people watching *Moana*. She made me want her.

She was wrong earlier. She didn't win.

When a fake relationship developed into a legit heart-pulsing, breath-catching connection, both parties won.

Cruise champion was a shared title.

My back pocket buzzed. Lauren's must have too, because she broke the kiss and leaned back, pulling out her phone. Her face glowed from the light of her screen before she put it away. "They're not coming."

I stood, reaching for her, and she took my hand. "Pizza time."

We walked toward the buffet room, skirting around one of the many hot tubs on this ship.

"Oh my gosh, Jack," Lauren whispered, pulling my hand to get my attention. "Is that Sydney?"

She sat in the hot tub, snuggling up to a guy we didn't know, his blond hair spiking from the water and sporting a gold chain around his neck.

"Walk quickly," I muttered, pulling Lauren away before the queen of drama could notice us.

"Maybe now she'll leave us alone."

I sighed. "One can only hope."

We walked along the railing of the ship to reach the buffet at the back. The half-moon gleamed overhead, reflecting on the inky ocean.

Lauren chewed her lip, worrying me.

I pulled her to a stop, and she faced me easily. "Are you stressing about Sydney?"

"No. I mean, yeah, just . . ." Lauren let out a small sigh. "You've kissed my sister."

My stomach dropped to the slick deck at our feet. This was bothering her? She hadn't seemed to like the revelation when Sydney had forced it upon all of us, obviously, but she also never brought it up again. Seeing Sydney and the hot tub together must have resurfaced it for her.

"It was barely even a kiss."

"But you have. I mean, it happened."

I swallowed, nodding. "Yeah. We went to that Alphi Phi party with a girl Kevin had kind of been seeing, so I was on my own that night. I met Amelia, and she seemed a little young to me, but we got talking and I kissed her. She met Kevin that night too and he asked her out the next day, so nothing ever came from it."

"But you wanted it to be something?" she asked, tilting her head to the side a little.

"Honestly? I didn't think twice about it. I wasn't looking for a relationship. I'd just started my master's program, and I'd done the college thing the last four years, so I was really just along for the ride that night. It didn't mean anything, and I didn't think about it again. Especially not after she started dating my roommate. We never really talked about it. She'd told Kevin, apparently. But I think it just wasn't a big deal to either of us."

"Because kissing isn't a big deal to you?"

Oh. So that's where this was going. Lauren wondered if I was just a . . . what? A womanizer? Someone who made out with any beautiful, willing woman and didn't think twice about it? I swallowed. Maybe that's who I used to be, but I wasn't that person anymore.

"It is now," I said. "My past isn't perfect, but I'm not that man anymore. People can change."

Lauren nodded, but she looked uncertain. "So being with me isn't weird for you?"

I laughed. "No. It's not. Amelia is one of my good friends now, and it took like five minutes of watching her with Kevin to see how perfect they are for each other. I'm not hung up on anyone, if that's what you're wondering."

Her shoulders relaxed. "Okay."

"You feel better?"

"Yeah." She chewed on her lip, scrunching her nose. "I didn't want to be a consolation prize."

I took her hand and pulled her toward the smell of pizza. "Don't let Sydney get in your head. You're no consolation, Lauren. You're the grand prize."

Maybe I was the winner, after all.

CHAPTER TWENTY-ONE

JACK

WHEN DID you know something was too good to be true? Because I was only a week into this fake-then-real relationship, and I was pretty sure Lauren was *the one* for me. It felt too perfect. Like *win the jackpot on your first spin* kind of perfect. Could I just be that lucky?

I was an idiot for letting that waitress kiss me during our first date two years ago instead of going after Lauren. Now that I'd convinced Lauren to give me a real shot, I wasn't going to screw it up.

The rest of the cruise had gone by in a happy blur. Something in Lauren had been unlocked, like she wasn't fighting her thoughts so hard and was free to enjoy herself. We still stayed out of the sun while her burn healed, but Sydney had found a new group to hang out with while we'd been gone at the wedding—the guy in the gold chain came with a slew of friends, apparently—so we didn't have to put up with her anymore.

Kevin, Lucas, and I had participated in the Sexiest Man contest by the pool, which Lucas won, fairly. None of us spent as much time in the gym as he did. We'd invited Annie and Levi to join us for lunch and spent a few hours in the arcade battling them in Pac-Man and Skee-Ball. Lauren showed me how it was humanly possible to eat multiple ice cream cones a day and not get sick. She read her mystery books by the pool in the shade and I napped. I showed her how to haggle with street vendors while shopping on the islands. Okay, fine. She didn't need much instruction there, but it was fun to walk the market with hands intentionally entwined and Sydney nowhere in sight.

Then, my favorite part: each night I tucked her in—despite her laughter or protests—and went to sleep on my side of the bed, pillow wall intact. Because I was a *gentleman* now and trying to prove it to her.

Basically, we were meant to be.

Getting off the boat at the end of the week was bittersweet. Regardless of how well everything had gone before, real life was never like vacation, and there was some settling and calibration we were going to have to do together once reality snuck back in. I wasn't naïve. I was prepared. But I wasn't looking forward to it.

Maybe if I moved my flight, I'd get a few more hours of Lauren in vacation mode. The Lauren with her hair down and nose not stuck to her phone screen.

"What time do you take off again?" I asked when we got in the shuttle to drive to the airport. Cara, Lucas, Sydney, Amelia, and Kevin were already in the van, along with a young couple and their baby.

"2:05," she said, without needing to consult her phone.

I pulled mine out while buckling my seat belt. I navigated to my flight and found hers. "What's your seat?"

She looked over my shoulder, her breath tickling my ear. "You aren't changing your flight."

"Yes I am."

"You guys are, like, annoyingly cute," Cara said from the row behind us.

Lauren blushed.

I felt victorious.

Sydney scoffed from the backseat, but we both ignored her.

Lauren pulled up the airplane seat map. "There aren't open seats near me."

"I'll just grab the closest one." I leaned over to see her phone and found a seat a few rows back. It was easy to move onto her flight. What had gotten into me? I really was obsessed. "Done."

Lauren rolled her eyes, but she looked happy about it. Or, at least, I hoped she was.

"I won't take it personally that you just moved off our flight," Kevin said from the back row, "when it would have been just as easy for Lauren to move onto it."

I shrugged. "I'll see you tomorrow morning when we move those boxes, right?"

"And you won't see her?"

Would I see Lauren so soon? Instead of answering, I put my arm around her and pulled her closer.

Maybe I didn't want to know the answer to that yet.

She looked at my new seat. "This is good, actually, because we have a few business things to sort out anyway."

That got my attention. "Like what?"

"The conference." She lifted her hazel eyes to me.

Right. The conference. I should have loved the stupid thing for bringing Lauren and me together, but really it just made me nauseous, the merest mention tightening my stomach. Until it was settled and the contracts were signed, I would stay uneasy.

I withdrew my arm and looked down at my phone. "I'll get started right away, boss."

She tensed. Maybe I shouldn't have used that term.

As it turned out, drafting the email to my actual boss was harder than I'd expected. I was glad he'd already told me he was open to the idea when I had texted him at the beginning of the cruise, but this was important to Lauren, and I didn't want to mess it up.

We grabbed lunch with our friends in the airport before parting ways to find our gate. I thought about the best way to formulate the request to change venues for our conference. This late in the game, I had difficulty putting to words why it would be a good move for us.

I'd pretty much headed up the entire conference board on my own, so MediCorp probably couldn't execute it without me. They needed me, which meant my job was safe.

But still, it was an awkward request, even though I'd warned Brad at the start of the cruise. I'd made a promise to Lauren though, so I needed to find a way to make it happen one way or another.

"Jack!" Annie called, bouncing across the walkway and appearing out of *nowhere*. She pulled me in for a hug, hitting me in the chin with her pink cowboy hat, and I noticed Levi push up from his chair across the aisle and cross toward us at a much slower pace. "I didn't think we'd see you again. Are you flying Delta?"

"No."

"Darn, I was hoping we'd be on the same flight." She smiled up at me, and my heart tugged with affection for my cousin.

Then her husband stepped into my line of sight. "Good to see you, Jackson."

"Still not my name."

"If you ever feel like swinging by, I'll take a look at your teeth."

"Thanks for the weird offer."

Annie pulled Lauren into a hug. "Don't be a stranger."

"It was really nice to meet you," Lauren said.

Annie smiled before swinging her attention back on me. She folded her arms in a stance I'd seen my sassy momma take many times. A wave of foreboding swept over me, predicting an incoming lecture. I could feel it in my bones.

"Tucker's party is tomorrow night, and you should be there."

Her eyes bore into me. "Your parents' house. Six o'clock. Don't be too late or you'll miss all the good cake."

"Annie, I can't—"

"Nope," she said, cutting me off. She turned to Lauren. "You should make him go. He'll be glad he did, and everyone would love to meet you."

"Annie," I said again, firmly. "Don't be telling the whole family about Lauren."

"Why not?" She narrowed her eyes.

It wasn't that our delicate relationship was too weak for any definition. It was my cowardice and lack of desire to face my mom's questions. "We just aren't ready for that yet."

"Fine. If I promise not to tell everyone about your girlfriend, will you come to Tucker's party?"

"*Annie.*"

Her lifted eyebrows were a language all their own. I could read them well.

"I'll do my best to convince him," Lauren said.

Hey, whose side was she on here?

It worked to snap Annie's attention her way. She smiled brightly. "I'm so glad we've met! Don't let him keep you away from us."

"I think we're boarding now," I said, gesturing to the gate behind my cousin. The airline employees had been announcing first class boarding for a few minutes already, but our group was close enough.

She pulled me in for another hug. "Love you, Jack!"

Levi patted my shoulder in his condescending way. *I am the same age as you,* I wanted to shout. He wouldn't listen.

We were quiet while we stood in line, showed our tickets, and boarded the plane. When we reached Lauren's seat, I squeezed her arm. "See you in a few hours."

She bit her lip. "You know, you should really think about going to that party."

My stomach clenched.

She continued. "It sounds like maybe your brother just forgot to pass on the information. Annie seems to think there will be a lot of people who would be happy to see you."

A man waited in the aisle behind me, so I slid into the row across from Lauren to let him pass. "I don't think I can, not without being invited. It just feels weird."

"But it's your family. Aren't they supposed to welcome you with open arms?"

"It's not really that simple." It was hard putting myself out there. Just showing up. Pretending I wasn't the one who'd ditched all of them for Dallas the moment I graduated. I didn't know how much resentment they'd held onto all these years.

"Just think about it," Lauren said. "I told Annie I'd try, and I tried."

"Well done."

She rolled her eyes playfully. "For what it's worth, I agree with her. I think you should go."

Maybe they were both right, but that didn't make it easy. "I don't think I could do it alone."

"Go early and arrive with Annie and Levi."

"That's not the same."

She held my gaze.

A throat cleared in the aisle. "I think you're in my seat."

I looked up to find an older woman gesturing to me. "Sorry, ma'am. I'll just get out of your way."

I started down the aisle toward my own row, walking backwards.

Lauren pivoted to watch me. "Just think about it," she repeated.

"Okay, fine."

Her mouth split into a grin. "And finish that email while you're at it."

I laughed, shaking my head. "See you in Dallas."

THE EMAIL WAS SENT. I'd done it the moment we touched down and I was able to take my phone off airplane mode. My reasons for requesting the change in venue sounded valid. When Lauren left her seat mid-flight to use the restroom, I commandeered her for a minute and had her tell me the top five reasons my bosses would like her hotel better than the one we were already contracted with. Turned out, they were pretty good.

To say nothing of the steep discount she was offering and the fact that I'd already promised this to her. I wanted to make her happy, and she seemed to think this conference was the answer to her prayers.

We filed off the airplane and walked through DFW toward baggage claim. Once we retrieved our bags and walked outside, the cold hit us like a wall. I froze on the sidewalk, but not just because of the biting wind.

It was time to part ways.

Our cars were parked in completely different lots—mine in the garage, hers in the cheap uncovered parking that required a shuttle ride.

"I'll drive you to your car," I offered.

"It's okay. The shuttle guys know right where to go."

So did I, but I wouldn't push it. I made sure my suitcase wouldn't roll away before stepping toward her and pulling her in for a hug. Her arms went around me, and I closed my eyes, resting my head on top of hers and inhaling the scent of her lemon shampoo.

"You can't expect things to change if you don't make an effort," she said, her voice muffled against my shoulder. "You should really just go to the party."

She was right, but I didn't want to go alone. It would be hard and awkward for me. I was sure Tucker would be embarrassed that he never invited me. Or, worse, if he had a reason for not wanting me there—and Wyatt had a reason for not inviting me to his birthday just before I left for the cruise—then I didn't want to be around.

But if it was a matter of me making an effort and proving I'd drive out to Arcadia Creek just for a party, then Lauren was right. I needed to take the first step. It would be much easier if I wasn't alone.

"I'll go if you go with me." The second the words were out of my mouth, my body tensed in self-conscious second-guessing, but I also realized how much I meant it. I could introduce her all around as a *friend* so she didn't get drilled by all the southern mommas, and it would be easier to face Tucker, Colt, and Wyatt if Lauren was by my side.

Lauren laughed. "That's moving a little fast."

"You don't have to come as my girlfriend."

"I'm not sure that title is real anyway."

It *was* kind of soon, I had to agree, but it felt right to me. I wouldn't push it though. "You could just be a friend. They might make assumptions, but my family is mostly harmless."

"Mostly?"

"Well, you already met Annie."

She nodded against my shoulder as if that was explanation enough. "I can't go with you, Jack. I have to get back to work. Jerry has already sent me a hundred emails about things he needs help with for this lawyer conference coming up."

Had to? Or was that an excuse? I decided to prod a bit. "Tomorrow is Saturday. Arcadia is an hour away. We could leave at five and be home by ten if we wanted to, and that still gives you most of the day to catch up on those emails."

"I don't know."

That wasn't a *no*. I leaned back, looking into her golden green eyes. "Actually, this is a great idea. You already know Annie, so you won't be a total fish out of water, and if I have you beside me, it'll make me feel like I can face all of them."

"You make your family sound terrifying."

"They're amazing. I'm the one who dropped the ball the last few years." I lifted my hands to cup her face. Her hair was half-down, falling around her shoulders in gentle brown waves. "Please come with me, Lauren."

She couldn't look away. Her voice grew quieter, more vulnerable. "I'm not great with families. I've never had a big one, and I don't know how I'm supposed to act around them."

"Just think of it like a networking event, then. I'm guessing you rock those."

"I can work a crowd pretty good at a professional mixer," she agreed.

My smile came unbidden.

"This just feels so couple-y," she said, biting down on her bottom lip.

"It doesn't have to be. It can just be you helping a friend out."

She rolled her eyes. "Fine. I'll go. But we leave at—"

I cut her off with a kiss, gratitude building in my chest until it spilled over. Lauren wasn't a passive bystander, though. She kissed me back until we both had to come up for air.

"We leave at five," she said, finishing her thought, "and we're home by ten."

"Deal." I kissed her on the nose. "Thanks, Lauren. You won't regret it."

CHAPTER TWENTY-TWO

LAUREN

JACK WAS WRONG. I already regretted it. He picked me up ten minutes after five, and we drove out of Dallas, away from the light pollution and high-rise neon buildings and car washes on every corner. The interstate spaghetti bowl and toll roads were behind us, with nothing outside my window now but wide fields spotted with cows. I pulled my sweatshirt sleeves down over my hands and leaned back against the headrest.

Wasn't it just yesterday I was cursing his name, and now I was going to meet his parents?

"Everything okay?" Jack asked, glancing at me before putting his attention back on the road.

"Isn't this a little fast?"

The car immediately slowed.

"Not the car's speed." I gestured between the two of us. "*Our* speed. Meeting the family."

"It's kind of a complicated situation. I'm not really bringing you as my girlfriend, right?"

"Complicated is a good word for us." I shut my eyes. I'd left my hair down, trying my best to give it beachy waves. Regardless of how much I wanted order and keeping flyaway hairs out of my mouth, I also loved how much Jack loved my hair. But it turned out more frizzy than wavy, and I just felt silly. Like a seven-year-old checking the mailbox for birthday cards from family, like the kids at school all got, but not finding anything and just hoping no one noticed my efforts.

Jack snaked his hand over mine and pulled it onto the center console. "No pressure, remember? We don't have to be anything. You are my friend, aren't you?"

"I think we kind of skipped that step. We jumped straight from enemies to meet the parents."

"Not just the parents, basically the entire extended family."

I slumped in my chair. "You're making it worse."

"They're going to love you."

"You can't know that. Just change the subject. Distract me—"

Something jumped from the side of the road and hit the front of our car, the impact jolting us. Jack ripped his hand from mine to grip the wheel as a curse tore from his throat. We swiveled, the back of the car fishtailing before moving into a spin. My hair flew in front of my face while pressure pushed me against the door. The car thudded to a stop, nose down in a shallow ditch, jerking my neck slightly from the impact.

"Are you okay?" Jack asked immediately, panicked.

My seatbelt was tight, holding me back against the seat. I took stock of my body, and aside from my racing heart and what would probably be a bruise on my elbow later, I felt fine. "Yes. You?"

"I'm good."

We sat in silence for a few more seconds before I unbuckled my seat belt.

"Wait," Jack said. "You need to let the adrenaline come down first so you know if you're injured."

"There's no broken glass and the airbags didn't deploy, Jack. I'm fine."

"But it's safer to—"

"I need to find that deer and make sure it's okay." I opened the door, climbing out into the damp ditch on the side of the road. It only took a minute to get up to the road and see the deer lying on its side, its head on the ground.

Jack came up behind me. "I'm sorr—"

The deer—a male, given its antlers—jumped up, turning his neck to face forward and shaking out like a dog. He jumped, a little disoriented, before turning around and getting on his way.

My shoulders sagged in relief.

"Stupid thing is totally fine," Jack grumbled.

"You'd rather it wasn't?"

"That's not what I said." He groaned, turning back to face his car again, the front light crushed, nose-down in a ditch. Then he looked back, reaching a hand toward me.

I took it, letting Jack pull me in and wrap his arms tightly around my back, my breath shuddering onto his shoulder. "That was scary," I murmured.

"Yeah." He kissed my temple in a sweetly reassuring way. "I'm sorry."

"It wasn't your fault. No one got hurt." I looked back at his car, the angle and the jolt not boding well for it.

"Except my car, maybe."

I pulled away and started back for the ditch to retrieve my phone. "I have AAA. I'll get my card and give them a call. Do you know where we are?"

Jack followed me to the car. "There's no need."

"You have it too?"

"I have a cousin," he said, flashing me a small smile. He pulled his phone from the center console and made a call, putting it to his ear. "Hey, man."

Jack kind of spun away from me but kept talking. "Yeah, I'm good. Listen . . . no, actually, Annie told me about it. I was

189

coming to surprise Tuck . . . yeah, I *was* coming. But a deer ran out in front of us. My car's in a ditch."

I walked down the road a few steps. Fields went out in every direction, disappearing into a thicket of trees. The two-lane road spread forward both ways, with no sign of cars coming either way.

"Like twenty-five minutes east. You'll see us from a mile away . . . thanks, man. Okay, bye." He hung up the phone and looked at me. "Looks like we might not be getting any of the good cake."

"It's going to take a while for the tow truck to get out here?"

"Not the tow truck. Just Wyatt with a truck that tows. He should be here soon, but I don't know how long it'll take to get the car out of the ditch." Jack took a few steps closer, gripping me by the shoulders. He ducked his head a little to see into my eyes. "I'm really sorry."

"When I told you to distract me, I didn't mean like *that*."

He relaxed a little at my joke. "This is not how I imagined rolling up at my brother's party."

"In a truck that tows?"

"With no car. I don't know how we'll get home tonight, but I'll figure it out."

The idea of not being back at my computer by ten so I could keep working through Jerry's emails and my proposal for the MediCorp conference sent a sizzle of stress through my chest. "Will anyone be heading toward Dallas tonight?"

"It's unlikely, but we can probably figure something out." He looked over my shoulder. "Maybe my car will run perfectly fine. I'll have Wyatt take a look at it when we get to town."

JACK'S COUSIN, Wyatt, shook his head. He looked at Jack over the hood of the car. "One glance at that radiator tells me you aren't driving this home anytime soon." He'd towed us into Arcadia Creek, where we were now huddled around the front end of the car in his garage. His actual, attached-to-the-house garage, not an official mechanic situation. Apparently, they had nothing like that in town. Just a few hobby guys who knew a lot. If you needed something beyond their expertise, you had to drive to the next town over.

"That's not ideal," Jack muttered.

Talk about an understatement.

"Is anyone else up from Dallas?" he asked.

Wyatt leaned forward to look at something else under the hood. "No one else lives in Dallas."

"Okay." Jack ran a hand over his face. "I have an idea. But we need to get to the party first."

Wyatt pulled an orange degreasing wipe from the shelf and wiped his hands. "Hop in the truck. I'm heading over myself."

Jack took my hand, pulling me toward the green Ford that had come to get us off the side of the road. In the forty minutes we'd waited for Wyatt, six cars had stopped to ask if we needed help. "Don't worry yet. We'll get you home."

We climbed into the cab. I slid into the center seat, leaning toward Jack. His knees bounced the entire drive, displaying his anxious energy. Here I was worrying about whether I'd be home tonight to work on my proposal, and he was about to face his family, arriving uninvited to a party he was anxious about.

How could I have been so self-absorbed?

We stopped on the side of a long gravel road that ended at a farm-style house, trees butting all up around it and lights dangling from the wrap-around porch. Cars lined the entire road and filled the gravel space in front of the house. People milled around and country music blared. More than half of the vehicles lining the road were trucks.

We were not in the Metroplex anymore, Toto.

Jack stopped in the middle of the road. Wyatt glanced back once but kept moving, giving him space.

I took his hand, overwhelmed by the desire to lessen his burdens. "Don't stress about the car thing. We'll get home eventually."

"But you have to catch up on work." He looked so beaten down. "I made you a promise."

"You had no control over that deer." I squeezed his fingers. "Besides, when your conference is transferred to the Hunnam Group, I'll be able to offload some of my smaller events to coworkers. Most of them are pretty well in hand already, anyway." And I could always tell Jerry to just handle his issues himself. It's what I did, after all.

"I'm not surprised, Spreadsheets." He sounded fine, but his voice was still tight.

I hooked a thumb toward the house. "Should I enter doing the moonwalk while shouting the national anthem?"

His eyebrows pulled together. "Why?"

"To take the attention away from you."

A smile spread over his lips. "How sweet of you to offer to make a fool of yourself for me."

"There's nothing foolish about the moonwalk or the national anthem."

"You may fit in here better than you think."

Jack pulled me toward the house. He seemed more relaxed now, so I considered that a job well done. When we climbed the steps and opened the door, pretty much everyone in the room stopped what they were doing and turned to look at us. But while the general buzz of conversation had dropped to a cricket level of silence, the attention in the room wasn't on Jack. It was squarely on me.

He dropped my hand.

"Lauren!" Annie called from somewhere out of sight, her arms in the air while she ran through the crowd and pulled me into a hug. "You made it!"

Never had I seen so much plaid in one room or been so happy to have a friend. She unlocked the silence. The noise started up again as people surged forward to greet Jack.

"There are a lot of people in here," I said.

Annie took my arm, pulling me away from Jack and all the people swarming to hug him. "It's too cold outside or half of us would be on the porch. Come on, let me introduce you around."

I watched Jack over my shoulder as a tall guy with dark brown hair wrapped him in a hug and lifted him from the ground. Jack wasn't small, but this guy was much taller.

"Who's that?" I asked.

"Oh." Annie stopped. "Colt. The youngest Fletcher boy."

"*He's* the youngest?" He was bigger than Jack.

"That's the other one, Tucker," she said, pointing to a guy with wavy brown hair who came from behind, hugging Jack around the chest and sporting a wide grin, revealing a perfect row of white teeth.

"The man of the hour?"

"The very one." Annie looked from me to the Fletcher boys. "On second thought, let's go introduce you to them first. I'm just so glad you got him to come." She pulled me toward them, but it didn't fall on her to do any of the introductions.

Jack slid his arm around my shoulders, bringing me close to his side. "Colt, Tucker, this is Lauren Foley. Her sister just married my friend Kevin."

My gut reaction was to ask them not to tell anyone about the elopement, but by now I was guessing it wouldn't matter. Kevin and Amelia planned on approaching his parents tonight to give them the news.

"Congratulations," I said to Tucker. "I hear it's a big accomplishment."

"Thank you." His smile looked like Jack's, but the rest of him was pretty different. He was built more like a linebacker than for a suit and a boardroom. Neither of them were as tall as Colt.

Tucker faced his brother again. "Didn't expect you, though."

"I thought I'd surprise you after Annie told me about the party."

Tucker's neck went pink. "I just didn't want you to feel obligated to come out, man. Everyone's making a big deal out of it, but—"

"It *is* a big deal," Colt said, cutting him off. "You worked hard to get here, Tucker. Don't minimize your accomplishments."

I liked Colt already.

"Says the slacker." Tucker grabbed Colt by the head and bent it down into his armpit or somewhere in that region. I wasn't quite sure what was happening, but it looked like some sort of brotherly wrestling move. "It doesn't take much to impress you."

A woman stepped from the kitchen, wearing a cherry-dotted apron. Her blonde hair reached her collar bone, but the back was teased high and kept in place by at least half a bottle of hairspray. She had dainty features, and I could see a resemblance with Annie right away. "My boys," she said, lifting her arms until Jack returned the hug.

"Hi, Momma."

Well, melt my little urban heart. Who knew a man could be so attractive for openly loving his momma in that faint Texan drawl? I was pretty sure it had gotten thicker when we entered the town boundaries.

"Who'd you bring?" she asked, turning eagle eyes on me that carried the weight of one of the longhorns we'd passed coming inside.

"This is my friend, Lauren. Her sister just married Kevin on that cruise I told you about."

Mrs. Fletcher's eyes lit up. "Congratulations. We like Kevin."

"He's pretty great," I agreed.

"Well, don't be staying out here too long. We have cake in the kitchen, drinks in the coolers. We are a bit casual," she added, leaning close and squeezing my shoulder. "And always happy to have one more."

I felt it. I felt the way she was welcoming me, a complete stranger, into her home. The warm smile she gave me that slid back over to her son was authentic. Her subsequent scowl was just as fierce. "Now quit standing around here and get this girl a piece of cake."

"Yes, ma'am." Jack led me toward the kitchen.

Annie had disappeared, but I saw her sitting on Levi's knee on the end of the couch. Everyone was so comfortable with one another here, one giant mash of people who were happy to spend the night chatting and munching on treats.

It was so relaxing, the vibe in the room comfortable. This was what a big family felt like? It was exactly what my dreams had been filled with for the last twenty years, but I hadn't even known it.

The kitchen was the same farmhouse chic as the living room, except a little heavier on the farmhouse. This place wasn't decorated from a trip to Waco and Joanna Gaines's warehouse—it was the type of house that inspired people like Joanna Gaines. The farmhouse and the chic were both here, authentic and warm and clean. Three pans of Texas sheet cake lined the counter surrounded by a mishmash of cookies and bars and things people had brought with them.

"Which one's the good cake?" I asked.

Jack lifted an eyebrow, cutting and dishing up a portion of the Texas sheet cake and handing it to me . . . of which there was quite a lot left.

I took a bite. Mmm delicious. "Why are y'all calling it a cake? You know this is a brownie right?"

"Brownie isn't in the name."

"Everyone knows it's a brownie, though," I said.

"Then why is it called Texas sheet *cake*?"

"Not relevant."

He grinned, cutting himself a piece and taking a huge bite.

"Who's up for Celebrity?" someone called from the front room.

Jack lifted his eyebrows in something of a question, or maybe a challenge. He seemed more relaxed, like the initial arrival had been dealt with and he'd survived, so now he could breathe. "My family is crazy about games, so play at your own risk."

I gave him a shrug, taking a bite of the best Texas sheet cake I'd ever had. The icing melted in my mouth and the brownie was chocolate perfection. "Only if I get to bring another piece of this. Does that make me look like a greedy outsider?"

He cut another piece and plopped it on my plate, then leaned down and gave me a quick kiss on the lips while we were alone. "I think you fit in just fine."

CHAPTER TWENTY-THREE

JACK

EVERYONE HAD GONE HOME except for my brothers—and my parents, but it was their house. We sat on the sofas in the living room, picking at leftover treats. Lauren didn't seem thrilled about the need to stay overnight, but Tucker could drive us back to Dallas in the morning, so she wasn't going to be away for too long.

"Tell us about yourself, Lauren," my mom said, giving her a bright smile. She leaned back into Dad's side, but her eyes were wide and set on Lauren like a homing device. I knew what this was. She couldn't pretend to be innocent with me. She was about to drill Lauren for every piece of information she could. It wasn't a habit of mine to bring girls home, and everyone was acting cool about it, but I knew they were all dying of curiosity.

My mom's phone was going to be busy tomorrow when all the ladies called to find out what was going on with *Jack's new friend*.

Which meant we had to be strategic in our answers.

"Not much to tell," Lauren said humbly. "I work for the Hunnam Hotels Group as an event coordinator in Dallas, where

I've pretty much lived my whole life. I have one sister, and . . . that's about it."

"She also knows how to make a killer spreadsheet."

Lauren speared me with a *watch it* glare.

"And," I said dramatically, "she is the one who dragged me here tonight."

"I knew I had a good reason to like you." Mom leaned forward to pat her knee. "How long have you known each other?"

Lauren looked at me, so I answered. "A few years now, but I've known her sister since my first year of grad school."

"Is your family nearby?"

"I don't have much family." Lauren shifted on the sofa. "It's really just my sister and me. And now Kevin, the lucky dog."

"He is lucky," I said. My phone pinged, and I pulled it from my pocket to find a message from a guy at work and a few missed emails. One of them caught my eye.

I had gotten an email response about my request to move the conference.

Colt pulled a face. "Kevin might be, but now you have to put up with him."

"You're just bitter because he beat you in his TC," Tucker said around a mouthful of cake.

Colt scowled. "That car should *not* have handled so well."

Mom pointed her fork at her youngest son. "I said no racing on Alburn Road, Colt. It's not worth your life."

He put his arms up. "This was years ago." His side-eye gave him away. There's no way he'd quit racing.

Dad leaned forward to snag a cookie off the coffee table, then tapped the distressed white oak tabletop. "Jack made this," he bragged, graying eyebrows lifted.

"Restored it," I corrected.

But Lauren looked impressed. She ran her fingers over the

smoothed edges where paint was sanded away to give it an aged look. "It's beautiful."

"It's basic," I said, but the praise still lodged itself somewhere in my chest.

"He also did the dining table," Mom said. "And the hutch in the kitchen."

Lauren's approval did something weird to my stomach. I couldn't hold her gaze, so I lowered mine to the plate of cookies. "It was years ago."

Mom shook her head. "That hutch was last summer."

That was true. I'd brought it to her garage last June and spent a few weekends down here restoring it for her. It had been a little project to get my brain out of work when things had become overwhelming. It had done its job.

"That's amazing, Jack." Lauren grinned. "Now the HGTV obsession makes sense."

"I only tried to watch it once," I defended.

"Twice. The boat and the plane."

Oh. I hadn't known she'd noticed that. I guess it was paused on *Property Brothers* when I stopped her in the walkway on her way to the bathroom.

Dad yawned. "I better hit the hay."

"I made up Tucker's old room for you, Lauren." Mom pushed herself up in silent agreement. "No special Jack furniture in there, I'm afraid."

"But there's a great poster of Carrie Underwood," Tucker defended.

Dad took Mom's empty plate to the kitchen. She looked at me. "You're in your old room."

"Thank you, Mrs. Fletcher." Lauren stood and stretched. "It was nice to meet y'all."

"Come on. I'll get you a toothbrush and something to sleep in," Mom said, moving toward the staircase.

"You haven't seen the last of us," Colt promised.

I slugged him in the arm. "Don't scare her away."

Lauren laughed, following Mom up the stairs.

When the women had gone, I settled back down on my chair. My dad was still in the kitchen, doing the dishes if I had my guess, but Colt and Tucker were on the sofa, watching me. "What?"

"New girlfriend?"

"We're not really labeling things yet."

"You labeled her when you brought her to Arcadia, man," Tucker said, snagging a chocolate chip cookie from the plate and popping the entire thing in his mouth.

"She's more like an emotional support blanket than a statement to the town."

"You were that scared to come home?" Colt asked.

I looked at Tucker. "I didn't know if I was wanted."

"Don't do that to me, Jack. I'm not going to invite you to every little party one of the mommas throws, or you'd be down here every weekend."

Time to be honest. "This is different, though. You're my brother, and I want to support you."

"Well, come around more often, then."

I should. He was right. It was just as much my fault for staying away as it was his for not asking me to come.

"Or better yet, move home," Colt said with a grin.

Tucker laughed. "They don't have marketing executive jobs out here in big fancy offices."

I laughed, but the sound was hollow. True, they didn't have advanced, well-paying marketing jobs like the one I was doing in Dallas. But Arcadia Creek did have both of my brothers, my parents, my cousins, aunts, uncles. It had people I missed, that I hadn't realized how much I enjoyed being around until this evening. Why had I fought so hard to leave this place? Was my sterile, clean apartment really better than open fields and unimpeded sunsets and races down Alburn Road and Burgers at Gigi's Diner?

My heart surged with affection for my hometown while my stomach did a somersault. I pulled out my phone and swiped to my email, opening the one I'd gotten from Brad, my boss.

No dice, Jack. We can't move the conference this late in the game. Maybe next year.

No. No no no. How could he give me a flat no when his last text had made him sound so open minded? Besides, I'd had so many good reasons in my email. My motivation was to help Lauren, but the reasons I'd given Brad were solid. I typed up a response and sent it before I could think it through.

I really feel like Hunnam would be a better fit. Will you reconsider? I'm happy to put together a presentation for Monday if you want to sleep on it.

His reply was instantaneous.

You can come up with a proposal for next year. We aren't moving this conference. Too many things have already been put into motion, so it would be a hassle to move it all.

That was it. Lauren was going to kill me.

"He's distracted," I heard Colt say.

I lifted my head. "Sorry."

"Nah, we need to head out anyway." Tucker stood. "What time do you want to take off tomorrow?"

"Morning sometime?"

"I'll call you when I wake up, then."

My brothers both left. I sat in silence, listening to Dad finishing up the dishes in the other room. I had expected a little pushback about moving the conference, but not a flat no. Brad was not an unreasonable person, and when faced with a logical option, he was the first to jump on board a new idea. Presenting him with the opportunity to save the company a significant amount of money with the discounts Lauren had offered was supposed to make this situation a no-brainer. The location was prime for Dallas's night life, and the suites for the executives were a nice perk.

He must know something I didn't.

It also meant I needed to tell Lauren right away. I pulled out my phone and sent her a text.

JACK

Meet me on the front porch in ten?

LAUREN

Is this where you lure me out to the corn fields and murder me?

JACK

Don't know where you're getting that crazy idea. There are no corn fields around here.

She laughed at my text.

LAUREN

I'll be down soon.

My dad came out of the kitchen, wiping his hands down the front of his jeans. His plaid shirt was worn, familiar from years of use, and the lines on his tanned skin were well creased. "Good to have you here, son."

"It's good to be here."

He disappeared, leaving me in the dim living room alone. I fetched a blanket from the oversized basket tucked against the wall and let myself outside, closing the door softly behind me. The air was biting, but I was glad the sky was clear.

It didn't take long for Lauren to meet me on the porch. She was wearing one of my mom's flannel nightgowns under her thick sweatshirt and wool socks. It was quite the sight, and it only made me grin. "Well, don't you look adorable."

"Not another word, Jackson."

"That isn't my name."

She lifted her eyebrows. "Not even your full legal name?"

"Nope. Levi just says it to get under my skin."

"Good to know."

"All right, you," I said, pushing the blanket into her hand. "Hold this."

"Why?"

I leaned down and picked her up, one arm under her knees and the other around her back. She yelped, which only made my smile grow. "So I can do this." I stepped down the porch onto the stone pathway that curved around the house.

"Is this necessary?"

"You're the one who chose not to wear shoes."

Despite the grandma attire, she still looked lovely. Her hair fell over her shoulders, and her eyes glinted in the moonlight. The way she smiled up at me like she was trying to pretend to be annoyed but loved being in my arms nearly undid me. I didn't want to ruin that smile and wreck her mood.

The moment I told her about the conference, she was going to hate me.

The hammock was just behind the house. "Hold on to the sides when I lower you, or you could spin out."

"Okay." She gripped the fabric, and I set her in so her feet could hang over the side before I climbed in next to her.

We sat up, our feet hanging over the side, while I shook out the blanket and laid it over our laps.

"This is . . . fun."

"Just wait," I said, twisting my torso to spread the fabric of the hammock further behind our heads. "Now lie back slowly so we make sure our weight is distributed evenly."

"Lie back?"

"Just your head."

We both leaned back until I was sure we weren't going to

topple out of the hammock. I kept both of my feet on the ground to rock us gently.

Lauren gave a soft gasp. "The stars!"

"They're beautiful, right?" I felt a surge of happiness that she seemed to appreciate the brilliance of the sky out here as much as I'd hoped she would. "Watch for a shooting star. I'm sure we'll see a few."

"I don't think I've ever seen one before," she said.

"Light pollution makes it hard until you've left the city far, far behind."

"Speaking of leaving the city, why would you ever want to be anywhere but here?"

She wasn't holding back the tough questions. "I was kind of asking myself that same question tonight."

Lauren was quiet for a moment. "Your family is really incredible, Jack. And enormous."

"You haven't met them all. There's more."

"Good grief. Do Fletchers fill Arcadia Creek?"

"No. But I'm related to an embarrassing percentage of it one way or another." I laughed.

We swung in the silence, listening to the grass moving in the breeze. "Your parents made me feel welcome," she said gently.

"It's kind of their specialty. We always had a lot of people in our house growing up. My mom likes being one of the town mommas. Everyone's welcome, there's always enough supper prepared to add a plate to the table, that sort of thing."

"Next you're going to tell me your dad is the town pastor and there was a period of time when no one was allowed to dance."

"We're not quite *Footloose*, but my brother did drive an old Volkswagen Beetle in high school."

"Tell me it was yellow."

"Blue."

"So lame."

"Hey, Lauren?"

"Yeah?" She tilted her head back to look at me, her gaze direct, and I forgot what I was going to say. Something about crushing her promotion and breaking my promise? Her lips were *right there* and so soft—I remembered them vividly—and the sky was clear and the stars were bright. I didn't want my bad news to ruin this moment.

At this point, it wouldn't matter if I waited until tomorrow, right? There wasn't anything she could do about it right now, anyway. She had no way to get home to her computer tonight, which would probably only send her into a panic. I'd seen anxiety get the better of her once; I didn't want to push her into that again. No, it was probably better to wait for the sake of her ability to get any sleep tonight. I would still tell her before we left Arcadia Creek.

"Thanks for coming with me."

"Of course." She settled back, but I kept watching her. "I saw one!" Lauren pointed up at the sky, a smile spreading broadly over her lips. "A shooting star!"

"Make a wish."

"Really?"

"Yes. Hurry or the magic will leave."

She rolled her eyes before closing them tightly. "Okay, done."

"What did you wish for?"

She nudged me softly with her elbow. "I know enough about shooting stars to know I'm not supposed to tell you."

"Okay, fine." I found her hand under the blanket and wrapped mine around it. She'd seemed to relax a lot over the duration of the cruise. The Lauren sitting beside me now wasn't the same woman I'd approached in the airport before we went to Florida, manically checking spreadsheets and stuffing as much work as possible into the free minutes before boarding. It made me wonder why she was so married to her work if the separation from it only appeared to do her good. "Hey, what do you love about your job?"

"Planning."

"Of course."

"No, really. I love the planning and executing of events. I love problem solving and making someone happy with a wedding or retirement party or conference well done. It gives me a rush."

"It sounds more like a recipe for being stressed all the time."

She was quiet for a minute. "I am stressed most of the time, but only because I've worked so hard to prove I deserve this promotion. Jerry hasn't put the time in to really earn it, but he's a major contender. Until it's well and truly mine, I don't think I'll be able to relax."

My stomach flipped. "Kind of crazy to have your job influence your happiness so much."

"And you're so different?"

"No. I mean, my job is crazy stressful, too. I just don't want my whole life to be centered around work anymore. I've done that for a few years now and I guess I'm over it." The words were true, and as they left my mouth I realized how deeply I meant them. I wasn't happy at MediCorp. I wasn't happy promoting drugs and medical equipment at exorbitant prices people shouldn't have to pay. I wanted my work to mean something. "I guess I just want to be more impactful, less rat-racey."

"So . . . meditate more?" she suggested.

Not a terrible idea, but not what I was thinking. I shook my head. I couldn't quit my job anyway. What would I do? How would I afford my apartment? I couldn't. It wasn't an option.

"Can we just pretend there's no job to return to?" I asked.

"Only for tonight. My brain can't shut off longer than that. It's been in crisis mode since the car rolled, just knowing I was going to be separated from my computer even longer than expected."

My stomach clenched. She was not going to be happy when I gave her the news. I shoved the thought away. "Well, maybe *you* need to meditate more, Lauren."

"Okay." She faced me, slipping her hand over my cheek and turning my head until I was looking at her. She leaned forward and kissed me until I didn't feel the Texas winter anymore and all I could think of was this woman, this place, this moment.

Nothing else mattered.

CHAPTER TWENTY-FOUR

LAUREN

I WOKE up to the smell of bacon. Like the smell of actual, legit, sizzling bacon wafted into my room and woke me from the deepest, most comfortable sleep I'd had in a while. Sunlight streamed through the cracks in the blinds, highlighting dust motes floating lazily through the air, and the hum of conversation downstairs pulled at me.

But first, I had to get out of this *Little House on the Prairie* getup. I got back into my jeans and black T-shirt from yesterday, pulling on my University of Texas sweatshirt.

"Good morning!" Mrs. Fletcher sang out when I stepped into the kitchen. The table was set like this was some sort of sitcom and not real life. "Sleep well?"

"I did, thank you."

"Breakfast is on the table. You aren't gluten-free, right? Those pancakes are full of flour."

"I'm not allergic to anything."

She bustled over to the table. "Orange juice?"

"Yes, thank you."

Mrs. Fletcher poured for me. I moved around the table and

pulled out my chair. When I reached for a pancake, she stopped me. "A hot one is coming in two shakes, if you can wait."

"I can wait."

I loaded my plate with scrambled eggs and browned sausages.

"Jack is out with Roy. They should be in soon." She flipped the pancakes and looked at me over her shoulder. "Tucker was called into work in the middle of the night for some emergency. He thinks he'll be done by noon."

Noon. I looked at the clock. That meant killing four hours before our ride back home. If I started walking, would I make it home before that? Unlikely.

"Y'all are welcome to come to church with us, if you'd like."

I eyed the single yellow flower in the vase on the center of the table. This was growing more sitcom-like by the second. "Is your husband the pastor?"

She gave me a funny look. "He runs the farm here and drives bus for the local schools."

"Oh."

The door swung open as Mrs. Fletcher was putting two pancakes on my plate, steam rising from them and making my stomach grumble. Jack stepped in, wearing a red plaid shirt over jeans, with boots that almost reached his knees.

"Boots on the porch," Mrs. Fletcher said.

Jack turned right back outside and heeled them off before returning in his socks. He must have borrowed the outfit from his old drawers if the tight way the jeans fit was any indication. I didn't realize I was into cowboys, but apparently a soft, worn plaid and a pair of Wranglers made my blood hum.

"No ride to Dallas until noon?" I asked, getting Jack's attention.

"It's a hazard of Tucker's profession. If there's a power line down, he has to go out."

"Probably a drunk driver hitting a pole," Mrs. Fletcher mumbled, moving near the stove again.

"I had an idea while we're waiting though."

"Church?" Mrs. Fletcher asked.

Jack looked from his mother to me. "If Lauren's okay with it, yeah. Then I want to show her around."

It wasn't like I had any other choice, right? Besides, I liked the idea of seeing more of his charming town. "It's fine with me."

He bumped his knee against mine. "It's a date."

THE CHURCH WAS FULL. The music was familiar, like what you'd hear on the Christian radio station so many businesses played in the DFW area. I recognized a number of faces from Tucker's party, too, sprinkled on the pews. Jack stopped to chat with people as we slowly made our way down the aisle and outside, stretching our escape twice as long as it should have been.

It was evident Jack was a rare commodity here and people were eager to see him. It gave me plenty of time to admire the architecture of the old church. This venue would make for a killer wedding—so much richer than the sterile ballrooms I had to manage at the hotel. I was pretty sure this church had made a few appearances in various Hallmark movies. Or maybe Hallmark just really nailed the whole small town vibe.

When we finally reached the grass, he waved at his parents and took my hand, pulling me in the opposite direction.

"Didn't realize I was with a celebrity."

Jack's neck turned red. "Just my old teachers and neighbors. It's been a while since I've seen most of them."

"Maybe you should visit them more often."

He gave a noncommittal huff, tugging me down a tree-lined

main street, though the branches were still pretty bare. Chilly wind nipped at my nose. I curled the ends of my sweatshirt into my fists while a shiver swept through my body.

"We can head back." Jack shot me a side-eye.

"We have hours to kill."

"But we don't have to kill them outside."

I looked from him to the idyllic main street, where it was possible to see both ends from where we were standing, it was so short. The road continued on both ways, dotted with trees and houses as far as I could see.

"This place should go on the front of a greeting card for small-town America."

"Who's buying greeting cards about small towns?" he asked, amused.

"Probably people from big towns who yearn for this slow life but won't do anything to change their suburban ways."

"Are you speaking from experience?"

"I've never yearned for dirt roads or lack of Target, actually."

He gave a dramatic sigh. "You don't know what you're missing."

"Didn't you run away from all this?"

Jack was quiet for a second, walking down the sidewalk before his shoulders gave a shrug. "Yeah."

I wanted to press. To find out what was hidden in the silent stretch before he admitted it. There was a weird tension in his shoulders today, but I didn't know why. He wasn't acting differently toward me, just more like something was on his mind. When we nearly reached the end of the road, I took his hand.

He closed his fingers around mine and glanced up at me. "What's that for?"

"Isn't this one of my perks?"

A genuine smile came over his face. "Perks, huh? What else did you have in mind?"

"Homemade pancakes in the morning, stargazing in hammocks, MediCorp Conferences. Just to name a few."

Jack's smile tightened. He pulled me along until we reached an alley, totally ignoring the opportunity for banter. "Want to see my favorite place on Main Street?"

"Yeah." Surprise curled around my chest when it occurred to me how much I *did* want to see his favorite place on Main Street, how much I was enjoying the bits and pieces coming together to make up Jack's background. Every new thing he showed me was like another brick torn away from the window to his soul. I wanted to learn every little piece of information until there was nothing else, no more bricks, and I understood who he was.

We followed the lane between the buildings and came out the other side, where a road ran parallel to the businesses and led to what appeared to be houses. But we kept following the alley lane straight back until it turned into a tree-lined drive.

"Is this where you bring all your victims before you make them disappear?"

"If I did, would I tell you?"

"Good point."

The alley had been narrow but wide enough for a car. The lane itself was not much wider and led directly to a dilapidated house on a shallow hill. The house was noticeable from the alleyway, but the overgrown trees gave it enough privacy that it wasn't standing out too much.

It was worn and beaten, the wraparound porch broken in places. The windows were boarded up.

"You were joking about the victims thing, right?" This was definitely a perfect murder spot.

"Why are you so obsessed with murder?"

I laughed. "It's the small town bringing it out in me, I guess. I can't stop thinking about *Signs*."

"Well, good thing there's no threat of aliens here," he said, chuckling. "You have life security, anyway, so you don't make a good victim. If you went missing, Amelia would hunt me down."

Now *that* was funny. "You act like she would notice if I went missing."

"Is that a joke? Amelia would hunt you down and then anyone who played a part in your disappearance."

"Wow. You have a lot more confidence in my sister's opinion of me than I do."

He stared at me. "Are you joking?"

"I think she'd be sad if I disappeared, obviously, but I don't picture her as the dad from *Taken* or anything. Our relationship isn't like that."

"But if she went missing, you'd *Taken* the heck out of the situation."

"Of course I would."

Jack crossed his arms over his chest. "You hear the double standard, right?"

"I'm the older sister, the caregiver, the grandma. Obviously I don't expect Amelia to see me the same way I see her. She wasn't the one making my lunches and getting me to the bus on time for all those years."

"Or tucking you into bed at night," he said, so quietly I wondered if he was saying it to himself more than me.

"Exactly. You get it."

"No. I understand why you see it that way, though." He peered at me too long, his X-Ray eyes boring through my skin to all the yucky, misshapen parts underneath.

"So," I said, a little too loudly, my smile a little too bright. "What's so special about this place?"

He watched me for a minute, and I could see the moment when he decided to trust me. It made me straighten my spine and pay close attention, because this didn't seem like standard hometown date protocol for Jack.

He looked briefly at the house. "It's my Narnia."

"As in—"

"As in my secret escape closet when I was a kid."

I tilted my head a little to the side. "I didn't take you for a reader."

"My mom read to us a lot when we were kids, so I know the whole walk through the closet to another world part well. This" —he swept his arm up toward the house—"is the doorway in my closet."

"In plain speech?"

"I used to come up here a lot as a kid and play with my brothers. The house was haunted or a shipwreck or an orphanage we needed to escape from or whatever suited our purposes that day."

"You're giving me less reason to feel sorry for your child-hood, you know."

Jack's gaze shifted to me. "I never wanted you to feel sorry for me. My childhood was amazing."

My heart tweaked at that. I could see how it was, and being around his family, witnessing their genuine warmth for one another, was really a beautiful thing to behold. "Then what happened to make you want to leave all of this?"

"My ego was too big? The bubble that is small towns felt stifling. It can be claustrophobic."

My eyes swept over the large, open sky and the quiet street on the other side of the trees. Houses dotted the road that ran perpendicular to the buildings and ended at an elementary school or daycare down on the end—something with a play-ground. But claustrophobic? It felt far from that. Inhaling the crisp, fresh air, I faced him again. "I have a hard time seeing anything negative about this place."

"Just wait until you break up with your high school girlfriend and it makes front page news."

"Maybe the issue is less that the town is nosy and more that you needed to learn how to set boundaries."

Jack dipped his head, holding my gaze. "Don't get all philo-sophical now. I was trying to bare my soul to you. You're supposed to be impressed or want to soothe my inner child. Either of them work for me."

He was deflecting. "You know I'm right, Jack."

"If I tell you you're right, will you come over here?"

"Depends on what'll happen to me when I do."

He lowered his voice. "I think you'll like it."

My pride hummed softly. "I am right."

"Yes, you are." He reached for me.

I stepped to the side. "You don't actually mean that."

"Of course I do." He reached for me again.

I stepped back again until my feet bumped into the bottom step of the porch.

Jack lunged for my arm, pulling me back before I could climb the steps. "Don't!"

I landed in his arms. "What the heck?"

"It's not safe. The entire porch is rotten, so you could fall through at any point."

"Yeah right. You just wanted to rescue me so I'd feel beholden to you."

His arms tightened. "Did it work?"

"Kind of."

Jack shifted so his hand was free, and he pushed my hair behind my ear. "You look pretty today."

"I'm in an old sweatshirt and jeans. The same ones I wore yesterday."

"My compliment stands."

It was hard not to reciprocate his smile in kind. He was a charmer, but his eyes were steady and green and sincere.

He twisted a lock of my hair around his finger, his face hovering just over mine. "Do you want to go around to the back entrance? It's safer over there and I can give you a mini-tour of the house."

"Yes." I was eager to see the interior. The exterior was obviously deteriorating, but the house still had a romantic quality to it. Or maybe that was just the warmth buzzing through me, putting romance-colored glasses over my perception.

"Okay. But first . . ." Jack leaned down, pulling me flush against him, when his pocket started buzzing. He pulled it out and released me to answer, his voice tight. "Hey, Tuck. What's up?"

I still wasn't used to kissing Jack on the regular. It was a treat that had been denied me, and I felt a little salty toward his brother for calling.

"Oh. Now? Okay. Yeah, sure." He looked at me before hanging up the phone. "Tucker's ready when we are."

"Ready for what?"

"To take us home."

"Oh." Oh. Why was I disappointed? I needed to get back to my laptop and lists and the PowerPoint I was developing to show Hal the reasons I deserved this promotion. The main feature was the MediCorp conference, of course, but I felt like there were enough other things to add to fill a presentation. It wasn't desperate. It was me trying to make up for my utter lack of facetime around the office in the last week and a half.

I called it strategy.

Jack must have picked up on that weird underlying disappointment though. "We can always come back sometime," he said, his voice heavily laced with hesitation. "You didn't get your tour of the house." Jack took my hand and started pulling me down the lane back toward Main Street.

"Sure." Noncommittal. Cautious. The opposite of enthusiastic. "Maybe after the MediCorp conference is over and my promotion is in the bag, then I'll have the free space to think again."

He stopped, his hand dropping mine like a hot iron.

"What is it?"

Jack couldn't meet my gaze, which started a whole slew of anxiety in my stomach. He cleared his throat. "About that conference . . ."

Silence nestled around us, fraught with tension. "What, Jack?"

"It's not—" He cleared his throat. "They aren't willing to move it. It won't be coming to the Hunnam Group."

The world beyond our little conversation grew deathly quiet. "What do you mean?"

"I mean," he said, his voice warming while he took a tentative step closer. "My boss messaged me last night and—"

"*Last night* and you're only telling me now?"

"I didn't want you to stress unnecessarily."

I scoffed. He'd known for *hours*. If I'd known that long, I could have at least started making a plan. A backup plan. Anything to try to save my promotion.

Jack looked helpless. "It's out of my hands, Lauren. I'm sorry, but I can't give you the conference."

CHAPTER TWENTY-FIVE

JACK

IT WAS STILL undecided whether Lauren was ever going to speak to me again. The woman had massive skill where the silent treatment was concerned, despite the fact that she'd spent an entire hour in the middle seat of Tucker's truck, her leg pressed up against mine.

She'd been nothing but smiles and gratitude when we were saying goodbye to my parents, and at the beginning of the drive she'd answered Tucker's first few questions with perfect manners. But the man wasn't known for his chattiness and the conversation had quickly died.

I knew I'd messed up. Promising the conference had been stupid when I didn't actually have the final word. Clearly my opinion wasn't as heavily weighted with Brad as I thought it was, since he'd disregarded it out of hand.

It stung.

Now Lauren was ticked—rightfully so—and I had nothing to say that would absolve me. I'd screwed up. Plain and simple.

"You coming back for the Easter parade?" Tucker asked.

"I'll be back sooner than that for my car," I said, a little hurt that he thought the next time he'd see me would be a month from now. Though if you looked at recent history, we'd gone a lot longer than that between visits more often than not.

Being home in Arcadia Creek and surrounded by so many people who were happy to see me, who made me feel wanted there, had been the boon I didn't know I'd needed. I was eager for my own bed after over a week away, but I wasn't looking forward to my empty, quiet apartment anymore.

We were in Arcadia longer than we'd meant to be there, but it still hadn't felt like long enough. Waking up before dawn to feed the cows and move pipe with the sunrise had filled my soul. Eating Mom's pancakes after working the muscle in my arms organically, without the help of machines and weights, had given me a sense of nostalgia that left me wanting more. But above all that, showing Lauren my dream project . . . that had been the highlight for me. Only, I never got far enough to explain the whole dream project part to her.

"It's just up here on the right," Lauren said, directing Tucker through the parking lot of her apartment complex.

The truck pulled to a stop.

Lauren faced Tucker. "Thanks for the ride."

"No problem."

I got out of the truck and held the door for her. She passed me, swinging her bag over her shoulder, and I caught my brother's eye.

His eyebrows rose, speaking their own language. *You done messed up, didn't you?*

Yes, Tucker's eyebrows, I did. Royally. "I'll be back in a minute."

I shut the truck door and followed Lauren toward her building.

She glanced at me over her shoulder. "You don't need to walk me in. This wasn't a date."

That was news to me. "Lauren, listen. Give me a chance to explain—"

"It's not a good time." She walked through the front doors to the building.

I followed her. If we didn't talk about this now, I was afraid I'd lose the opportunity to talk about it at all. "This project has been mine since the beginning. My boss had to sign off on everything, but that was only a formality—"

Lauren stopped walking, her gaze drawn to the grouping of couches in the lobby.

This was progress. "My proposal was solid, I swear—"

"Not a good time," she said again through her teeth, her eyes narrowing on the couch. "Is that . . . ?"

A figure sat up on the small loveseat, where she'd been previously curled up in a dark ball swathed in a plain violet dress, the honey-brown hair matted to one side of her head proving she had been laying there for a significant amount of time.

"Amelia?" Lauren asked. It took half a second for her to cross the lobby and pull her unsteady sister into a hug. "What happened?"

Amelia clung to Lauren, black mascara smudged beneath her eyes. Watching them felt like an intrusion, but walking away would be abandonment. I swept the lobby quickly for Kevin, but he wasn't here.

Lauren pulled back a little, searching Amelia's face. "Where's Kevin? Is he hurt? Are you okay?"

"He's fine," she said, her shaky voice watery. "Probably. I don't know."

"You aren't making any sense, Ames."

Amelia gave herself a little shake, pulling away from her sister. She wrapped her arms around herself, and I noticed her ring finger was empty. Well, this screamed crisis.

"It's over," she whispered. "And I didn't know where to go."

Lauren tensed. "How long have you been here?"

"Just since last night. But I couldn't go home to get that spare key, so I just waited."

"Oh my gosh." Lauren put her arm around Amelia. "Why didn't you call me?"

"My phone died."

"Come on, let's get upstairs."

"Can I do anything?" I asked, desperate to help, or at least understand what the heck happened.

Lauren speared me with a glare. "Not the best time, Jack."

I could see that. My hands went up in surrender. "I'll call later."

Lauren ignored me, steering her sister toward the elevator. I watched them walk away, disappearing behind the sliding doors, my eyes glued to Lauren's face.

She didn't look at me once.

TUCKER'S entire truck rattled when I slammed the door.

"Hey," he said, closing his own door softly. We'd reached my apartment complex and parked in the garage beneath the building. My blood still hummed from the scene I'd witnessed in Lauren's lobby and the implications that stacked on top of it. I needed to call Kevin. The man was probably in need of a little emotional support or a sparring partner at the gym. I could provide either of those things.

"Sorry," I muttered. I led the way silently toward the elevators.

"Did something go down in Arcadia?" Tucker asked.

I stepped into the elevator and scrubbed a hand over my face. "I made a promise to Lauren, and I couldn't keep it. She has a right to be mad."

"But you're the one slamming doors."

"I have a right to be mad at myself." I shook my head. I told him about finding Amelia waiting in the lobby and the lack of closure it had given me and Lauren.

Tucker gave a low whistle when we reached my floor, then followed me toward my apartment. "That has to be a record in short marriages."

"We don't know what happened. They could be completely fine and her ring could be getting cleaned or something."

"Do you really think that's the case?" he asked, his eyebrow lifted.

I tossed my keys in the bowl on the coffee table and dropped on the sofa, lowering my face into my hands. She had said *it's over*. "No."

Tucker took the recliner, watching me. "Are you happy here?"

"Of course I am."

He put his hands up. "Fine. Lie to me."

"I screwed up with my girlfriend, and my best friend's marriage of less than a week could be on the rocks. Both of those things are not normal. This is not a typical weekend for me, Tuck."

"Maybe not, but I haven't seen you as relaxed as you were last night in ages. There was something about you that was just different. You haven't been that chill in years."

Years? A little dramatic. "Maybe that has more to do with the girl I was with and less to do with where we were."

"I'm guessing it was probably both, but if you want to disagree with me that's your prerogative."

"All I want right now is to get back into my own clothes and find out what's going on with Kevin."

Tucker stood. "I can take a hint. But don't be a stranger, man. I want you around. We all do."

"You're leaving already?"

"You say that like you weren't just kicking me out."

"I don't want you to hang with me in the shower, but I still have an Xbox. You can stay as long as you want."

Tucker looked out the window. "Nah, I need to get home. I only slept like two hours before getting called in last night. If I don't head out soon, it won't be safe to drive anymore."

"Take a nap here. We can grab dinner or something before you leave." My breath stalled a little. It hadn't occurred to me how badly I wanted Tucker to remain until he was leaving. It had been years since I wrecked him at Super Smash Bros. I really wanted to smash attack a Donkey Kong right now.

Indecision passed over his face. Then it clouded again. "I really need to get home. I told Aunt Marnie I could paint her porch swing today. I should start sanding it at least."

"Did she get a new one?"

"No, she wants to refinish the old one."

My chest buzzed. That was something I used to be asked to do.

Tucker must have realized this at the same time I'd thought it. "Of course she'd prefer if you did it. You're so much better at sanding than I am. You're just not local."

"I'm always happy to drive back," I defended. "It's not that far."

He gave a dry laugh. "No one's gonna ask you to drive to Arcadia Creek to paint a swing, Jack. Think about it."

I didn't really want to. I just wanted hot steamy water to wash away the farm dirt and clean clothes that hadn't been sitting in my teenage closet for almost ten years, getting musty.

I stood to give him a hug and walked him to the door.

He paused, looking at me over the threshold, his eyes narrowing slightly. "You know no one would ever think you failed if you come home, right?"

"I didn't think that would be the case."

He shrugged. "Fine. If you wanna play it like that. See you around."

I watched him walk down the hallway and closed the door behind him while regret pooled at my feet. Shrugging off the way his parting comment made me feel, I dialed Kevin's number. I filled a glass with water and drained it on the way to the bathroom. No answer.

I texted him.

JACK

> I saw Amelia today. What's going on, man? Call me back.

I put down the phone and started the shower.

When I got out, there was no text and no missed call waiting for me. I took an Uber to his house instead.

The windows were dark. The driveway was empty. I called again and it went almost straight to voicemail.

Something was definitely wrong.

CHAPTER TWENTY-SIX

LAUREN

AMELIA HADN'T SAID a word since entering my apartment except to tell me which of my loungewear sets she wanted to borrow after her shower. I threw a container of premade soup into a pot on the stove and stuck some frozen bread in the oven. Maybe I wasn't the best cook, but premade food saved my butt from hitting up takeout practically every night of the week. My freezer was *stocked*.

If we ever had another storm, with the power grids failing our entire state like they did back in '21, at least I wouldn't starve.

I won't tell you how many weighted blankets I bought after that blizzard, either. It never hurt to be prepared. Besides, I got use out of them. Like right now, when Amelia was curled up on my couch in one of Joanna Gaines's *Homebody* lounge sets, her dripping wet hair on the lavender weighted blanket cocooning her.

She was also staring at a blank wall with a frown. I spooned out two bowls of soup and brought them to the couch with a plate of bread and all the proper silverware.

"I can't eat," she said quietly.

"You need to." I pushed her bowl into her hands. "Keep your blood sugar up."

She reluctantly obeyed.

I waited until she had taken a few bites before leveling my gaze at her. "Are you going to tell me what happened?"

Her face crumpled and silent tears started rolling down her cheeks.

I put her soup back on the coffee table before it could drop on my floor and took her by the shoulders, pulling her in for a hug. "You're scaring me."

She sniffled. "I don't know how I can stay married now."

My body froze. "Did Kevin do something?"

A look of horror splashed over her face. "Gosh, no. Of course not. He's amazing."

"So . . . his parents?" I remembered she was supposed to go to their house yesterday and tell them about the wedding. "You told them about the elopement."

"Yeah," she said, the word silent, her mouth forming around it. "They were furious, which we expected. But I guess I thought once the wedding was over, they would at least take us more seriously. I was wrong."

I couldn't really imagine Kevin throwing Amelia to the wolves, but he wasn't here, and neither was her ring.

She caught me looking at her hand. "They wanted the ring back."

"Can they do that?" I tucked my chin. "Like legally?"

"It's a family heirloom. Technically, it wasn't Kevin's to give."

"Seriously?"

"Well, if he'd offered it to a pre-approved woman, it would have been fine," she said bitterly. "I'm not on that list."

I had no words. What was wrong with these people? So what if Amelia lacked the private prep school training and oil-dirty hands in her lineage? She had a golden heart and sincerely loved their son. "I still don't understand why Kevin isn't here."

"I left. I put the ring on the table and walked out while he was arguing with his dad. He doesn't know where I went."

"It won't take him long to figure it out."

"Maybe, but he's leaving me be. I got him on the phone before it died and asked him to give me a few days."

"And he agreed?"

"He respects that I need time to come to terms with this."

That was hard to swallow. I wanted to pull my phone out and check it to see if he'd checked in, but I refrained. I'd look later. "So, what now?"

"I don't know. They're going to disown him if he stays married to me. Kevin won't leave me, but I could leave him."

"You won't, though."

She lifted her gaze to me in a challenge. "I haven't decided yet."

"You can't tell me you think Kevin would take his inheritance over you."

"Without me, he could still afford to rent yachts or fly to Maui whenever he wanted to. Married to me, he would have to let go of some of the things he's lived his entire life with. He says he doesn't care, Lo, but the truth is he doesn't know the difference."

I hated what a good argument that was. "Shouldn't love trump all, though?" I was about as cynical as they came, but never once had I questioned Amelia and Kevin. Yes, I thought they were too young to be married, but that didn't mean I thought they wouldn't still be married one day. I just thought they could take a few more years to do it.

And maybe a small part of me didn't want to admit that my younger sister had her life together better than I did.

A loud knock at the door startled both of us, and I almost kicked Amelia.

"Ames!" a man's voice called.

Kevin. It had to be.

"He'll give you a few days, huh?" I challenged.

He yelled again. "Ames! I need to talk to you."

I waited for her to respond, but her wide, round eyes were sad. "I can't face him now. I need more time."

"Are you sure? Maybe talking is just what you need for a little perspective."

"I'm not ready," she whispered weakly.

"Okay, I'll send him away." I pushed up and padded to the front door, which was down a short hallway and wouldn't afford Kevin a view of Amelia on the couch. His fist pounded on the door again, and I waited for a lull before sliding open the lock with exaggerated sound so he wouldn't accidentally knock into my face when I opened the door.

I got it open two inches before stalling. Kevin looked like he hadn't slept in days. His hair was wild, his eyes wide and wary. "Is she here?"

"Yes, but—"

He started to push in, but I stood in front of him.

"Wait. She needs time."

His face contorted. "Time? She's my *wife*. I need to speak to her. To see her. To make sure she's okay."

"You can't take my word for it? *Mine*, Kevin?"

That seemed to stall him.

I gently pushed his chest until he was back out in the hall. "She's shaken, but she's safe. I'm making her eat, then I'm putting her to bed." I lowered my voice. "Let her get a good night's sleep and try again tomorrow."

"I just want to see her."

"She asked for some time, Kevin. I don't know what more you want me to say."

He blew a breath out through puffed cheeks. "Okay. One day."

"She didn't leave you. You know that, right?"

Kevin narrowed his eyes. "What else would you call this?"

He had me there. And apparently he felt he had nothing more to say, because he turned around and left. I watched him trudge away, my heart reaching out to him, but what else could I do? It wasn't my place to force Amelia to do anything. The most I could offer her was my support and a safe place to land.

Her eyes were alert when I locked the door and returned to the couch. "How did he look?"

"Miserable."

That only served to make her cry again.

I pulled out my phone and checked my messages, finding fourteen texts from Kevin within the last hour—nothing before that, though. I also had a message from Jack.

JACK

Is Amelia okay?

LAUREN

No. That family has issues.

JACK

You're telling me. Kevin isn't home and he's not answering his phone. I'm worried.

LAUREN

He just stopped by. Amelia wouldn't see him, so I'm betting he's on his way home now.

JACK

She turned him away?

LAUREN

She wants time. Whatever that means.

Three little dots showed up and disappeared over and over again before his next text finally came through.

JACK

Do you need time as well?

My job. The promotion. It all came crashing down on me with swift, blinding anger. I waited for my vision to clear.

LAUREN

Yes.

I put my phone away and picked up my soup. "If we're going to wallow, do you want to at least put on a movie?"

"Yes."

"What sounds good?"

"I don't care."

I thought maybe staying away from romance would be smart, so I toggled onto my movie app and played *Mean Girls*. Then I pulled another weighted blanket onto the couch and nestled in. By the sound of Amelia's revived crying, it was going to be a long night.

I DIDN'T GET to bed until after one in the morning, and when I woke up and tiptoed out to the kitchen to grab breakfast the next morning, Amelia was zonked out. I had a feeling she would still be like this when I checked in on her during my lunch break. It was tempting to stay home and take care of her, but I'd already been out of the office for over a week, and my promotion was on the line.

Tucking my blouse into my pencil skirt, I analyzed my hair through the reflection of my microwave. It wasn't weird to have professional hair at work, but Jack made me second-guess the bun I typically wore. My eyes closed, shutting out the image of his face and smudging the sharp edges of my memory.

Jack's opinion was irrelevant here. The man had made me

believe he could help me, and he didn't. He persuaded me to drive way the heck out of Dallas to go to a party when I could have been home making a plan. Or he could have at least informed me as soon as he had the rejection. Instead he made out with me and gave me a tour of his town.

I shook thoughts of Jack away, pulled a protein drink out of the fridge, and gently walked outside, locking the door behind me.

I had a promotion to save.

Something felt weird when I got to the office. I was greeted kindly and asked about my vacation. Heather from accounting offered me a *welcome back* donut from her bag. Nothing was outwardly wrong. But something *felt* off. No one held my gaze for long.

A message popped up on Slack from Hal. *Mandatory staff meeting at 9. I want everyone there.*

Thirty minutes. Okay. I went through the PowerPoint I had been working on and deleted the slide for the MediCorp conference that was supposed to be my biggest selling point. Without it, there was just a pathetic list of things I'd done over the years, projects I'd headed up, teams I'd overseen . . . actually, if I just beefed up the slides with more bullet points defining the work I'd done, maybe throw in a few more of those events I'd begun listing while on the cruise, the PowerPoint wasn't as weak as I'd thought.

I spent the next twenty minutes filling in the gaps and adding a few more key points that identified why I deserved this job. Camila had trained me specifically for this role before entering maternity leave, and that had to count for something.

Even if Jerry was heading up the lawyer conference this week, my resume for this company alone was three times longer than his.

Ten minutes before we were meant to meet in the conference room, I shut my laptop and carried it under my arm while I clicked my way across the cheap vinyl floor to Hal's office. I didn't need to knock for him to glance up and see me.

"Meeting's at nine."

Was it just me or would he not meet my gaze? "I hoped I could have a minute of your time first."

"I really need to prepare for the big announcement—"

"It will only take a minute, I promise."

He sighed, looking over my head at something behind me. "Lauren, it's not a good time. Schedule something for later this week."

But later this week we'd be swamped with the lawyer conference. "After the meeting? I only need a few minutes."

Hal held my gaze. I could see his jaw working in tandem with his mind, moving and thinking. Finally he nodded. "After the meeting, but then I'll need to run out. You can't have more than ten minutes."

"I won't need it," I said, feeling victorious. My phone buzzed, and I pulled it from my pocket while I made my way to the conference room. It was Jack.

JACK

How is Amelia?

LAUREN

Probably still asleep on my couch. I don't think she slept well last night.

JACK

Neither did Kevin.

LAUREN

You stayed with him?

I didn't know why that surprised me, but it did. Maybe because I'd been doing my best to paint Jack as an awful man who lied about conferences and didn't respect my work.

234

JACK

Someone had to. He was a wreck last night.

I sat on a swivel chair near the head of the table, debating what to say next.

LAUREN

I don't know how they'll come back from this.

JACK

They will. Kevin won't let his parents or their money dictate his life. He never has.

I didn't respond, and my phone buzzed with another message.

JACK

How are you?

LAUREN

Working.

JACK

Any news on the promotion?

LAUREN

I have a plan to state my case later this morning.

JACK

Complete with a few charts and spreadsheets, right?

They were sprinkled in my PowerPoint, but there was no way I was telling him that.

JACK

Can I bring you dinner tonight? I want to talk.

Dinner with Jack? I hated that I wanted to accept the offer so badly. He hurt me, and my job needed my attention right now. *It's not a good time.*

LAUREN

I don't know how long Amelia will be with me.

JACK

I'll bring enough for three.

My heart hammered. Did he deserve an opportunity to explain himself? Yes. Did I need to give him that chance *today?* No. But did that make me want to see him any less? Also no.

It was almost scary how badly I wanted to tell him to come over as soon as possible, preferably with Torchy's tacos and a giant tub of queso. Amelia could really pack that stuff away. But I was scrambling right now to put together my argument for why I deserved this promotion, and if Jack hadn't forced me to avoid work for the entire cruise and got me stuck in a podunk town for the weekend, I wouldn't be in this position.

LAUREN

Not tonight.

I put my phone away while people filed in for the meeting. Hal came in at nine o'clock on the dot and strode to the front of the room, taking the seat at the head of the table.

"You all know that Camila decided to make her maternity leave permanent."

My breath stalled. Oh, no. He could not be doing this now. It was far too soon. He hadn't even seen my PowerPoint yet.

"And while she hasn't been working, we did ask her to make a recommendation for her replacement. Who she found qualified and why they fit the criteria." His gaze swept over the occupants in the room, not settling on any one person for too long.

When he'd mentioned the announcement he had to make, I'd assumed it was something along the lines of *Fridge cleaning week! Everyone take your moldy Tupperware home and throw away expired yogurt!*

I caught Jerry's eye across the table, and he looked smug. His shiny forehead was lined and his cheeks ruddy with pleasure.

Chill out, Jerry. No one's offered it to you yet.

"But Camila's word wasn't the only one we took into consideration while making this decision. I'll have you know that while there are multiple qualified members of this team who we would love to offer the position to, there can only be one lead events manager. The candidate we settled on has shown exemplary management skills while maintaining a willingness to learn."

That was me, right? I'd been managing teams for over a year now and Camila had done nothing but teach me while she was still here. My heart beat faster and faster.

"The offer was extended and accepted last Friday. Please join me in congratulating our new lead events manager, Jerry Coolidge."

I started to stand from my seat when the name registered, and it occurred to me that it wasn't mine. My legs froze in their half-up position, incapable of moving one way or the other while Jerry stood and shook Hal's hand in the front of the room, his wide smile passing over me briefly.

Kind of like the way Hal had passed over me for the promotion I deserved. I sat hard in the chair, avoiding pitying looks from my colleagues. Then I lifted my gaze and caught Hal's. This was not over yet.

CHAPTER TWENTY-SEVEN

LAUREN

HAL FOLLOWED me into his office when the meeting ended—or was it Jerry's office now? When would Hal return to his old job and leave us under Jerry's shiny-headed guidance? I clutched my laptop with its useless PowerPoint to my chest for comfort.

"There is something you'd like to discuss?" he prompted.

Really? I sat, stunned that Hal could face me and pretend he didn't know I had a right to be angry right now. The least he could do would be to acknowledge my situation.

"Yes," I said tightly. "I wanted to discuss the promotion."

Hal cleared his throat. "This decision was left to the committee. No one person got to make the call."

"Did Camila recommend Jerry for the job?"

His side-glance was enough to tell me she hadn't.

Frustration simmered in my veins. "I have been with Hunnam in events two years longer than Jerry has, and I have been specifically trained for this role."

"There are other qualifications to consider—"

"Didn't Jerry come here from a finance job?"

"That is personal information."

That was side-stepping the question.

Hal folded his arms over his chest. "Jerry has spearheaded the lawyer's con this week and shown remarkable ability."

How many events had I spearheaded before that, though? How many times had I held Jerry's hand through an event? How many emails had he sent me *last week* alone? I was beginning to see my qualifications meant nothing. They wanted him, and they didn't want me. I must have been quiet too long, because Hal decided to fill the void.

"You are vital to this company, Lauren. We work as a team to accomplish the many, many events that come through our space here, and that won't change."

Vital. Me? Not vital enough. My body became light, like I was floating up above the office looking down on it from a bird's eye view. Jerry's promotion proved I wasn't vital, or I would have been offered the job. All it proved was that they didn't care if they kept me happy, that there was no more room to grow within the Hunnam Events team.

With no more room to grow, why should I bother staying at all? My mind ran down a list of reasons that might be worth giving more of my life and time to Hunnam Hotels Group, but the list was sadly empty. Camila, gone. Opportunity for growth, gone. The respect to admit that I was an equal contender for the position? Absent.

Well, I guessed that only meant one thing. I stood, holding my computer a little looser to my chest. "You can expect a formal resignation sometime in your email tomorrow."

"Okay, Lau—wait, what?" Hal looked up, his eyes wide. "You aren't quitting over this promotion?"

"I am valuing my own worth. If this company won't do that, then it's up to me to find one that will." I turned to walk away, but my deeply ingrained sense of proper business etiquette stopped me at the door, where I turned back. "Thank you for your time."

Then I gathered my purse from my desk and walked out.

Jack

I WASN'T sure if Brad was trying to avoid me or if he really just had back-to-back meetings all day. By the time my workday was over, though, I'd only seen him in passing a handful of times, never long enough for a decent chat. Not that we needed to discuss what had happened, but something about the way things had gone down hadn't felt right to me.

Now, the office was closing up, people were heading out, and Brad was still at his desk. Thanks to the glass walls, I could see he was clearly not in a meeting or on the phone. I slid my laptop into its bag and hiked it over my shoulder.

Time for a chat.

My fist knocked loudly on the glass door. Brad looked up and hesitated only slightly before waving me in. "I'm about to jump on a conference call," he said by way of greeting.

"I'll be quick." I closed the door behind myself and took one of the chairs in front of his desk. "I wanted to talk about the venue."

His attention flicked from me back to his computer screen. "Have you put together a proposal for next year? You can show the board, but the chances of them accepting it are pretty slim."

"Why?"

"Because the Dallas Event Center has a longstanding relationship with MediCorp."

"Those contracts change all the time—"

"No, you misunderstand." He clicked something on his computer before giving me his attention again. "They have a *relationship*."

"Outside of the business world?"

He flashed me his teeth in a grimace. "Like I'm talking Olivia Johnson is the niece of Howard Peele."

I only knew one of those names. "Our CEO is the niece of the Dallas Event Center's . . ."

"Owner."

"Ah." I leaned back in my seat, feeling the deflation in my mood even further. It was followed swiftly by a flash of anger. "You never told me I was up against nepotism."

Brad tilted his head side to side, pushing out his chin a little. "You could call it that. Or you could call it maintaining and utilizing trusting, established relationships."

"Which is fancy for nepotism," I argued.

Brad didn't disagree, which still didn't change the fact that my proposal was doomed from the start. I was never going to be moving the conference to the Hunnam Hotels Group. I'd been sunk from the beginning.

The unfairness of it all tightened the discomfort in my chest. Brad's text from when I was on the boat no longer made any sense. I shifted uncomfortably in my seat. "So when you told me it was worth discussing, you didn't know about the relationship between our company and the event center?"

Brad's attention flickered away before landing back on me. "I mean, it is always worth discussing potential improvements."

That didn't answer my question, though. An unpleasant feeling hummed through me that could really only be described as icky.

"I hate to do this, but I really have to run," Brad said, pointing to his computer, where the conference call was probably coming soon.

I stood to leave, my body and mind trying to reconcile the truth of what I just learned: my boss was a liar.

"Oh, Jack. You've been coordinating volunteers, right? If you need to send another blast to fill in the openings, go right ahead. And if you have time to assign the board to keynote introductions, that would be great. Just make sure Alex gets put on Michael Chen. They have a preexisting professional relationship."

"Sure thing." I walked numbly from the office, adding that task to my already overloaded to-do list.

Amendment: my boss was a liar and a user. In that he would take advantage of others, not drugs. Probably.

When I finally got an Uber home to my dark, empty apartment, I tossed my computer bag on the edge of my bed and fell back on the mattress, staring at the ceiling fan above me. The silence pressed down on my chest until I was practically scrambling for my phone and locating Lauren in my contacts list. My finger hovered over her name before I swiped down to Kevin and gave him a call.

He picked up after a few rings. "Hey."

"How are . . . things?"

"No different. She won't see me. I don't know what to do."

"Get the ring back?" I asked. He'd told me how surprised his mom was to find it on her table.

"No chance of that," he grumbled.

"Then get her a new one?"

Kevin went silent.

"Or not," I said quickly. "I know how important your grandmother's ring was to you—"

"No, it's brilliant." There was some sort of shuffling sound. "Freaking brilliant. Is anything open this late?"

"You want to go *now*?"

"Why would I wait?" he asked, the simplicity of the question proving how deeply he loved Amelia. There was silence while he seemed to be distracted—probably looking up jewelers—and I waited for him to remember I was on the phone.

His answer settled into my uncertainties, bouncing around in my head. *Why would I wait?* I had been giving Lauren space because she'd seemed to need it. But Amelia had asked for the same thing. Where was the line between respecting her need for space and fighting for her?

"Tiffany!" Kevin shouted, making me jump. "They're open until eight. You coming with? I could use your help."

"Sure." What else would I do? Wallow? Sit in the dark and imagine how I could have handled things better? Count the tiles in my bathroom? Might as well be Kevin's emotional support. "Wait. I still don't have a car."

"I'll pick you up. See you in ten." Three beeps sounded in my ear, telling me Kevin had hung up. The man was not messing around.

I went back to Lauren's name in my contacts and pressed the call button, muttering a prayer under my breath that she would not ignore me. After two rings it was sent to voicemail. I waited for the robot to finish giving me instructions. "Hey. It's me. I just wanted to check in and see how you're doing and how Amelia is holding up. Call me sometime. Or text me. Or loop me in on a spreadsheet. At this point, I'll take anything."

Was that desperate? Probably not my finest moment.

"Anyway, hope to hear from you soon, Lauren. Bye."

I hung up and scrubbed a hand over my face. There was definitely no chill in that voicemail. Maybe it would have been better off deleted.

Kevin and I were halfway to Tiffany & Co when I thought that maybe I should have insisted on driving his car. The man was on a mission and his speedometer reflected it. But we made it to the store in record time and without causing an accident.

Choosing the ring, it turned out, took much longer.

"What does the young lady like?" the shop assistant, Peter, asked, putting glasses on to look down at the jewelry counter. He had white hair and a patient smile.

"I don't know." Kevin looked at me for further help, but I shrugged. "It was always the plan for her to have my grandmother's ring, so we haven't talked about it much."

"Do you want to find something similar to your family ring?" Peter asked.

"No." Kevin's brow creased as he surveyed the rings under the lights. "I want this to mean something to us, independent of the other ring."

"So, you'd like for it to be completely different?"

"Yes."

There were crickets in the shop after this. We were no closer to finding something.

Peter's soothing voice filled the store. "Why don't you walk around the shop a bit and think of your wife and tell me which rings really speak to you. We can go from there."

That sounded time-intensive to me, but Kevin seemed into the idea. I took one of the padded chairs and sat quietly, watching him pass over the rings slowly, failing to settle for long on any one.

It took another forty-five minutes for him to choose. He stopped, stared for a ridiculous amount of time, and then said, "That one."

"Which features do you like about it?" Peter asked.

Kevin blinked. "It. I like it. That's the ring I want."

The jeweler's brow creased. Neither of us expected this to go so easily.

I moved to stand beside him. "Which one?"

"That." He pointed to a flat oval diamond on a thin diamond-encrusted band. There were probably technical terms for all those things, but I didn't know them. It did look good, though. And crazy expensive.

Kevin looked up. "Can I take it with me now?"

"All of our rings come in a standard size six but can be resized. Do you know your wife's ring size?"

"No."

Peter hesitated.

"If I bring her back will you resize it?" Kevin asked.

"Yes, but she could be without the ring for a few weeks."

At this point, I doubted he cared. Kevin just wanted a ring in a box in his pocket on his way to her house. Which only took another thirty minutes to make possible.

"How are you going to do this?" I asked when we pulled onto the freeway toward Lauren's apartment.

"I have a plan." Kevin looked at me briefly before putting his attention back on the road. "And I could use your help."

CHAPTER TWENTY-EIGHT

LAUREN

"I'VE NEVER BEEN UNEMPLOYED BEFORE."

Amelia gave me a wry, disbelieving look. "You only quit your job like six hours ago. This isn't going to last long."

More like eleven hours, but there was no point correcting her.

"Do you know what you want to do next?" she asked.

"Be appreciated." I sank lower on my chair and brought my chunky sweater sleeves down over my fisted hands.

"You could teach music to children. There really isn't anyone who will love you more than a first grader will. Kind of makes me wish I hadn't taken these next few days off for my honeymoon staycation." Amelia leaned her head back on my sofa, letting out a sigh. Then she turned to look at me. "Will you braid my hair?"

It had been a *long* time since she'd asked me to do that. Like, junior year of high school maybe. "If I remember how to do it on someone else."

She hopped up. "I'll get a comb."

We had the live action *Cinderella* playing in the background, though neither of us were really paying much attention. We'd also watched *Ella Enchanted, Roger and Hammerstein's Cinderella,* and *A Cinderella Story* with Chad Michael Murray was on deck. It had always been Amelia's favorite fairy tale, and I kind of wondered if she related to it a little extra right now with the super-rich husband. Her life was almost a rags to riches story. Maybe the crazy in-laws felt like a wicked stepmother? Either way, she needed comforting, and Cinderella in all her many forms was providing it tenfold.

If only there was also a major fairytale about a woman who got screwed over at work and lied to by her boyfriend and was left feeling directionless and unappreciated. I could really go for a happy ending to that story right now.

Amelia settled on the floor between my knees.

"Two braids or one?" I asked.

"Two."

"Dutch or French?"

"Dutch."

I got to work, brushing through her damp hair from her earlier shower and dividing it into sections. "Have you talked to Prince Charming yet today?"

Amelia's shoulders slumped forward. "He's tried to call a few times, but I didn't answer."

"He's probably a mess right now, Ames," I said gently. It was easier to be blunt when she was facing away from me. I didn't have to look into her puffy, sad eyes to deliver these opinions. "You say you're doing this for him, right?"

"Right."

"Then maybe you should talk to him about it. He's half of the equation of your relationship. Doesn't he deserve a say in the matter?"

"Does the same go for Jack?"

My fingers tightened the braid on impulse.

"Doesn't he deserve to have a say, too?" she pressed.

"How do you know about that?"

"It's obvious from the way you're sulking and not returning his calls. Did he make out with another waitress?"

I flinched, glad she couldn't see me. "He made me a promise, and he didn't keep it."

"Must have been a big promise."

"It kind of was. But more than that, it was how long he'd known he couldn't keep it and still didn't tell me."

"Hmm." Amelia didn't say more. She didn't really understand the whole situation.

It became important to me for her to understand, to not think I was being overly dramatic. "Men don't know how to do anything but let me down. He's just like the rest of them."

"Or maybe he made a mistake because he's human, and you just dug your talons into it like it's proof he's the same dirtbag who left you that voicemail ages ago."

"I'm not still holding on to that," I said, tying the band on the end of her hair.

She turned to look at me over her shoulder. "Oh yeah? You've deleted it from your phone then?"

My cheeks flushed.

Amelia faced forward again so I could do her second braid. "Thought so."

"It's bad, Ames." It helped to hold on to proof of how awful men could be.

"It *was* bad. He's not the same guy he was then, which you obviously agree with, or you wouldn't have dated him again."

She was right. I wanted to argue that we hadn't been in a real relationship, but that wouldn't be true, would it? It might have started out as a farce, but we'd both chosen to give it a real chance after the wedding. I'd obviously trusted him enough to give him a chance.

I *did* trust him enough for that. He wasn't a bad guy. He just wasn't reliable enough for me, either.

"Maybe you should delete it now." Amelia scooted a little

away from me, the bit of braid I'd started on the second half of her head unraveling, her hair falling limp against her face. "Pull it up! Let's laugh at it, then get rid of it forever. I bet it would be good for you. Like a release."

Her eyes were shining, and I didn't really want to be the reason they dimmed again. Listening to Jack identify all the reasons I was not worth his time after that terrible date two years ago didn't sound very good either, but maybe it would help to delete it. I pulled out my phone and navigated to the voicemail app, scrolling all the way down to my old voicemails. There were a few from my grandma I listened to occasionally when I missed her, and Jack's was nestled right in the middle of them.

My finger hit the triangle play button.

There was static while he held his phone, not realizing he called me. Maybe it was in his pocket? It was slightly muffled from something. "Nope," he was saying to his roommate. "Worst date ever. It started out all right, but she's kind of stiff, man."

I closed my eyes, remembering how lowering it felt to hear this for the first time. The pain was sharp, the humiliation of it agonizing.

"Maybe if she lightened up a little."

"So she's nothing like Amelia?" the roommate asked.

"Nah. I don't know. I guess I just didn't expect her to be so uptight. Like, no fun at all. She's intelligent, so the conversation had potential in the beginning, but I was way off. Kevin should have warned me, that's all I'm saying. What happened to the bro code?"

"It's outdated," his roommate said.

"You know what I mean. Kev knows Lauren. I don't know why he thought we'd be compatible. It's no wonder she's single."

It went on for a while after this, but the conversation shifted to A&M's football season, so I turned it off.

"That was brutal," Amelia said. "I forgot how bad it was."

"Yeah." I couldn't say more. My stomach had twisted over itself, making me regret the extra fries that had come with my DoorDash order.

Amelia looked at me meaningfully. "You gonna delete it?"

Was I? There was no point in holding on to it, of course. It would probably feel good to let it go. Maybe on some level I'd kept it because it allowed my anger free rein. Each time the irritation had started to ebb over recent years, all I had to do was pull up Jack's voicemail and righteous indignation swooped in again, reminding me that men were the pigs I thought they were.

That was probably just as unhealthy as it sounded.

Amelia was right. It was time to let it go and move on. "Okay. Yes. I'll—"

The doorbell rang, and both of us turned to look at the door.

"Did you order something?" I asked.

Amelia shook her head.

"Should I answer it?" We both knew what question I was really asking: are you ready to see Kevin?

Amelia hesitated.

"Just talk to him," I urged. "You might feel better."

She closed her eyes and nodded.

I got up. "Maybe do something with your hair," I said over my shoulder. I'd only gotten half of it braided.

When I swung the door open, I wished I'd had the foresight to do something with my own hair, too, besides twisting it super tight and shoving a claw clip over it. Jack stood there, his hands in his pockets, his head tilted down a little. He wasn't facing me as the tall, confident flirt I had known last week. This guy was carrying a burden, and I hated that it was probably emblazoned with my name.

His green eyes met mine, making my legs unsteady. "Is Amelia here?"

"Yes."

"Kevin's up on the roof. Any chance we can convince her to go talk to him?"

The roof? My roof, where it was something like forty-eight degrees? "He knows it's March, right?"

Jack's mouth tipped in a smile. "Yeah. It'll be worth the cold. Trust me."

My emotions flinched, but my body remained as uptight and wound up as ever. I turned away from him but didn't shut the door. Amelia was still sitting on the floor beneath the couch when I reached the living room, her brow clouding with uneasiness as I passed on the message.

"Want to borrow a thicker sweatshirt?" I asked.

"Just come with me. I don't plan on being up there long."

We followed Jack down the hallway and to the elevator. The ride up to the roof was awkward and long, though it probably only took twenty seconds in real time. I avoided Jack's gaze, but it was impossible to avoid the scent of his cologne. It triggered a visceral reaction in me, caving in my chest and making me yearn to step into his arms.

The first thing I noticed when we reached the roof and stepped into the cold was the addition of white twinkle lights strung haphazardly. Kevin stood in the center of the roof in a sweatshirt and jeans, watching us approach with intensity.

Jack took my elbow, pulling me back slightly so Amelia would walk ahead on her own. I leaned back a little too far, my shoulder resting against his chest before I thought better of it and took a step away. His arm dropped.

"What is he—"

"Just watch," Jack said quietly. They'd planned something. From the lights, I guessed it was a big romantic gesture.

Amelia approached Kevin, and he immediately dropped to

one knee, pulling out a Tiffany blue ring box and holding it out to her, opened to show a gorgeous diamond halo ring.

"That's not the heirloom," I whispered.

"We just went and picked it out a few hours ago."

I looked at Jack. He was already watching me, trapping me in his gaze. I fought the impulse to lean toward him and tore my attention away, settling it back on Kevin and Amelia.

"I need you, Ames," Kevin said, his voice desperate. "It doesn't matter if my parents can't appreciate you or what we have. That's their loss. The thing that matters to me is *you*. Please come back to me."

Amelia was already crying. "You think you're okay with that now, but I'm the one getting between you and your parents. It was supposed to be different. Our wedding was supposed to make them take us seriously."

"Yeah, that failed," he said softly. He reached toward her with his non-ring holding hand, but she stepped back.

Amelia looked at the ring and cringed. "You think you won't care, but you don't know how to live without your parents' money."

Kevin stood, wiping down his pant leg where he'd been kneeling. "You think my parents have been funding me all these years?"

"Of course."

"I have a job, babe."

"I know you don't live off them. It's everything else. Your Jeep. The vacations and restaurants and *wedding yacht*. The way you live is not sustainable on a normal income. I don't want you to resent me for making you give up a relationship with your parents *and* the lifestyle you're accustomed to. I couldn't bear it."

Kevin stared at her until he started to laugh, a crazy sound that had all three of us staring at him like maybe he'd gone a little mad. "I haven't gotten a cent from my parents since I graduated college."

Amelia drew in a quick, surprised breath. "How much debt are you in?"

"None. I made some solid investments back in high school with some birthday money, and it's grown quite a bit." He said this so nonchalantly, like it was normal to be gifted enough money to make the kinds of investments he must have made. But if that was the case, then Kevin's current wealth was entirely his own.

She looked down. "So your parents' money didn't buy this ring?"

"No." He took a step closer to her. "That was all me. At least now I know you didn't marry me for my money."

She slapped his arm, but she was smiling. "*Now* you know?"

"Come back to me," he said quietly, holding out the ring.

"But it's not your grandmother's. You wanted me to wear that one so badly. *I* wanted to wear it."

"That would have been nice. She was an amazing woman, and she would have adored you. But this is even better, babe. This is from me to you. No one else influenced or got a say in it. It's ours, and I think it's a good representation of *us*. We can move forward now together and there won't be any negative associations with this ring or our wedding."

"But your parents—"

"They'll come around eventually. They do love me, even if I messed up their plans. They're just being stubborn now."

"And if they don't come around?"

"I don't think they'll be able to resist grandbabies. If they can, that's their loss. We'll just have to create our own little family and teach them what love is really about."

Amelia fell forward into his arms. I patted my pocket to grab my phone and take a picture but realized I'd left it downstairs. "Grab a picture for them?" I whispered to Jack.

He got his phone out and snapped a few.

"Oh shoot, her hair." It was still half-braided. At least the pictures from this angle didn't make it that obvious.

Kevin slid the ring onto her finger. I heard him mention something about going into Tiffany & Co tomorrow to get it sized, but she cut him off with a kiss. Jack moved to the door and held it for me as we silently slipped away.

I hit the button for the elevator to take us down, and Jack reached for my hand. "Is it our turn, now?"

"You also bought me a ring?" I quipped before realizing that it wasn't funny. "Don't answer that. It was a joke."

The last thing I needed was for Jack to think I'd jumped to marriage after only a week-long relationship.

The elevator doors opened and I stepped inside. He followed me, stopping way too close. But, somehow, still not close enough. "I'm sorry, Lauren. I should have told you about the conference right away. It was stupid of me to hold on to it, but I didn't want to ruin our stargazing, and I thought it would stress you out to realize you needed to work but you had no way of getting home until the next morning. Then Tucker was called in and our ride was delayed, and I wanted to wait until you were actively heading home so it didn't ruin your morning."

It all made sense, but it was still dishonest.

The elevator doors opened. I pressed against his chest to push him out, which turned out to be a terrible idea. Jack didn't budge. He covered my hand with his own, flattening it against his heart, which I now felt to be hammering just as hard as mine. "Hear me out? Please?"

CHAPTER TWENTY-NINE

JACK

LAUREN'S EYES WERE WOUNDED. She was a puppy that had been kicked too many times, so my gentle bump had thrown her for a loop, naturally.

She stepped around me and down the hall toward her apartment. "Come on, I'm freezing."

I took that to mean *yes* she would hear me out, but she wanted to warm up first. Win.

Lauren unlocked her door and stepped in, so I followed her inside. She made it to her couch and curled up on the end, pulling her blanket around her. It probably served two purposes: warmth and a shield.

Hint taken.

I sat on the opposite end of the couch. "I messed up. I should have told you the truth. I will do whatever I can to help you get this promotion and make it right."

Lauren shook her head. "I already lost it. They gave it to Jerry last Friday, but announced it to the team this morning—though I suspect by the way everyone treated me that Jerry had already told most of them. So I quit."

That took me a minute to process. "Quit your job?"

"I have savings. I'll be okay for a minute."

I shook my head, sitting up and leaning slightly toward her. "What made you decide to do that?"

"There was no room for growth anymore. Jerry took it, and there's nothing else in that company I want to do. I saw how they'd taken advantage of me over the last few years and how it would only continue to happen, so I took myself out of the equation. If they think Jerry's so qualified, then he can do the job on his own."

"Until he can't anymore and they crawl back to you?" I asked.

"No. I'll be busy doing something that doesn't make me want to pull my hair out."

"I thought you liked your job."

"Parts of it, yeah. I like the event coordination part and running a business and making people happy on their special days or pulling off a huge conference."

"But you can do that in a lot of other places."

"Exactly. Probably. That's the hope, at least."

I leaned back on the couch, surveying her. She was the same Lauren, her hair pulled back and a thick sweater on, but the resilience in her eyes was bright, and I had no doubt she would bounce right back, probably into a situation that was even better than before. "It must have hurt when they chose the other guy."

"It did, but I was more angry than hurt. He's not as qualified as I am. If they want to run their company like that and not choose promotions based on merit, then they don't need me."

My breath hitched, envy filling me at how she'd been able to walk away. It felt similar to the situation with Brad. How would it have felt to tell him the same thing? If he wanted to support nepotism over good business, then he could find a different lackey?

"What is it?" she asked.

"I kind of dealt with something similar today. I went to talk to my boss about the whole venue thing and found out that we never stood a chance anyway. The owner of the Dallas Event Center is my CEO's uncle."

She nodded. "I doubt all of corporate America is this flawed, but I don't have a whole lot of faith in them right now."

Neither did I, to be honest. Or maybe I'd just lost faith in Brad. And our CEO. And the delegation system that had made me plan most of the conference but failed to give me any actual power.

The conference wasn't even the job I had been hired to do. I was in marketing. How did I reach the point where I was pushed onto the committee and then did everything myself?

I shook the thoughts. "I'm sorry, Lauren." I leaned back, rubbing my hand over the back of my neck when I bumped into something on the armrest and it skittered across the floor.

The sound of my recorded voice filled the room.

"I don't think they have a chance, man," I was saying in a muffled recording.

My old roommate, Alfie, responded. "As long as they win next weekend, I don't even care about the rest of the season."

I sought Lauren's face for an explanation, and her cheeks went scarlet. She leaned down, fumbling for what I came to see was her phone on the floor, but I was closer. I picked it up in a fluid motion and found it was a voicemail playing. It must have gone off when the phone hit the floor.

"This is from me," I said, looking down.

Lauren didn't respond.

I scrubbed it back to the beginning and hit play. My voice filled the room, louder than before, though still a bit muffled. I cringed, shutting my eyes while the voicemail got worse and worse. *Worst date ever. She's kind of stiff. So uptight. Kevin should have warned me. It's no wonder she's single.*

Each new phrase heaped more shame in my belly until I felt sick. I turned off the voicemail and stared at her phone, reading the date. But I didn't need a timestamp to know when that conversation had taken place. "This was after our date."

"You must have butt-dialed me," she said.

When I looked up, I saw the pain in her eyes, and her vehemence toward me these last few years made sense. She'd had every reason to hate me then and now. Every reason to reject me out of hand when I'd asked her to pretend to be my girlfriend. But she swallowed whatever disgust she must have felt so she could get the conference, and I'd let her down there, too.

"I'm so sorry, Lauren. I just . . ." My hands went out to the sides, then fell. "I am *so* sorry."

"It was a long time ago."

I stood up, trying to shake off the sense of failure permeating me. "I'll go—"

She heaved a sigh. "That's unnecessary. I've already forgiven you, Jack."

It didn't compute. I'd hurt her. That was very clear. I gestured vaguely to her phone. "There's nothing I can say to take that back. I was angry you'd ditched me during our date, and I complained, but I never knew you'd heard it. I had no idea." I shook my head. "I didn't even mean half of those things. I was just venting."

I was antsy to be gone, where I could loathe myself in solitude. It wasn't just that I'd done something stupid, it was who I'd hurt that killed me. She deserved better than what I'd offered her so far. My car was still gone, so I'd have to call an Uber. But I could do that from downstairs.

Lauren shrugged off the blanket and followed me down the hall. "You don't need to leave, Jack."

"Yes, I definitely do. I came here to beg you to take me back, and now I see why you have every reason to turn me away. So I'll just make it easier for you."

Lauren took my hand and pulled me to a stop, tugging until I turned back to face her. There wasn't a lot of room in this small hallway, forcing us to be close. "Beg me, then."

I shook my head.

"I'm pretty sure neither of us are the same person we were on that date two years ago."

"Why didn't you tell me?" I asked, but my voice came out as a pathetic whine.

"What would I have said?" Her hand tightened around my wrist, unlocking a deep need within me to have her in my arms.

What was I doing? I didn't want to run from her. I wanted to hold her tightly and infuse her with all the overwhelming feelings battering me right now.

Lauren came willingly into my arms. I wrapped them over her back, pressing her to me and lowering my head so it rested on top of hers. Her shampoo smelled clean. She let me hold her. I closed my eyes and ran my hands over her back.

"I've never felt as awful as I have since Tucker and I dropped you off. I know I don't deserve you, but I can't help but feel like I might be falling in love with you."

I felt her breath catch, her chest expanding against mine. She tilted her head back. "Then be different."

"From what?"

"My grandpa, who left. Everyone else, who died. My boss, who can't respect me. Just be *here*, Jack."

Her standards were so simple they made me ache. "I can do that."

Lauren slid her hand up my chest until it cradled my jaw. "That's a relief, because I'm pretty sure I'm falling in love with you, too."

She reached up, brushing a tender kiss over my lips. Tension and failure and shame seeped from me the longer her lips moved over mine, healing the parts of me I'd heartily regretted until all I felt was warmth. Abandoning any hesitation, I backed

Lauren up until she hit the wall in her narrow hallway, tilting her head to deepen the kiss.

My lips might have said I was falling in love with her, but my heart was already there, jumping in with both feet and not looking back.

Lauren leaned back, her breath coming raggedly. "I don't really have to guess how you feel."

"I can still keep proving it to you, if you want," I said, pressing my lips to the tender skin beneath her ear and eliciting a shiver.

She pulled me back for another kiss. When I straightened, I dropped one on the top of her head and hugged her tightly.

She hugged me back. "I'm going to delete that voicemail right away."

"Thank you." I shut my eyes. "I can't believe you agreed to the fake relationship, even after that."

"What fake relationship?" someone else said. I looked up to see Amelia and Kevin in the doorway, staring at us.

Amelia narrowed her eyes, looking from her sister to me.

Lauren pushed gently on my chest until she could stand straight, facing her sister. I stood close behind her, waiting for her to take the lead.

Amelia lifted her eyebrows. "What fake relationship, Lo?"

Lauren sucked in a breath. "I can explain."

CHAPTER THIRTY

LAUREN

IT TOOK ALL of twenty minutes to explain that we had begun the cruise as a fake relationship and watch the newly restored joy drain from Amelia's face. We all stood around my tiny kitchen island, no one relaxed enough to sit—me and Jack on one side, Amelia and Kevin on the other.

"So you lied to us?" Amelia asked, her lips turning downward in a perfect, depressed rainbow.

My instinct was to promise I hadn't, but that wouldn't be the truth. She was right. I'd lied to her. Of course I knew that, but I'd thought it was helping her out, that I wasn't the only one who benefitted from this arrangement.

I wouldn't lie to her anymore. "Yeah, we did, Ames."

"She was trying to help me out," Jack said. "Sydney was overwhelming when we broke up, and she got a little handsy when we first ran into each other in the lobby. I was worried about the rest of the cruise."

Um, okay. He hadn't told me that part. He also made me sound far more selfless than I was. "I got something out of it too." I caught his eye and held it for a second. "Well, I was supposed to. It didn't pan out the way we thought it would."

Kevin had been silent through the entire conversation, watching us go back and forth. "What were you getting out of it?"

"Jack promised to try and move his MediCorp conference to Hunnam Hotels so I could manage it, but they wouldn't move it."

Amelia shook her head, looking from me to the ceiling. "What I guess I don't understand is why you couldn't tell *me* the truth. If you wanted to be in a fake relationship to keep Sydney away like you're in some cheesy movie, that's your choice. Why keep me out of the loop?"

Jack didn't take this one. He couldn't step in now and explain something he didn't understand, either.

A million moments flickered through my head of Amelia letting me leave, telling me I wasn't required to stick around, of her friends not vibing with me or our interests not aligning. When I was with Kevin and Amelia, we were fine. We got along great. But add in her friends and I became the old lady, and it was clear she didn't want me there.

Amelia crossed her arms over her chest impatiently. There was fatigue behind her wan eyes. The girl deserved to go home.

The more honest I was, the faster this conversation would end. "I didn't want to add stress during your wedding."

"Knowing you were trying to be a buffer between Jack and Sydney isn't very stress-inducing."

"No . . . but you knew how I felt about Jack, and you just seemed so relieved when he said we were dating. Which I totally understand. If I dated the guy, then we wouldn't be fighting the whole time." I rested my hands on the counter. "Ergo, we wouldn't be adding any stress to your wedding."

She wasn't speaking, her eyes tracking me like they wanted to follow every word I said. Silence permeated my tiny kitchen.

"So all those times you two were off on your own, it was to

put space between you and Sydney?" Amelia asked. "I thought you just didn't want to be around us."

Wait. That wasn't fair. She was the one who was constantly giving me an out. "Partially. I was also trying to give you and your friends space."

"Space?" Amelia scoffed. "That's what you call avoiding us half the time? Or leaving early every night? Or not coming out with us in Miami for my bachelorette party?"

"I'd planned a spa night like you wanted!"

"I didn't want that. You just suggested it and I didn't want to be rude."

That hurt. Her words slammed into me like a heavyweight champion. "But you were so relieved when I said I would stay at the hotel. Same with the hot tub when I left after Sydney made things awkward. You were always relieved when I left."

"Because I didn't think you wanted to be there, so I was glad you didn't feel obligated to stay! You're always so busy working or thinking of work or talking about work. I feel like an obligation to you and it sucks. I don't ever want you to feel like you're a burden, too."

Suckerpunch right to the gut. Man, she could really deliver painful blows. My hands dropped from the counter when I took a step back. Yes, I had been a bit of a workaholic before, but I had always cared about my sister. I didn't avoid her or resent spending time with her. "Why didn't you tell me that?"

"You're not really in a position to ask that question right now."

Fair enough. "It's not true. You aren't a burden or an obligation."

"Just not as important as Hunnam Hotels?"

My chest constricted. "That's not . . . Amelia, I care about doing well at my job. That doesn't mean I don't care about you too."

"You have a funny way of showing it."

"Not anymore," I muttered. Now that I was jobless.

Kevin and Jack shared a look before slipping out of the kitchen and down the hall. I didn't try to stop them.

Amelia was tired. She'd gone through a lot this weekend and it was evident in the weary bend of her shoulders. She sucked in a breath and shakily let it out. "So you didn't think I wanted you to hang out with us?"

"You were always telling me it was fine to go and then looking massively relieved when I agreed."

She shook her head.

How did we get here? The age gap and the way I'd always cared for her had given me a motherly relationship, but we were sisters above all.

"I'm not a child anymore, Lauren. You don't need to constantly take care of me. Just be honest. If we can't talk to each other about how we're feeling, we'll never be close."

"You know that goes both ways, right?"

"Yes. I should have told you that I thought you cared more about your job than you did me."

"I'm sorry you ever felt like I wouldn't want to be around you, Ames. I just felt like a grandma around your friends. But I like Cara, and I always like spending time with you. I don't care about anyone or anything more than I care about you."

"I know," she said. "Despite all this, I really do know that." She groaned, rubbing her eyes. "I wish we could redo the cruise. I would never send you away. It was so nice *finally* getting to spend time together without your stupid laptop between us."

"Hey," I said defensively. "I haven't brought my laptop out at all since I quit this morning."

She laughed, shaking her head. "It's okay that you like working. We both just need to communicate more." She came around the island and pulled me in for a tight hug. "Just . . . maybe when you're picking your next job, find something that doesn't suck your life away."

"I'll put that on my LinkedIn."

She smiled at me, and I felt the weight of our conversation lift away. Her explanations were valid, and my interpretations still made sense, but now we could move forward without all the wrong assumptions we each held. I never wanted her to feel like she mattered less than work, and she obviously didn't want me to feel like I was less important than her friends. Having the truth out in the open was promising, and while I felt raw from the last few days of emotional ping pong, I also had hope that things could only get better from here.

"All better now?" Kevin asked, coming back from around the corner.

"Your idea of privacy is eavesdropping from the hall?" Amelia asked, swatting her husband's arm.

Jack followed, leaning one shoulder on the wall and crossing his arms over his chest. His gaze was steady on me, making my body tingle with awareness.

"Like you wouldn't have told me everything when we left?" Kevin took Amelia's hand. "Now you don't have to try and remember the details."

No one had an argument for that.

"Let me grab my things."

"You've been using all of *my* things," I reminded her.

She looked down at the yoga pants and oversized sweatshirt she was wearing. "Oh yeah. I'll get these back to you later."

Kevin lifted his eyebrows to Jack. "You coming?"

Jack slid his gaze to me. "Yeah. Can you give me five minutes?"

They left, and Jack immediately crossed the room to slide his arms around me, pulling me in for a hug. "You okay?"

"Actually, yeah. It was good to clear the air. But now I'm drained." Like someone had pulled the plug from my feet and let all the emotions slip out. With mental and physical exhaustion combined, I was now as limp as a deflated balloon.

"Should I give you a few days to decompress?" he asked, his hands roaming over my back.

What did I want? Aside from him, of course. The idea of space away from him didn't provide the relief I would have expected. "I don't need space."

"Then I'll call you tomorrow after work?"

"Yes." I leaned back, pressing my lips to his. "Tomorrow after work is good. I'll plan something for dinner."

"Okay. I better go or I'll be walking," he said, pulling me in for one more hug. He pressed a kiss to the top of my head. "See you tomorrow, Lo."

I walked him to the door. Maybe I still didn't have any direction for what I wanted to do or where I should put my energy now that Hunnam was behind me, but I knew one thing: reconciling with Jack was the best decision I'd made this week.

CHAPTER THIRTY-ONE

JACK

FOUR DAYS HAD PASSED since my conversation with Brad at work, and every minute I spent in the office drove indecision and unease deeper under my skin. The majority of my daily work tasks were in some way related to the conference, which made sense since it was such a huge moneymaker for the company. But I couldn't handle the conference without resentment building in my chest. I was glad it was Friday, because I wasn't sure I could take much longer in the MediCorp offices this week.

Brad waved when I passed his office to leave for the weekend, and I smiled back. This was a phase. It would pass, and then I would get back to what I was really at MediCorp to do: marketing.

My phone rang as I was sliding into the back seat of the Uber to get home, and I answered it. "Hey, Colt."

"Don't hate me."

My stomach sank. "You can't pick me up tonight, can you?"

"Have you tried Mom or Dad?"

"They're leaving pretty early to drive out to Amarillo, so I don't want to put this on them too."

Colt made a disgusted sound. "Why Amarillo?"

"To look at a trailer." I rubbed my tired eyes.

"They couldn't find one five hours closer?"

"Guess not. What came up for you?"

"A work thing. I can come out tomorrow afternoon if you can wait."

Did I have a right to complain when he was literally driving over two hours round trip just to help me pick up my car? I intended on hanging out in Arcadia Creek over the weekend anyway. I wanted to see how Aunt Marnie's porch swing looked and maybe start a project of my own. I was itching to sand something down to its original state. It was just so satisfying and completely in my control.

"That's great," I finally said. "Just let me know when you hit the road."

I thanked the Uber driver and got out of the car, hanging up the phone so I could tip the guy and find my apartment. It was the first night this week I hadn't planned to see Lauren, but maybe now that didn't have to be the case.

I sent her a text.

> JACK
>
> My trip was delayed. Any chance you want to come over? I make a mean spaghetti dinner.

> LAUREN
>
> The car isn't ready?

> JACK
>
> My ride was delayed. He can come tomorrow, though.

> LAUREN
>
> I can give you a ride tonight.

> JACK
>
> Are you just trying to get out of tasting my spaghetti?

LAUREN

You caught me. What time should I be there to pick you up?

I stared at the message. She was an actual angel.

JACK

Thirty minutes? I'll feed you first, though. Consider it partial payment.

LAUREN

What's the rest of the payment?

JACK

You'll see.

LAUREN

See you soon. 😙

Yes, please. I showered off the work grime—it was mostly mental, obviously, but the ick factor was there—and threw a pound of hamburger on the stove with some chopped onion and garlic. This was the one thing I could make reasonably well, and I wanted to dazzle this girl. Maybe a touch of oregano, too, or was that overboard on the spices? I was planning to mix it with jarred sauce, but don't tell anyone.

When the knock came on my door a little while later, *Farmhouse Fixer* was playing on HGTV, sauce was simmering on the stove, and the pasta was almost done boiling. I buttered and sprinkled garlic salt on a few slices of bread, then tossed some asparagus in the oven with olive oil, salt, and lemon juice.

I opened the door to see Lauren in jeans and a black jacket, her hair held back by a sage green headband. She'd never definitively said she wore her hair down for me, but it hadn't been arrested into the tight knot since we gotten together, either.

"Smells good," she said, kicking off her shoes.

I leaned in and hugged her. "Yeah, you do."

"Stop." But she was grinning, and her cheeks were turning pink.

"Come on, Spreadsheets. It's almost time to eat."

Lauren set the table while I put out the food. We sat, piling our plates while the TV was on in the background.

I spun my fork in the noodles. "Any new job leads?"

"One, actually. I had an interview for it today."

"What?" I lowered my fork full of pasta. "Why didn't you tell me?"

She twirled her fork, speaking calmly. "It happened really fast. I submitted the application last night and they called this morning to set up a Zoom interview." She shrugged, eating the bite of pasta.

"And?"

"It went well." She wiped her mouth and finished chewing. "They offered me the job."

"Lauren, that's great." I stared at her, but she didn't seem very excited about the prospect. "What's the job?"

"Event managing for a small firm in Plano."

"And the commute is bothering you?"

"No. I mean, it's not ideal, but it's not too bad."

I pushed my plate away and leaned closer to her. "What is it, then? You don't seem happy about this at all."

Her hazel eyes dropped to her plate. "It's not the job . . . I guess it just doesn't feel satisfying to go back to doing the exact same thing I did for Hunnam. I've been wondering if I should do something else entirely."

"Like what?"

She wrinkled her nose. "I have no idea."

"Did they give you time to make a decision?"

"I asked for the weekend, so I have to let them know by Monday."

My hand snaked across the table to take hers. "Since you don't have to return to Dallas after you drop me off, do you want to spend the weekend with me in Arcadia? Maybe clear your head?" I held my breath, suddenly worried that the idea of being in my quaint little hometown wouldn't sound like much fun for her.

"Yes," she said quietly. "I'd like that a lot."

Within twenty minutes we'd finished eating, shut off the TV, grabbed my bag, and were on our way. "Don't you need to run home for clothes?"

Lauren shot me a sheepish smile while she pulled on to the toll road. "I came prepared."

A laugh tore from my chest. "Of course you did."

"Hey," she said, her tone defensive. "I didn't want to be stranded if we hit another deer and then be forced to wear your mom's nightgown again."

"I liked it . . . in an 1800s farmwife sort of way."

"Don't get me wrong. It was comfortable. But it wasn't mine, you know?"

"I get it."

She looked at me briefly before putting her gaze back on the road. She seemed hesitant, if not a little nervous. "Are your parents going to be okay with me coming?"

"Are you kidding?" I leaned my elbow on the center console. "My mom has asked almost daily when you could come back for another visit. If anything, she'll be mad they have to leave while you're there."

Relief was palpable in Lauren's soft exhale. "Good. I like your mom."

"I think she likes you, too."

Lauren

IT DIDN'T TAKE LONG to pick up Jack's fixed car from the shop in Beeler. I followed him back to the Fletcher homestead and parked on the gravel behind his sedan. A weird sense of familiarity came over me, like I was returning home. I had been to Jack's childhood home a total of once, so this wasn't exactly warranted. I shook it off to greet his parents on the porch.

Mrs. Fletcher welcomed me with a wide hug. Her hair was still perfectly teased, though it looked a little blonder, if that was possible. "Y'all come on inside, now. It's cold out here," she cooed, her voice like warm honey drizzled over cornbread. "What did I do to deserve visits two weekends in a row?"

Mr. Fletcher dipped his head stoically behind her, and I returned it with a smile.

"Had to pick up my car in Beeler," Jack explained while we were ushered inside, our jackets taken and hung near the door. "Can we stay the weekend?"

"As though you need to ask." Mrs. Fletcher sounded mildly offended. Her warmth and sense of welcoming was unmatched. She was exactly the sunny, glowing soul who made you want to take your shoes off and stay a while.

"We're heading to look at a trailer tomorrow," Mr. Fletcher said. "Afraid it'll take all day."

Mrs. Fletcher frowned. "We can be home tomorrow night, can't we?"

"Might be late—"

"That's fine."

He nodded, walking away. "Better see if I can cancel that hotel, then."

"Thanks, love," Mrs. Fletcher called, unapologetically.

Jack merely looked amused. "I will choose not to be offended that you were fine being gone through Sunday when it was just me visiting, but now that Lauren's here, you're gonna hightail it home tomorrow night."

"I can't stay gone with a guest in the house, honey. You know that. Who would make Sunday breakfast?"

"Lauren?" he asked.

I laughed, but Mrs. Fletcher swatted her son. "Don't pretend you were raised to have no manners."

"Yes, ma'am."

Mrs. Fletcher took my arm, pulling me into the family room and onto the sofa. "Now, Lauren, are you hungry? I have left-over shepherd's pie or I can fix you a sandwich real quick."

"I ate before we came, but thank you. Jack made dinner." I thought she'd appreciate that extra tidbit.

Her gaze tracked over to her son, her blonde eyebrows lifting. "Guess you're using those manners after all."

"Yes, ma'am." He grinned. "I'm not hungry either, in case that was relevant information."

Mrs. Fletcher sent him a soft smile before turning it back on me. Being in the middle of their playful, jovial banter was soothing. I was swept up in the homey, comfortable feeling they provided. What made this house different from the rest? Why did stepping inside give me the impression that I could take a load off and breathe? It was nothing particularly special, the sofa no more comfortable than anyone else's, the smell no more pleasantly distinct.

I looked around the family room while Mrs. Fletcher and Jack chatted about a few mutual acquaintances in town, Jack's mother doing her best to fill me in on who was who to whom. Not that I was paying much attention or remembering anything she said. Nothing here was new. It wasn't beat down or aged in a noticeable way, more worn from use and care. That was part of what set this house apart. It had to be. It was thoroughly lived in.

The Fletchers, though—they were the biggest reason.

"Borrowing another nightgown?" Mrs. Fletcher asked me.

"I packed a bag this time." I caught Jack's smile and looked away. "I like to be prepared."

"It's one of the things I love about her."

My eyes shot to his, noting their almost imperceptible widening. Phew. It had been a slip of the tongue. Time to joke us back to normal. "Of course it is. How else would we have avoided an extra half-hour in traffic on our way here?"

"Because you looked ahead and figured it out," he guessed. "That's actually a pretty normal thing to do."

"Don't take my moment."

"Anyone up for a game?" Mrs. Fletcher asked when her husband had joined us again, sitting close to her on the sofa.

Jack's brow wrinkled. "Don't you two need to be up early tomorrow?"

Mr. Fletcher shot a side-eye glance at his wife. "I can swing one round of Uno."

"He's been on a winning streak," Mrs. Fletcher said, rising to fetch the cards. "Hasn't lost a game all week."

Jack interlaced his fingers and stretched them high above his head like he was preparing to enter a sport. "That's about to end."

If I thought the house and Jack's parents provided the warm, gooey feeling of home, I hadn't expected the rush I'd feel playing cards at their kitchen table. One round swiftly turned into five, and it was almost midnight by the time Jack gathered all the cards.

"One more won't kill me," Roy said—his insistence after I called him Mr. Fletcher while forcing him to draw four. Evidently not going easy on him had endeared me to him somehow. They were now Roy and Jan, and I was overwhelmed by how comfortable I already felt with them both. It made me anxious in a weird way. I didn't like having something to lose.

Jan pressed her hand over her husband's. "You won't be singing that same tune when our alarm goes off at four."

I winced.

"Farm chores," she explained.

"I can take care of it," Jack offered. "It's been a while, but I helped Dad last week. I'm pretty sure I remember most things."

Roy appraised his son. "I'll accept that as my due for continuing to hold the title of undefeated Uno champion."

Jan rolled her eyes good-naturedly, leaning closer to me while the men cleaned up the cards. "We'll never hear the end of this."

"I'll hide a few cards in my sleeve tomorrow," I promised. "We'll take him down."

We said goodnight and went outside to fetch our bags from my trunk. The night was overcast, the stars clouded over, the air crisp and biting. When Jack tugged on my arm and pulled me in, I didn't resist.

"I think I'm in love with your family."

"I'll take it." His arms tightened around me like a compression sock made from a weighted blanket.

I couldn't think of anything more perfect than being held by him. I could feasibly be here and do this for the rest of my life. It was so idyllic you could pluck this night from a Norman Rockwell painting. Did that mean it wasn't sustainable, though? I couldn't imagine Jack would want to stay away from a family like this for long. The sudden image of him packing his apartment and moving away from me dropped in my mind, turning my stomach.

Most people left me, but Jack had promised he wouldn't. That was much easier to believe when I wasn't being charmed by his family and his hometown.

His husky voice drifted into my imaginings, putting a pause on the visions of him leaving me behind. "So, about that L-word earlier—"

"We don't have to do this," I said, burying my head against his firm chest.

His body froze. "Okay." After a minute of stilted silence, he pulled back. "We should get some sleep."

I'd said the wrong thing. My stupid insecurities had gotten in the way. Whatever I'd cut him off from saying had clearly messed up the mood, because Jack took both of our bags from the trunk and walked ahead. He didn't seem angry, but we were definitely off. When he squeezed my hand in the hall between our bedrooms, I frowned. I hadn't even gotten a goodnight kiss.

CHAPTER THIRTY-TWO

JACK

LAUREN WAS OFFICIALLY INTRODUCED to the town by way of brunch at Gigi's Diner. She looked a little dazed when we left, probably from the dozen people who stopped at our booth over the course of our meal to finagle a nosy introduction. Levi was there getting a coffee, so she knew one familiar face, but the majority of the others were old friends, teachers, or neighbors I hadn't seen in a while.

It was overwhelming, even for me.

"You are very loved," Lauren said when I took her hand and tugged her down Main Street. We passed the bakery, dentist, and hair salon before turning up the alley leading to my favorite abandoned house. Her open smile and easy comfort in Arcadia Creek was just another reason she was perfect for me. Last night when I'd mentioned one of the reasons I loved Lauren, I'd slipped the L-word in there entirely by accident. But on reflection over the course of the evening, it occurred to me that maybe I'd said it because my subconscious had recognized something my conscious brain wasn't ready to admit.

It was too soon in our relationship to throw around such strong feelings; the last thing I wanted to do was scare her away.

But that didn't mean I wasn't feeling, somewhere deep inside, that tiny little green sprout coming out of the earth of our relationship. It was springtime in my heart, and that sprout was the very beginnings of love.

An exciting and terrifying prospect, if I was honest.

Lauren looked warily at the house. "Bringing me back to your favorite murder spot?"

"You're not supposed to figure that out yet."

"Not until I've dug a big hole in the back garden?"

"No, Miss Morbid. Not until I've gotten you inside the house. Now watch your step." I pulled her along the outside of the wraparound porch. "Don't want to fall through any rot on the front porch."

"I'm not morbid," she muttered. "I just read a lot of cozy mysteries."

We rounded the house, picking our way through overgrown grass and unruly bushes. Lauren stopped when we reached the cement steps at the back door, tugging on my arm. "This view," she breathed.

It was incredible, which was one of the reasons I loved this place. The sky was open and wide, despite the slight gray overcast, and trees stretched out for miles. It was our own little oasis. I pointed to a thicker section of trees just beyond the first shallow hill. "Arcadia Creek runs down there. We can walk to it next time we visit if it warms up."

Lauren intertwined her fingers with mine. "I'd like that."

I keyed in the code for the lock and opened the back door to the house, then stepped in first to make sure it was safe. The floor still felt sturdy. It was dirty, the walls peeling and covered in graffiti from bored teenagers before we had upped the security. I wouldn't be surprised if we found rodents, but Tucker changed out the rat traps for me regularly. The bones of the house were solid—even if it needed to be rewired and the plumbing was likely shot.

"You really love this place," Lauren said, watching my face with a hint of suspicion.

"Yeah, it's beautiful."

She lifted her eyebrows, making me laugh.

I stepped further into the house. "I don't see what you see. I mean, I'm not crazy. It's old and probably needs a truck bed full of Brillo pads to clean up the mess." My fingers grazed the gorgeous carved banister, leaving a line in the dust. "But my mind washes over all the imperfections and I can visualize what it would look like restored to its former glory."

Lauren walked past me into the kitchen, relics of the 50s I didn't have the heart to dispose of dotting the room, covered in dust. "This is amazing." She opened the once light blue (now faded to gray) Frigidaire, rending an angry squeak from the rusty hinges, then looked back at me. "You want to flip this place, don't you?"

My heart jackhammered against my ribcage. "Not exactly."

"You want to restore it, though, right?" she asked, shutting the fridge and coming closer.

"Yes, but not to sell." I swallowed. No one knew this, not even Tucker, and he'd been the one helping me keep the kids and rodents out. All I'd ever told him was that it was a project house, but to keep it on the DL. Telling Lauren now was opening up my heart and letting her peek inside.

Plus, the only thing she'd ever asked me for was not to leave her, so I was terrified of what this would mean to her. I wasn't planning on going anywhere, but revealing my intentions with this house would also reveal my long game, and that didn't involve staying in Dallas forever. I swallowed roughly. But the way Lauren waited now, patiently looking at me with zero judgment and an open mind, gave me courage.

I looked up at the crown molding on the ceiling. "It's kind of a distant dream, honestly. I don't live here, so it was meant to be an ongoing project for my weekends, but it doesn't make much sense. My job and my life is in Dallas."

"It's okay to daydream, Jack," she said carefully.

"Trust me, I do that plenty."

Lauren passed me, stepping through the archway into the dining room. The blinds were shut but light streamed through them, a thick slash of light falling over us where a few blinds had broken or were missing. "Tell me what you would do with this room, then."

My heart sped up. "Really?"

She shrugged. "Yeah. I want to hear it."

"The wallpaper needs to go, but I'd replace it with something close to vintage in a sage green, maybe? Do all the crown moldings in white." I pointed. "Put in a long sideboard against the wall. I used to have the perfect one, but I sold it years ago, so I'd have to hunt estate sales for a similar piece. Then tables would dot the room, every shape and size I could find and feasibly fit."

"Sounds more like a café than a dining room."

"Kind of." I swallowed. It was all or nothing now. Might as well jump into the deep end of my crazy fantasy. "I think this place would make an ideal bed & breakfast."

A slow smile curved over Lauren's face. "That's the most adorable daydream I've ever heard."

"I'm not finished yet," I said, grinning. I was already pretty deep; might as well tell her the whole of it. "It would also function as a showroom. There's a big unattached garage in the back that would easily convert to a workspace for my restoration projects. They could be utilized in the B&B, but it would be heavily advertised that everything is for sale. If someone loves a piece, we offer to ship it to them. Once it's purchased, we just replace it with something else."

She stared at me, her eyes carefully shuttered. "So you could constantly restore furniture and have revolving stock for the hotel."

"After I get the house into shape."

Her eyes widened.

"Got. I mean after I *got* the house into shape, in this totally hypothetical slash unrealistic situation."

Lauren ignored that last part. "Why haven't you done it yet? Is the house not available?"

"No, it's not."

"Oh." Her face fell for me.

Deep breath in, Jack. "It's not, because I already own it."

Lauren laughed, walking through the open archway into what was probably a family room. When I didn't laugh with her, she stopped and turned back to face me. "You're kidding, right?"

"No."

"What?" Pure confusion swept over her face when she came back toward me. "You mean you own this place, you have a solid business plan and the skills to restore it, and you haven't even started?"

"I've started . . . kind of. But it needs time and my job doesn't give me much of that outside of the office."

Lauren stared.

I was beginning to itch under her disbelief. "It's not like I can just quit my job and move out here to devote myself to it full time, and that's what it would take to turn this place around. I was overeager when I bought it, didn't consider how much time it would take. It'll be more than a full-time job."

Weirdly, Lauren looked hurt. She swallowed. "Are you happy at MediCorp?"

"Gosh, no," I said, the words tearing from me with sudden, stark truth. The more they settled on me, the more I realized how deeply I meant it. "I hate it there."

"Yet you own this place and you have somewhere to stay in

town until this house is habitable. What's stopping you from following your dream?"

I reached for her waist and pulled her toward me until she was in my arms, her head tilted back to look into my eyes. I could feel how tense she was. Did she worry that I'd walk away from her? "Well, for one, you live in Dallas, and I'm finding that I kind of like you."

That earned me a little smile. "Nope. Our relationship is a newborn baby. You don't get to use me as an excuse."

That was fair. I drew in a musty, dust-filled breath. "To be honest, I was hesitant because I didn't know how I'd fit in here again. I bought the property a few years ago on a whim and put it in my back pocket to deal with later. Aside from a few security issues, I haven't really had to think about it yet. But lately, with the way Brad handled the venue issue and how he'd been taking advantage of my position in the company, I've felt less and less like I need to remain with MediCorp. Then with you dragging me out here for Tucker's party, I realized how much I missed Arcadia and the people here."

Lauren listened intently, never interrupting, allowing me to vent my feelings about this property and town. They had been building in me for some time—long before we had gone on the cruise—and I was ready to face them. Lauren allowed me to feel strong enough. Her open mind and interest in what I had to say made it easy to admit things I'd been afraid to even admit to myself.

"I love my life in Dallas, and my friends, the food, the culture. The way the buildings light up like they're trying to outshine the Vegas strip. Torchy's Tacos and something new to do every night. There is so much culture in the city, and it's been a wild ride. But," I said, hesitating, "I've come to realize that lifestyle isn't something I want to keep up for the rest of my life."

Lauren stepped out of my arms, holding my gaze. "So you

would really quit your job to move out here and follow your dreams?"

My heart thudded, blood pulsing in my ears. Did I want that? It was a pointless thing to ask myself, because I knew immediately, deep in my gut, that it was exactly what I wanted to do. I was done with corporate marketing. I was finished with stupid conferences and doing all the menial jobs Brad didn't want to handle.

A soft chuckle escaped my throat. "Yeah. It is. I think I'm going to quit."

"Just make sure you start a new Instagram handle for this place." She gave a defeated smile and wrapped her arms tightly around her waist. "People love huge renovation projects like this. They'll eat it up."

"That's a great idea." I'd thought about starting an account for my furniture with the hope that it could grow into another advertising avenue or place to sell finished pieces. Maybe it would be better to create a brand that encompassed both the house and different furniture projects, one that could roll into advertising for the bed & breakfast once it was finished and ready to accept bookings.

Lauren walked toward the window, then her gaze took in the whole room. "This place is going to look great."

"Don't sound so enthusiastic."

She tried to smile. "It's bittersweet. I love your dream. I just wish it was closer to Dallas."

My throat grew tight. "I'm not leaving you, Lauren."

She took a step back.

I walked toward her. "I'm not. Even if I decided to take this seriously, I wouldn't move right away. And Dallas isn't that far. We could make a plan."

She drew in a breath and let it out. "You're right. There's no point grieving our lost relationship yet."

Yet. I didn't like the sound of that. I took her hands and pulled her back in, breathing in the scent of her hair.

We stood like that for a minute, surrounded by floating dust mites and bits of ideas.

"You could probably create an event space in the backyard, you know." Her voice sounded normal now, which relaxed me further. "Another stream of revenue. The view is unreal."

It was a brilliant idea. I leaned back to look into her hazel eyes, the green bright in the natural light. "Not to sound like you or anything, but I kind of want to head back to my parents' house and start crunching numbers."

Lauren's hands dug into my shirt, fisting it until it pulled taut across my back. Her voice was breathy. "Oh my gosh, please let me help."

I laughed. "Maybe I can hire you to be my project manager. Then you can manage events once the place is ready to go. I think you're right. This would make a great wedding venue someday." I'd spoken facetiously, but truth laced each of those ideas, raising my heart rate with each one.

Lauren leaned up and pressed a kiss to my lips. "Don't say things you don't mean, because I just might take you up on it." She chuckled, taking my hand and pulling me toward the back door again. "Come on. Those spreadsheets won't fill themselves in. Have you utilized the graph options for Excel? They're beautiful."

I locked the door behind me, my heart free from burden for the first time in as long as I could remember.

CHAPTER THIRTY-THREE

LAUREN

NOT TO BRAG, but my spreadsheet skills really were unrivaled, and since I no longer had a job to occupy my brain, I threw myself into helping Jack figure out his business plan with everything I had. Something about Jack following his dream made me hesitate to jump into a similar job to the one I'd left at Hunnam. The small event firm in Plano was kind when I told them I wasn't ready to make a decision but informed me they were going to consider other applicants.

I took it as a good sign that my stomach wasn't sick when I got off that phone call and turned my attention back to formulating Jack's budget. Well, *budgets*, since there were plural. The house renovation was its own thing, the B&B as a business was a totally different form, and then Jack needed an idea of living expenses while he worked to get his business up and running. I was in data and calculation heaven.

It was a great distraction from the very real fact that my boyfriend was leaving me soon. Just like everyone else.

He'd delivered a two-weeks' notice to MediCorp first thing Monday morning—much kinder than I had been when I quit

Hunnam Hotels cold turkey—and served his apartment manager a 30-day notice. He was really doing it. He was moving to Arcadia Creek.

Needless to say, I had extremely mixed feelings about this. I didn't really need to analyze them yet, because I was busy acting as Jack's project manager. Today's focus had been calling Arcadia Creek's plumber and electrician to set up appointments for them to supply us with quotes and a basic rundown of what kind of work the house needed. Jack had done this when he first bought it, but those quotes were a few years old and needed to be updated. Jack's trust in both of those men was crystal clear when he'd permitted me to give them the house's door code so we wouldn't have to be present during their inspections.

It was Jack's last day with MediCorp, so I'd made dinner, and Amelia and Kevin were coming over to celebrate with us. They all happened to arrive at my apartment at the same time, which meant I'd have to fill Jack in on my progress later.

We clinked glasses over the slow cooked pork sandwiches and coleslaw. "To Jack, for following your dreams," Amelia said, and each of us echoed her.

"We'll miss you," Kevin said before biting into his sandwich.

"Arcadia isn't that far, man," Jack argued for the millionth time.

I filled my mouth with coleslaw so I wouldn't say anything to disagree. It wasn't that far, not really, but it wasn't feasible to see each other all the time, either. Jack's weird disconnection from his family in recent years proved that.

Amelia gestured between me and Jack. "You guys are doing the long-distance thing though, right?"

I tried not to sound worried. "That's the plan."

Jack reached for my hand and squeezed it once before returning to his sandwich. "Until I can convince her she's better off moving to Arcadia, obviously."

I choked on the coleslaw, grabbing my ice water to wash it

down. He hadn't mentioned that to me yet. I would know; I'd been having daydreams about it. Honestly, wasn't it the perfect solution? Jack restoring his furniture in the backyard while I cooked up breakfast for our guests and then spent my days coordinating the event space in our backyard. That view was legitimately unrivaled.

That dream also had a nice cushion-cut on my left ring finger and a few chubby babies crawling around, so it remained firmly locked in my mind.

Amelia pulled me from my daydream. "Cara and Lucas have gone out a few times since we got back from Miami. I think they might be a thing now."

"That's adorable."

"Now we know why they kept disappearing on the ship," Jack said, grinning.

"Have you heard from Sydney?" I asked, swatting at his arm.

Amelia cringed. "I decided it was time to let that friendship go."

Smart girl. Most relationships were worth occasional setbacks or putting up with irritating quirks, but some people were simply toxic. No one needed added toxicity in their lives.

We finished eating, the conversation moving between Jack's moving plans, Amelia's current school play for her elementary kids, *The Jungle Book*, and Kevin's latest bitcoin obsession.

Jack took over the dishes while I cleared the table. Amelia hopped onto a barstool at the island, and I couldn't help but think of the last time she'd been sitting there and the way we'd fought. I was glad our relationship had seemed to bounce back. Both of us were making an effort. If anything, we were doing better than before, now that we understood each other.

"How are things going with the in-laws?" I asked.

"Don't ask," Kevin shouted from the sofa, which wasn't even that far away.

Amelia gave an exaggerated cringe. "I invited them to

Sunday dinner and they've accepted. I don't anticipate them being anything other than frosty." She leaned in, lowering her voice. "Kev just wants them to see my ring, I think, so they know we aren't getting divorced like they recommended. I don't really care why they're coming. I'm just going to do my best to mend our differences."

"And if you can't?"

She shrugged. "I'll cross that bridge then."

"It's kind of ridiculous that the twenty-four-year-old has to be the adult in this situation."

"We can't all be humble and mature," she joked. It was the truth, though, as ridiculous as it was.

They stayed for another few hours before calling it a night, leaving Jack and me on the sofa, my computer between us, going over the updates I'd made while he was at work.

"You can see I upped your grocery allotment." I turned a little on the sofa to face him better, my shoulder pressing into his. "I wondered what you thought about working out a deal with Gigi's Diner so the guests had the option to go there some mornings."

"Maybe for special occasions, but I don't think anyone wants to book a bed & breakfast and then have to leave to eat."

"Yeah, maybe not." I screwed up my nose. "There are so many variables. It's hard to know what the final numbers will be."

He tapped the top of my computer. "At least this can help us get a loan."

"Us?" I raised my eyebrows, turning in time to see his cheeks mottle red.

Jack took my computer and put it on the coffee table. "Hear me out before you answer, okay?"

I nodded.

"I am not asking you to move in with me. I just want that to be clear from the onset. Our relationship is new, and that is something I want to protect." He took a breath. "That being said, I also know without even a little doubt in my mind that I love you and want to spend the rest of my life with you fixing up this little B&B and making spreadsheets and organizing events in our backyard."

My breath caught. He was listing all my favorite things.

"Moving to Arcadia Creek is an enormous ask, but it's not entirely selfish," he said gently. "I feel like you could flourish there, too. My parents have already offered *multiple times* for you to take a room at the house until the B&B is ready. If that idea doesn't give you enough independence, there are a handful of people in town who could potentially be looking for a room-mate. I could find you a situation. I would hire you as my project manager and events coordinator so you aren't coming to town without an income, which is necessary since it'll take at least a year to get the place open for business."

I wasn't quite sure if I was hearing him correctly, but he was addressing each of my worries about uprooting my life and moving to the country. First and foremost: crushing the fear that he wouldn't want me to do it at all. He was making his stance perfectly clear.

Jack slid his hand over my cheek, losing his fingers in my hair. "I love you, Lauren. We can take this one day at a time, so please don't feel pressured. I want to do this thing with you. Please say you'll come to Arcadia Creek?"

My body hummed, excitement beating a steady drum through me before deflating. "Amelia. I couldn't let myself be estranged from her the way you and your brothers became over the years."

"I've thought about that, and my solution is monthly dinners. We'll take turns going to their place in Dallas and having them come to Arcadia."

It was a good plan, actually.

"If I'd made more of an effort with my brothers, we wouldn't have grown distant. It's all about the choices we make and the amount of effort we put into the relationship. Kev and Amelia won't want to lose us either, Lo. It'll work."

"But my life is here. It has been here for . . . basically since I was born."

He leaned close, looking into my eyes with such focus and intensity. "Does it have to stay here?"

I let my heart answer him. "No. It doesn't. I want to come with you. I'm just scared."

"Trust me, then."

He said it so easily, I wanted to agree at once. I closed my eyes and nodded. "Okay."

Jack's hand went stiff against my jaw. "Okay? Like yes?"

I nodded. "Yes."

A grin stretched over his face before he crushed his lips to mine, kissing me with a ferocity I had yet to experience since we made up against the wall in my entryway. I kissed him back, telling him without words just how *in this* I really was. He had proven in the last several weeks how deeply he cared, how careful he was with my heart. I had no doubt the man wouldn't let me down. The prospect of doing this project together, surrounded by a town I had quickly learned was more like a huge, extended family, filled my soul in a way I never thought would be possible.

Jack pulled me tighter against him until I was sitting across his lap, kissing me like I'd just promised him a 200-year-old bureau in need of restaining. I cupped his face in both hands and leaned back, holding his love-drunk gaze. "If I live at your parents' house, where will you be?"

"Tucker's."

"Does he know this yet?"

"No, but he'll be okay with it. He has space, and as soon as the first room is ready at the B&B, I'll be moving in." He nipped at my lips, smiling. "Only one thing left, Lauren."

"What's that?"

"The bed & breakfast. We need to come up with a name."

I leaned in for another kiss. "I'll think on it."

EPILOGUE
LAUREN

I TURNED off airplane mode on my phone and it immediately pinged three times with voicemail notifications. I'd be nervous there was an emergency from the way Jack's missed calls filled my screen, except this was his habit. Every time he knew I would be unreachable—on airplanes, out of service, or when I turned off my phone for things like the brunch meeting I'd just had with Camila, my old boss—he'd call.

Turned out she was starting an online event coordinating business—meetings and workplace clientele, mostly—and wanted to know if I was interested in joining her team. As a new stay-at-home mom, she wanted to be with her daughter, but she missed working. Enter this entirely remote company.

I was clear with her about my plans for the future, but having my own job and income meant I wouldn't be leeching off Jack or his company yet. I'd still help him manage the project, but I also liked the idea of supporting myself. Someday the B&B would take priority, that didn't have to be now. We weren't married yet, at least.

I got in my car to drive home and told my phone to play my voicemails.

Jack's voice filled the car. "Hey babe. Hope the meeting is going well. Is she begging you to take your job at Hunnam back? I'm guessing she'll be devastated when you tell her about our little project. Poor lady."

He didn't sound contrite in the least.

"Mom started washing peaches for cobbler, but I guess she's waiting for you to help her finish making it. Something about promising to teach you Grandma's recipe." He lowered his voice. "I'm not sure if that was a joke, but if it's real, then I hope you realize the honor she's bestowing on you. If she's giving family secrets away, you're really one of us now. She doesn't share that with *anyone*. Flora has been asking for years. I'm sure you'll get the talk from Mom, but if Flora corners you at the grocery store and bribes you for the secret ingredient, you zip those pretty little lips and run away. She offers everyone free haircuts, but don't buy it. It's a scam. She expects a huge tip."

I smiled, pulling onto the freeway. I had at least an hour in the car before I made it home, but it wasn't bad. The drive was super pretty.

And I had Jack's voice to keep me company part of the way. Then an audiobook after that.

The voicemail continued. "Speaking of those pretty lips. You got plans tonight? After the whole cobbler situation, I mean. I want to show you the new wallpaper in the dining room. We can take a pizza and a few candles and make a date of it if—"

The voicemail cut off. I started the next one.

"Someday they'll realize that limiting the length of a voicemail is just rude. At least warn a guy. Anyway, as I was saying, I want to show you the wallpaper. Also, I got my hands on this cute little number that's going to make you and all your morbid myster—*ahem*, I mean *cozy* mysteries very happy. Don't judge it based on how it looks now, okay? Keep an open mind and remember how skilled your man is."

I laughed. The furniture he found was probably water-warped, with peeling paint and a hole in the back. I'd come to see over the last few months how Jack found absolute junk and transformed it into beauty. Kind of like what he had done with me.

Okay, so I wasn't junk before. But I liked how he saw through all my junky bits to whatever he was able to fall in love with underneath. I'd followed him to Arcadia Creek two months after he moved, and that separation had been good for us. It had led to a lot of FaceTiming and getting to know each other without physical attraction cutting down our conversations. The last two months I'd been living at the Fletcher homestead, though, had been even better.

I'd never lived in a house with a mom and a dad that I could remember, and while the Fletchers weren't trying to parent me, they were filling in the empty places in my heart. I loved learning Jan's recipes and secrets in the kitchen, and I loved hanging out with Roy and his favorite longhorn, Steve. To be fair, Roy was doing legit farm chores; I was the one hanging around and petting the animals.

I forced them to accept rent, but it was such a small number I wasn't sure it even qualified. My expenses weren't high in general, so taking the job with Camila wasn't totally necessary —my savings could get me another six months, honestly—but now I could contribute. I wasn't doing much for the B&B yet anyway, and it would be good to occupy my mind so fully again.

Plus, it was a part time job. So, perfect.

Jack's voicemail finished up and I turned on the third one, loving how his rich voice filled the car speakers. He told me about his run-in at the mailbox with Tucker's dog, Sadie, who hated him, then sighed. "You're probably on your way home. I would tell you to hurry back to me, but you should probably watch out for deer instead. I'll just sit here patiently waiting to see you again. Love you, Lauren. Bye."

He hung up, and my heart was full. Then I did a sweep of the grassy areas on either side of the road. No deer in sight.

I forced myself not to speed anyway. Those little butts came out of nowhere.

Turning on my audiobook, I sighed. This was what contentment felt like.

Jack

TUCKER LET DOWN the tailgate on his truck and pulled the blanket-wrapped dresser toward us. "You're going to start paying me for deliveries soon."

"Sure will," I agreed, untying the ropes holding it down. "Right when I start paying you rent."

"Don't worry." We heaved the heavy furniture on its side. "I've been keeping a tab."

I laughed, but the weight of the dresser cut me off. It was one of the things I loved and hated about old furniture: everything was made from solid wood. Which meant I could restore it, but also that it was heavy to lift. Enter: Tucker and his guilt-riddled assistance.

At least it was fake guilt. He was kidding. I'd tried to pay him rent more times than I could count. It was now something of a joke between us, but I got him back by filling his cupboards and bringing him leftovers from Mom's pretty regularly. Guaranteed the guy hadn't eaten this well in years—all thanks to Lauren moving in with Mom and Dad and my inability to stay away from her.

We neared the front porch of the Hansen residence, where we were delivering a refinished dresser that had been in their family for generations, when voices curled through the front screen door, stopping both of us in our tracks.

"You think Jack's gonna marry this Dallas girl?" Mrs. Hansen was saying.

"Well, you never know," another female voice replied. "She's a cute little thing, but Jan is tight-lipped. Can't get a word out of her mouth about them."

Mrs. Hansen made *hmph*. "There used to be a code between us gals, you know?"

"Mmhmm," the woman agreed.

"We *shared* with each other. Now we have to wait and hear the news with the rest of this nosy town."

Tucker caught my eye over the dresser. He lifted his eyebrow. I nodded once, like *let's get this over with*.

"I really think they oughta put a ring on that finger soon. We all know it's gonna happen," Mrs. Hansen said.

"Well, maybe," the other woman replied. "But you never do know, do you? We all thought Tucker would marry June, and look what happened there."

Tucker stopped, forcing me to grapple with the dresser, the weight straining my arms. We got a hold of it and I looked at him sharply, but his eyes had clouded over, his brow turning dark and thunderous.

No one mentioned June without getting a Texas storm out of Tucker. I swallowed, hoping he wouldn't take it out on this poor dresser. She'd never done anything to hurt him, and I didn't want to have to return to my shop to redo all my hard work.

"Just set it down softly," I said, as if I was speaking to an enraged bull.

Tucker shook his head, clearing it.

"You're right," Mrs. Hansen continued, her voice getting louder. "Best not to say anything until there's a ring on that finger." She pushed open the door to find us standing just before her front porch steps. Her plump face paled. "Boys," she squeaked.

"Good evening, Mrs. Hansen," I said, trying to regain a good hold on the dresser. "Just making a delivery."

"Come on in," she said pleasantly.

Flora poked her head through the doorway before stepping back to allow us to pass. I should have known it was her. Bunch of busybodies.

"Jack, that is just beautiful," Mrs. Hansen said, admiring my work as we set it down in her entryway.

"Where would you like it?"

She showed us where to put it, and Tucker and I got the dresser situated for her.

"I'll be off!" Flora called, disappearing while our arms were full. Coward.

Mrs. Hansen looked from me to Tucker, clearly wondering how much we'd overheard. "I'll just get my checkbook."

I waited for the payment while Tucker turned and walked out of the house, letting the screen door slam shut behind him. Yikes.

Mrs. Hansen gave me the check. I thanked her and went out to Tucker's idling truck, glad he hadn't left me stranded. The sun was going down and twilight fell over the quiet Texas evening. Well, as quiet as it could be with cicadas buzzing every-where, like broken sprinklers mixed with radio static.

Tucker didn't seem to notice me approach. Any mention of June made him a little unpredictable. When I got in, he was glaring at the steering wheel.

"You okay, man?"

He looked up sharply, like he had forgotten I was there, then started driving back to the shop where I'd left my car. I really needed to invest in my own truck. Since I needed help moving most furniture, it hadn't been necessary yet.

Tucker didn't respond; he just drove. When we reached the

B&B, I could see Lauren was already inside. I slid out of the truck, holding onto the door. "Want me to bring you dinner?"

"I'm good."

"Thanks for the help."

He looked at me, and I could see the struggle on his face. It wasn't me he was mad at. It was the women and their gossiping and them dredging up something he didn't like to think about. "See you at home," he said.

I shut the door and walked away while he drove off.

My feet stomped up the cement steps at the back of the house and Lauren opened the door, flooding me with light from inside. She grinned, holding a plate of peach cobbler in one hand and wearing a gingham apron.

I whistled. "When did you tap into my brain?"

"Your mom told me this cobbler is your favorite."

"I meant the fantasy of a woman feeding me cobbler."

She shoved the plate in my hand and started untying the apron. "That one's staying in your dreams."

I laughed, shoving a bite into my mouth. *Mmmm, heaven.* I put the plate down and pulled her in for a hug. "Missed you."

Lauren laughed. "I was gone for one day."

"One day too long," I muttered, leaning in to kiss her. For all the shortness of our almost five-month relationship now, I knew she was my person. I had the ring in my dresser to prove it, too, but I was waiting until she'd been out here at least six months. Then it wouldn't feel like I was rushing her into anything. As impatient as I was to get a ring on that finger so I really could come home to her every night, Lauren was worth waiting for.

She leaned back, her eyes sparkling. "Thanks for the voicemails."

"Did you enjoy the list of reasons I like you?"

"Yeah. My favorite reason was probably how cute you find my fascination with morbidity. You know cozy mysteries aren't actually that—"

"I know, I know," I said, pulling her arm. "Speaking of unrealistic fiction, I have something to show you."

I led her toward the shop to show her the bookcase I was going to refinish, but we walked slowly, enjoying the warm air, the cicadas, and the contentment.

"I love you, Lauren."

She smiled at me. "I love you more."

NEXT IN ARCADIA CREEK

Falling in Line

Tucker's heart was broken, stomped on, chewed up and spit back out. But that was five years ago. He's had time and space to come to terms with being left behind, to heal his heart. It's helped that June has stayed away from Arcadia Creek.

Except now . . . she's back.

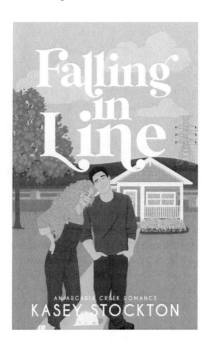

ACKNOWLEDGMENTS

Love on Deck is my 30th published book (five novellas, twenty-five novels) which means I've done a few of these acknowledgments pages before. After a while they become redundant, just me thanking the same people over and over again for their help, work, and support. But I kind of love that, because it illustrates how wonderful my support system and publishing team are.

So, without further ado, many thanks goes to all the people who were part of the process in getting Love on Deck from idea to paperback.

Thanks first to Lauren for letting me steal your name. I miss our B&N weekends, fangirling over *Twilight,* and epic Mario Kart tournaments. Mostly, I just miss you.

Thanks to my critique group, Martha Keyes, Kortney Keisel, and Ashley Weston, for helping me iron out the beginning, making Jack flirtier (I'll pass on your thanks for that, too) and reminding me to describe what people look like.

Thanks to my alpha and beta readers for your feedback, ideas, and dislikes, you made my story stronger: Nancy Madsen, Melody Williams, Rebekah Isert, Emily Flynn, Martha Keyes, Maren Sommer, Melanie Atkinson, and Brooke Losee.

Thank you to all the ARC readers, bookstagrammers, and readers who leave reviews, post about the book, or tell your friends to pick it up. You are the reason I can keep writing these, and my gratitude knows no bounds.

Thanks to Melody Jeffries for the most perfect cover ever.

Jack started out blond, but my brain saw him as brunette and you still made both versions of Jack look amazing.

Thank you Karie Crawford for your polish and editing, your notes and reactions are my absolute favorite. Your grammar edits are pretty stellar, too.

Thanks to my favorite cruise buddies, Jon and my kids, for putting up with my incessant need to talk about the book I'm working on.

And finally, thanks to my Heavenly Father for blessing me with the ability and grit it takes to be an author.

ABOUT THE AUTHOR

Kasey Stockton is a staunch lover of all things romantic. She doesn't discriminate between genres and enjoys a wide variety of happily ever afters. Drawn to the Regency period at a young age when gifted a copy of *Sense and Sensibility* by her grandmother, Kasey initially began writing Regency romances. She has since written in a variety of genres, but all of her titles fall under clean romance. A native of northern California, she now resides in Texas with her own prince charming and their three children. When not reading, writing, or binge-watching chick flicks, she enjoys running, cutting hair, and anything chocolate.

Made in United States
North Haven, CT
31 October 2023

43424397R00188